"THE WILD WILD WIND"

The life & times of a frontier lawman
and a preacher undercover deputy
with a daughter that could out shoot most men.
"An Outlaw turned Lawman"

Rebecca Ra'Chel

LOOSE CANNON ENTERPRISES
Petaluma, CA

2014 Edition
Print ISBN 978-1-9398126-5-0
Also available as an ebook

Published by
Loose Cannon Enterprises
www.loose-cannon.com

Acknowledgments

I wish to acknowledge & thank the Frontier Gun Leather Company for their permission to use the "Desperado" model gun belt and holster, as part of the cover of my novel.

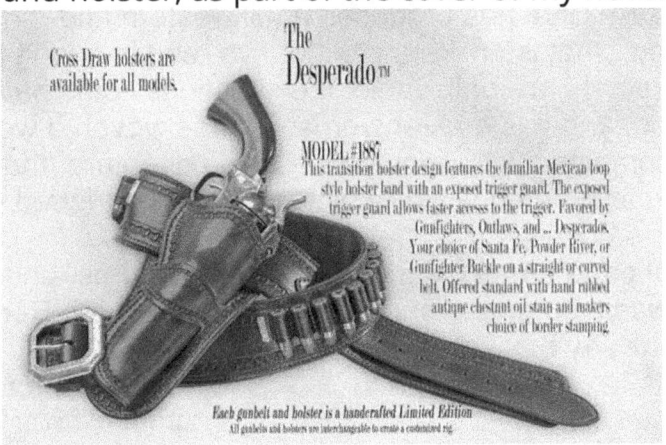

Cross Draw holsters are available for all models.

The Desperado™

MODEL #1887
This transition holster design features the familiar Mexican loop style holster band with an exposed trigger guard. The exposed trigger guard allows faster access to the trigger. Favored by Gunfighters, Outlaws, and ... Desperados. Your choice of Santa Fe, Powder River, or Gunfighter Buckle on a straight or curved belt. Offered standard with hand rubbed antique chestnut oil stain and makers choice of border stamping.

Each gunbelt and holster is a handcrafted Limited Edition
All gunbelts and holsters are interchangeable to create a customized rig.

For information, they may be contacted at:
www.frontiergunleather.com

I would also like to thank Cy-Quest Media Services, for all of their help as well. Not only have they created my website, they are the ones who created the cover for my novel as well. You can contact them via their website:
www.cy-quest.com.

Background painting for front cover by Mira Sudarevic. You can see more of her work at: miras46.deviantart.com

Further, I wish to acknowledge and sincerely thank my very special editor-in-chief, Scott Freemen, for his hard work and dedication to my work...

Inspiration

I sincerely dedicate this book to my grandfather (grams), who took on a near impossible task of raising a rebellious girl and guided me to this point in my life to be a responsible woman and author.
I needed the inspiration and faith he so freely and lovingly provided. Thank you grams, I Love You !

I do further acknowledge and appreciate my Uncle Tony for giving me several situational ideas to research of which I have used sparingly. Thank you as well Uncle Tony.

TABLE OF CONTENTS

CHAPTER 1

The Pardon

The sounds of horses and a wagon sloshing through the rain-soaked street of Durango, Colorado was all you could hear through the thunder and crackling of lightning as the storm raged on. The only lights in the near vicinity was streaming out of the saloon, and the Marshal's house farther up the street; and all was still, the main street was empty, not even a stray dog barking, as the wagon had reached the livery and the team put up for the night.

Daisy, the good Marshal's wife was preparing their evening meal and looking out the window at the tempestuous storm and wondering when it was going to end, as it has been storming now for two solid days. Yet, through it all she was humming to herself, lost in a revelry of bygone years, when her son Noah, sitting at the table, fifteen years of age and full of questions, broke the moment.

"Ma, why isn't Pa home yet? It's raining terrible outside and I can't imagine Pa a wasting time out there. Do ya think you know for sure where he is Ma?"

"Yes son, I'm quite sure I know where to find him, suppers nearly ready and I'll go fetch him so we can all eat together. Now you just sit right there, I'll be right back. I don't want you catching any more cold than you already have. Your cough seems to be getting worse."

Thunder boomed, shaking the house as lightning again streaked across the night's sky. Daisy hurriedly slipped on her raincoat and wet-weather boots and left the house with the wind whipping at her and through the open door before she could close it. The heavy rain and wind making it difficult to hurry as she first intended. Looking on down the street the only light visible was coming from the saloon as the light was streaming through the open bat-wing doors and the one dirty glass window onto the boarded street-walk and on out into the street. By squinting, she could see some shadowy figures lurking near the doorway, and wondering why they did not go in, which was suspect to her, as this acclimate weather was not conducive to continue lingering outside. She stopped, looking around, spotted some old wooded staved barrels at the corner of the saloon and slipped quietly behind them within the shadows. Daisy decides she best wait this out to see what if anything is going on. So she huddles closer to the saloon wall to try and keep out of the rain. At this moment she is able to hear through the wind-swept rain some hollering from a shadowy figure in front of the open doors, but was unable to understand what the yelling was all about as a thunderbolt blocked everything out. But no sound of answering activity was prevalent from inside the saloon...then... suddenly, without warning the sound of a bullet ripped through the night's air.

The saloon doors burst open and Marshal August and Preacher Kennedy quickly slid through the doors with guns in hand, but the lone gun-shot had hit it's mark with a fatal wound between the eyes of one of the lurking strangers. And was now lying dead in the middle of the rain-soaked muddy street, as lightning flashed and thunder roared continuously.

Daisy could not help herself as a scream of fright escapes her lips. Looking quickly around the Preacher gives the Marshal some cover and starts shooting at a shadowy figure off to his left. At the same time the Marshal makes a tumbling roll out onto the street and takes aim at the third stranger. His shot goes wild because of the roll in the mud and his second shot never happened as his rifle jammed. Strange then, as he felt a jolt in his left upper arm and notices blood oozing out from a flesh wound and numbness sets in. Through the night's storm another blood curdling scream was heard and Daisy stumbled out from behind her hiding place behind the wooden barrels onto the street and collapsed.

Marshall August's eyes followed that familiar sound and saw Daisy lying in the street, rain plummeting down upon her. The

Marshall threw himself upright and raced to her as fast as humanly possible through the mud. He knelt down beside her, bending over to shield her face from the stinging rain and mumbling over and over...

"Oh dear god, why, why?" With tears stringing down his face.

Yet the shooting was not over, as Preacher Kennedy was intent upon taking down the second shooter and finally did so after exchanging several shots and that outlaw also lay dead only a few feet away from the first one. He looked up quickly at the sound of a horse running and saw the third gunman racing out of town.

The Marshal hears his wife's laboriously breathing and her eye's both flickering open and closed, a wheezing cough escaped her parted lips, trying to talk, and August cuddles her in his arms as she whispers in his ear with her last gulping breath,

"Take care of our son... my darling, he's going to need you now more than ever." And with a sigh she passes on.

August knows his wife just died, but answer's her with tears flowing freely, despite the rain. "I will Daisy, I will." Closes her eyes and picks her up out of the mud in his strong arms and awkwardly stumbles towards their home.

Inside the house Noah has heard the gunshots being fired and now runs through the door frantically in the rain towards him. Noah knew immediately his mother had been gun-shot and bursts into tears screaming, "No Ma, no, no, please God no."

Three days later, the storm abated, a solemn funeral was held and a multitude of towns folk attended, all were misty eyed as Daisy was known far and wide for the good Christian woman she was. Always willing to help her neighbor and was an excellent midwife to many women coming with child.

Preacher Ethan Kennedy provided a reputable service for Daisy August, it was so heart rending, the misty eyes turned to red eyes and flowing with tears, and gave Marshal Daniel August opportunity to reflect back over the years and how it came down to his beloved wife being killed. *The many years have seemed to vanish so quickly from the time he and Ethan was tried and found guilty of bank and train robberies, not to mention the murder of various train and bank personal during their sojourn in the life of an outlaw. The infamous pair had basically been forced into this nefarious cult of gangsterism after the civil war. But then again, as August continued to reminisce, it was their own fault, so here we stand on the gallows with the hanging rope around our necks; asking if we have any last words. Well, that's kind of a stupid thing to ask I thought...My words, at this point, wouldn't mean a damn thing to these deaf ears my words would fall upon; but I did end up saying,*

"Hey, just get on with it!"

Preacher just said, "God, forgive us both our sins. Now get on with it before I decides not to do this."

But apparently God had other things in mind for us, as just at this moment in time lost, the Governor of Georgia was present at our hanging, and had received a telegram from the Department of Justice in Washington not to hang me, but with conditions. The Governor approached the hangman, telegram in hand, so stating a Pardon may be granted if certain conditions are met unconditionally and immediately. The hangman held up the hanging and the Governor walked up those dreaded 13 steps to the platform of the gallows, and continued over to me.

"Daniel August? I have here a pardon for you if you will properly answer a few questions. The Department of Justice in Washington has held up this here hanging and gives me permission and authority to grant the pardon after you agree too and put into writing your sworn testimony to agree to live as a solid law abiding citizen the rest of your life and to further accept an appointment to become a U.S. Marshal and abide by all state and/or territorial and federal laws. Do you so agree Mr. August?"

"Well now, it would take a complete idiot and damn fool not to accept those terms, but does this also include my pard here?" nodding over towards his buddy Ethan.

"No, it does not say that, his name is not mentioned at all in the telegram."

"Well then on second thought Governor, since he is my pardner and we committed those crimes together, I guess I'll just choose to be hung with him." August flatly stated.

"Now Mr. August, wait a moment, I do have the power to grant a stay of execution or perhaps a pardon for him here in

Georgia, and perhaps he could be your backup, but unofficially. Would that satisfy you?"

"Well now Gov.," looking over at Ethan with a wink. "That sheds a new light upon it then. Take this damn rope from around our necks and I'll sign the papers. But I'm a still trying to figure out the why fore's and what not's of all this."

"Mr. August, let's go down to the sheriff's office, sign some papers and I'll tell you the further stipulations and reasons."

The papers signed and the firearm hardware was returned, August asked, "Gov. what's the rest of the story?"

"Ok August, and you listen carefully too Mr. Kennedy, since you both know how to handle firearms so expertly there is........ aaawww what the hell is that commotion outside?"

They all ran to the door and windows to peer outside and saw a gang of rough riders ride into town shooting their pistols in the air, designed to scare people to run inside, seeking cover; and they rode directly to the bank.

"Hey, damn... looks like our bank is about to be robbed. If you two can stop this, I'll grant damn near anything to you."

No sooner said and both new lawmen ran outside guns drawn at the ready and the bank was only across the street and 2 doors down. August shot the outlaw holding the horses and the horses scattered, but not far as they were not gun shy. Both August and Ethan knew and remembered four of the would be bank robbers, as at one time they had ridden with them. The outlaws were now emerging from the bank and Ethan shot the one carrying the money bags and August wounded one of the outlaws he knew well as the robbers scurried to their horses without the bank loot and whipped their horses out of town, but not before one of the outlaws yelled to August.

"What the hell August, you just killed my brother."

August hollered back in return, "Well, where in hell were you and the boys when we were about to get hanged?"

But they were now out of town, and no need at this time to form a posse and give chase as the money bags were laying loose on the boardwalk. August bent down, picked up both bags and walked into the bank and said,

"I know this may seem funny, but I'll make a depository contribution instead of a withdrawal." And handed the bags to the bank teller.

The Governor was waiting outside and was already praising Ethan for a fine job, offering him a big cigar and patting him on the back.

"Now Governor, what were you saying before we were so rudely interrupted by that little ruckus." August inquired.

"OK August, now let's go back to the Sheriff's office, you haven't been sworn in yet, and there is more I need to tell you."

Back at the sheriff's office, the Governor pulls out two badges and tells both men to to raise their right hands... no Ethan, your other right hand, now be serious damn it, this is serious business we're about to do. So, wiping a smile off their faces they became solemn.

"I've decided to let Ethan be a kind of undercover deputy, he will have a badge, but not to be worn openly. I'll clear this with the Justice Department. Now let's get on with the swearing... oh damn, now you two stop that a cussin I say, this is serious."

"Alright Governor, we are serious now." August said with a chuckle.

After the swearing in and pinning on the badges the Governor sits down and tells them of further stipulations that are necessary for this job.

"You will need to relocate your families to the Durango, Colorado territories, there's a mess of outlaw gangs hanging out there in the badlands...but the little town of Durango seems to be their sanctuary. They are a ruthless bunch not to be taken lightly. Now I know this doesn't give you much time, as I can only allow you one day to convince your families to do this and gather up only a few personal items to take with you to make the move. Wagons and draft horses have already been assigned and can be picked up at the livery stables tomorrow. Now remember Mr. Kennedy, your job is to be behind the scenes, do not wear your deputies badge openly. Oh, and by the way, two excellent saddle horses are also available. Do you both agree to these terms now?"

Both Augie (as he was often called) and Ethan nodded affirmative and said... "Let's do it Ethan, hell I don't like being on the run and feels damn good without that hangman's rope around my neck, besides we are now able to get with our families again without hiding."

Ethan had a favorite saying, "let's just do it!"

Picking up their saddle horses, Augie and Ethan rode out of town together, thinking of their new found lease on life; they came to a crossroads and had to part, each going to their own homesteads from over fifteen years back, not really sure if they still had a home or not.

August rides up to his old homestead, stops short, takes off his hat and rubs his brow wondering how much things would have changed after fifteen long years, landscape looks about the same, but doesn't see any actual signs of life. Doesn't even know for sure if his wife still lives here. Couldn't blame her if she moved on, after all 15 years is a powerful while and I only wrote a few letters or so. As he rides a bit farther he notices a man off to the side of the house chopping wood. Not recognizing him August slides down from his horse and silently approaches, takes his pistol out and says,

"What the hell, who are you Mister and what are you doing here?"

The stranger turns to August slowly with hands in the air and answers. "Please don't shoot, I'm just a neighbor helping out Mrs. August."

Just then Daisy appears from the back of the house, stops suddenly. "Oh dear Jesus, Augie your alive"... starts crying, nearly in hysterics, sobs uncontrollably. And through those tears she exclaims, "Daniel, oh dear God Augie, we didn't know if you were dead or alive all these years, since your last letter four years ago."

Augie rushes to her, enfolding her in his arms, and trying to comfort her, he says, "yes Daisy I am here and yes, for good this time, thanks to God. I love you my dear."

Daisy continues to sob, but those tears are slowly subsiding and a young boy walks from the front of the house, just standing there, watching and wondering who this strange man was. Finally Daisy looks up and motions the boy to step forward.

"Noah, I want you to meet someone very special. This is your father Daniel, and this is your son Noah, nearly a growed up now."

Noah looks him over carefully, extends his hand to shake, but asks, "Where in hell have you been, didn't ya know Ma and me a needing ya?"

Augie takes his hand and draws him close. "Noah, I've been derelict in my duties and a hoping you can forgive me now. I promise things to be different from now on, can you find it in your heart to forgive me?"

Noah hugged his father and burst into tears. "Oh Pa, I wasn't even sure you were real all these days. Kids a teasing me at school and all, and Ma would always tell me about you and said to never mind what they said, one day your Pa would come a riding in; and now here you are."

That evening after a fine meal that Daisy prepared especially for Augie, fried chicken, mashed potatoes and chicken gravy and corn on the cob, they sat around the slow burning fireplace and recounted bygone years of yesterday. Finally after a prolonged period of time, August tells them of his agreement with the Governor and asks them if they want to go with him to the Colorado territory. Without hesitation, both Daisy and Noah agreed.

"Oh Augie of course we'll go, we don't ever want to be separated from you again, but what about the homestead here and my sister is alone, can't just leave her."

"Well the Governor promised to buy this place at a fair price if we decided to go and we'll take your sister with us." Augie spoke matter of factually. "But you remember Ethan Kennedy, my friend that just became a preacher before we left to join the army, he and family will be going with us."

"Oh Augie, there is some sad news waiting for him there."

Ethan Kennedy rides up to his homestead, but before he gets there he notices a grave-stone off to the side of the rode under a big Black Oak Tree about a quarter of a mile from the house, that he never remembered being there. Gets down off his horse, takes off his hat out of respect to whoever is buried there... reads the marker and kneels,

"Mattie please forgive me, I'm so sorry, sorry again for not being here for you."

Then he looks up into the heavens, tears streaming abundantly, raises his fist and hollers,

"Oh God, whatever did I do, for you to take Mattie for my sins; I lost faith because my hands are stained with unforgiving blood... and you did not intervene then... you should have taken me, not Mattie. Did you not see that?"

Ethan stayed kneeling until the tears stopped flowing. "Forgive me God!"

Ethan Kennedy stood up, stared long at the marker and climbed upon his horse, he had to go to the house now and see how and what his daughter was doing, but dreading the confrontation, let's see she would be about 19 now, as I left 15 years ago, damn, she won't even know me now or I her.

"Hello the house, is anyone about?"

Out steps a stranger and answers, "Yes indeed friend, how may I help you?"

"Well who the hell are you Mister and where is my daughter and what are you doing on my land?"

"You must be Mr. Kennedy, yes sur, I'm Seth Young. Give me a minute sir and I'll tell you a what happened. After your wife died, the bank repossessed this here land and house, cause your daughter was unable to keep up the payments on the loan. She cried a lot but she's a strong one what wif being alone and all, she tried hard, but they finally took it... She moved in-to town and works at the livery stable and lives in a little shack behind the livery, people respects her cause she's aright pretty girl and not afraid to get her hands dirty, works real hard. I believe the ole livery man takes a shine to her and helps her along."

Thanks Mr. Young, you've been right nice, I'm obliged." Tips his hat and saunters off back towards town. Just before he enters town he stops at the livery, needing to put his horse up for the night anyway and wondering why he didn't see his daughter when he and Augie picked up their horses earlier today. But whoa, just now he hears a ruckus inside the stables and jumps down from his horse, opens the door, and sees a man evidently trying to have his way with this gorgeous girl, her shirt was torn, exposing an ample breast, hay in her hair and a cut-lip, Ethan immediately grabs the guy, knocks him down, draws his gun, and tells him to get the hell out and do it now. With a dirty look

9

that guy gets out as fast as he could. Ethan looks over at the girl and says, "Sorry Miss, hope your not hurt badly, here now please coverup the best you can. Is there anything I can do for you, Miss?" Want me to get the sheriff for you to press charges"

The girls stands there, breast still exposed, looks him over and says, "Well I'll be damned, I'd remember you anytime. I'm your daughter Charlotte." Walks up to him and slaps him hard in the face, slaps again and again, crying and yelling, "Damn you Pa, damn you all to hell, damn, damn you." And falls into his arms sobbing uncontrollably. "Oh daddy, mommy died, did you know?"

"Yes my sweet, I just found that out an hour or so ago, I know how you worked so hard and tried to save the farm, it wasn't your fault Charlotte, it was my fault, and hoping you and God can both forgive me, especially for not being here for your mothers funeral; or actually for not being here at all and if I had been, perhaps she wouldn't be dead now. Besides honey, you were so young then, when your mother Mattie passed on, it wasn't up to you to have to do."

"I know Pa but I didn't know what else to do or where to go."

"It's ok Charlotte, listen, I've just received a pardon from the Governor for all my past crimes and have been given a job, we can start over, but we have to go live in Durango, Colorado to do this. Will you go with me Charlie?"

"Oh daddy, of course I will, I have nothing here to tie me down now. When do we leave? Oh, I haven't been called Charlie since I was a little girl, I always liked it Paw."

"Tomorrow bout noon time or a bit after, we'll be a meeting up with my old friend and pardner and his family at the crossroads going into town tomorrow. Is that to soon?"

"No daddy, I only have another pair of work pants & shirt and one dress to my name to gather up, but I do own that sorrel mare over there in the last stall, saddle and tack. I can be ready in a moments notice."

"Good honey, get cleaned up now and we'll go to dinner at the cafe, then get us some rooms tonight at the hotel; and gather things up in the morning and be ready to go, we'll tag along with Daniel August and his family on the trail."

CHAPTER 2

Durango Bound

M eeting up with Augie at the crossroads was no problem and they all road back into town together. Nora Weber, Daisy's sister was glad to have come along as she had no one since her husband had died two years ago and she was barren of children. She had been living alone since then, but mending for herself as a seamstress, making just enough to survive, but managed to save a few dollars in that time. She was a very handsome middle aged woman and men were always trying to court her, but to no avail. She loved children and especially young Noah, her nephew, and always cutting and sewing a new shirt for him which he proudly wore to school. So both Daniel and Daisy were eager to have her with them, it was agreeable to all and she had her own wagon that her husband had and a team of horses and harness. She had few things to gather up and was ready before Daisy and August were; but now going into town, she was anxious for this new challenge and long wagon trek from The Breaks here in Missouri to this place called Durango.

They stopped in the middle of town at the sheriff's office as that was where they were to meet with the Governor, for the last time.

"Well folks I see your all ready, but am a bit discouraged that you'll be leaving us here at the same time. Ya'll would have been a big asset to stay here and help protect us from outlaws here as you did yesterday. However, it gives me great pleasure to have been a part of this, to grant you pardons, and to further award you with $200.00 dollars gold to settle in your new homes in Durango. Daniel August and Ethan Kennedy it has indeed been a pleasure in assisting you towards this new challenge in your lives. But Ethan, you will need a wagon and a team of horses to make this journey and take this note to the hostler at the stables and pick out a sturdy wagon and team of horses. Your trip needs to look like you are settlers to the Colorado Territory. Besides it will give Miss Charlotte a place to sleep. Nora sense you have your own wagon and team and no man, it may be a more difficult trail for you. I wish I knew of a man wanting to go west. Ha haa, here I am just continuing to spout off as if I am again running for office, sorry folks, just a habit, now get along with you and God's speed.

They now had three wagons to make this sojourn, plus four good saddle horses, Nora's dog Major, that was a crossbred wild Wolf, and didn't like riding in wagon's. He preferred to scout with either Ethan or Augie, which ever man was doing the scouting at the time, but even then sometimes he would just take off on his own. Turns out to be a big help, seemed to know what he should do when. They were now only about 25 miles, by estimate into their journey, but it was starting to get dusk and so they thought it best to make camp for the night. They could travel approximately 35 miles a day on a 10 hour day, depending on terrain and weather conditions. So if good luck remains with us throughout our journey, we should make it in less than a month, or perhaps a few days more. So we gathered wood that we would need for the night, plus a bit more in case we stopped for the night sometime and it was raining, always best to have a few dry pieces on hand, just in case. We cleared an area of any dried debris and started our fire, put on coffee first of all and permitted our ladies Daisy and Nora to start cooking. Nora brought out here dutch oven and proceeded to make bread and Daisy cut up a couple of rabbits the men were able to kill on the way here, to make rabbit stew with thick rich gravy. Major was out scouting our perimeter, and knew he would warn us of any intruders, so we settled down to a nice meal and fellowship. Friendly banter from one to the other ensued and we all got to know one another again. Over the years Ethan and I had been away our families had lost track of one another, so it was especially good to see fellowship renewed.

I had found an old map, hand drawn, at the livery before we left and I dug it out now so Ethan and I could go over it and try to make plans. In the morning we would head south down towards Siloam, Oklahoma about 2 days on the trail, plenty of water there and we can refresh ourselves there, it's right on the border of Missouri & Oklahoma, then we can point nearly due west to the town of Tulsa, that'd be another 2 days on the trail. We could buy more supplies as needed, cause we'll have a long trek to go from there about 160 miles or so to the closes point to the Canadian River. That 160 miles may be treacherous and just no telling what we'll run across to face.

"Hopefully, that won't take but 4 to 5 days, what do you think Ethan?"

"Well, it works for me Augie, I just need to know each day when I start out a scouting which way to go to find us the best trail."

"Yeah, I know and I'm just trying to keep us close to water. That's the one thing I fear about this trip is running out of water... I think when we get to Tulsa we better buy a couple of more water barrels so for when we start to cross the Staked Plains in Texas."

"Good idea August, probably each wagon should have 3 barrels each to carry, I think the horses can manage that load, as we're not heavily loaded now with things... only a few pieces of furniture."

I'll tell you what Ethan, I'm sure proud of the way the women are handling the horses, course we haven't come across any bad terrain or other problems yet, but their doing good, especially I noticed how Charlotte handles her team. Her a working at the livery the last couple of years has made her a fine hostler. She would be good to ride the trail with. You otta be proud of her Ethan."

"I am indeed August and I feel I'm a mighty lucky man for her to forgive me for not being there for her during her time of need, trying to keep the homestead an all, and especially so after her Ma died."

"Well I think we're both damn lucky the way things have turned out for us. Hey, time to eat, I see Daisy waving us over."

Our evening meal was a delicious rabbit stew, thick gravy and dutch-oven baked bread with lots of strong coffee. "Daisy and you too Nora are fine cooks and I for one thank and appreciate your efforts, but now I need to tell you how we can push on faster. Our breakfast will have to be on the trail, so may I ask you both to fry some bacon tonight and use the left over bread this evening to make sandwiches to be passed out for breakfast, and the coffee needn't be fresh, put a bit more on now and we'll keep it warm by the embers of the fire during the night. That way we can start out at first light, we have a heap of trailing to do in the morrow."

"We'll try to make about 60 miles tomorrow, we still have a few more miles to get to Siloam Springs heading towards the town of Tulsa in the Indian Nation, and hoping we don't run across any Indians or other hazards, well have to stop a few times to water the horses and rest our weary and tired arse's, (laughing), but I have faith we can do it." Ethan added.

"Ethan, if it's alright with you, I'll stand first guard tonight, I'll wake you later. Now we all need to hit the sack." I suggested.

The night passed smoothly this first night, and all slept well and the morning came in surprisingly well for a first morning on the trail... Ethan had everyone up and teams hitched to the wagons while Charlotte was passing out the bacon breakfast sandwiches and coffee. They were now officially on their trek and no turning back. Next stop for the horses hopefully would be until at least halfway to Siloam Springs. They didn't anticipate any difficulties and all were of good cheer. At Tulsa, another 3 or 4 days hence they would rest over a day, have the wagon axle's checked and greased, and make sure all was sturdy.

However, we did see upon a far rise some Indians following us along, were either Oto, Saukor Fox, not sure which as they were to far away to see anything distinguishable. Yet they did not appear to be threatening and obviously we didn't want to intimidate them in anyway. So we continued our trail driving as if they were not even there... but Major would stop occasionally and look in their direction as if to be measuring their strengths and weaknesses. I have the feeling if Major could talk he'd be able to tell us more about them. After another couple of hours we stopped to give the draft horses a break and a cooling drink of water and our lady teamsters a well earned break.

It was a little after dark when they pulled into Siloam Springs, which wasn't really a town at all, but simply a trading post with good clear water and that was the best thing about it. The trading post itself was nothing more than an oversized shack with a stinking bar, as a matter of fact the whole place stunk. It had half cured hides stacked inside which gave off a putrid odor, a couple of half drunk Indians which had lost their self respect, most likely just blanket Indians now just hanging around looking for a handout to get another drink of watered down whiskey.

Ethan & I could see no reason whatsoever to allow the women to come-in and witness this foul smelling place with dried tobacco spitting and probably urine all over the floor. The Trader himself was unkempt, dirty, disheveled and appeared to be a complete rogue. Ethan and I looked around at all of this and walked right back out, and luckily we stopped the ladies just in time.

"Ladies, this ain't no place for the likes of you women, there's nothing inside we want or need, let's just make camp her for the night and fill our water-barrels again in the morning and head on to Tulsa with an early start. This place smells to high heaven." I cautioned.

Without a word the women complied and we set up a quick camp, ate a nice meal and sat around the camp fire sipping on our coffee for a short while before settling down to sleep. Ethan and I debated about posting guard here and decided not to as we could sleep with just one eye open, so to speak, and would remain alert however to any strange sounds. Well this proved to be a wrong decision as along about four in the morning, we heard a ruckus starting up, the horses were snorting and stomping and Major was growling furiously. We jumped up immediately grabbed our shooting irons and ran to the horses. There we spotted two shadowy figures tying to steal our saddle horses.

"Ethan, take to the left, I'll go straight in. Go get-um Major." Augie quietly whispered.

Major was already upon them in a leap, at least one he had down and we heard a gurgling scream, then just a wheezing and the one other guy we only could hear running away in the dark. Charlotte came now with a lighted lantern and gun in hand and we retied the horses and settled them down, then checked on the one Major had downed. Blood was flowing freely from a deep gash in his neck, not wheezing anymore, he had died on the spot.

We carried the dead person over near the Trading Post and deposited him there; looking at him closely with the light of the lantern, we didn't recognize him, but Charlotte did.

"Pa, that's the guy back in town that attacked me, don't ya remember him. I'll certainly not forget so easily, and it wasn't the first time he tried to get at me."

"Well I'll be damned." Ethan said, "it is that same guy Charlie, I recall his ugly face now. Well he got his comeuppance now anyway and won't be bothering anyone else."

"Now why would he follow us all this way, just to steal a couple of pieces of horse flesh." I queried, "Gotta be more to it than that."

"Do you have any idea's Charlie?" Ethan inquired.

"Only thing I can think of Pa, besides him wanting to molest me, is if he heard that you and Uncle Augie was caring 200 gold each, but why would they go for the horses first if that was the case?"

"Well, it's seems that will remain a mystery for now anyway." I suggested.

"Charlie honey, is there a history with that guy we need to know about?"

"Ok, yes in a way there is Pa, but I assure you nothing ever happened at anytime. I guess I best tell everyone the story. When I first started going around looking for work after Ma died, I was just past sixteen and pretty well growed up in the places men like and the owner at the saloon said he'd hire me as a hostess... well needing the money and not knowing what a hostess was supposed to do or be I said ok. Well one of the other girls that worked there got me all dressed up in finery, put rouge and lipstick on me and perfumed my breasts that were halfway out of my dress and told me to go wait on the customers, flirt with them and get their drinks for them and have a couple watered down ones myself and they give you tips. Well, I was doing that and must have been doing pretty good at it and got lots of tips, nearly three dollars the first couple of hours.

Well I decided I best go put the money away in my room and so I went upstairs, unlocked my door and was suddenly pushed into my room and down on my bed. That same man was pawing me all over and I was hollering for him to get off a me, when the owner came into my room and asked what the problem was...I told him that man attacked me... He said honey he already paid for you downstairs, but if your really good to him he'll probably give you a nice tip...now get undressed and do your job. I was shocked, really I was and knew I had to think quick, cause I didn't want to be a .50 cent girl or any kind of girl like that. But I said... well ok, but please I'm a little shy, let me undress behind the printed screen divider, you go ahead and get in bed...I slipped outa that dress and into my old pants and shirt and was out the window as quick as you could say scat. I hid in the livery loft for 2 days and nights before the ole toothless livery man a found me. That's the truth of it, I never went back, and guess that guy thought I still owed to him a night of it."

"Mercy Child." Daisy proclaimed, "What else could you do?"

"You did right Charlotte," Nora answered, "Just wish Major coulda been with you. None of that woulda happened."

"Well now Ethan, that explains a lot, but still doesn't add up to them a horse stealing, and must have had their own horses stashed somewhere close by." August stated. "And right now we need to go ahead and break camp and move on towards Tulsa, it's still a 2 maybe 3 day trail ahead of us barring trouble that we need to from now on be thinking of and try to be prepared for. It's nearly dawn by now anyway, so let's all get a move on."

Breaking camp was easy and Charlotte wanted to do the early morning scouting. Ethan was reluctant to let her until she calmly took the 44 out of his holster and shot an old can off in the distance and then with two more shots kept that can a rolling. She damn sure knew how to handle a gun. Ethan didn't say damn thing then, but went to his bedroll and took out a gun and holster and ask, "Do ya handle a rifle the same way honey?...I have a 44/70 you can stick in that boot and use if necessary. Now scat girl and find us the easiest route and watch for what ever. Somehow I don't think I need to tell ya damn thing, 'ceptin, be careful."

Ethan and I both watched her ride out of sight, then I said, "I'll take the left flank and be a watching out fer her Ethan, don't you worry yourself none, I think you got a right smart gal there, knows her business more 'n we think. You take her wagon and the lead, with Nora at the tail-end. Let's move out Ethan."

About 2 hours into trail, Charlie comes riding in hell-bent for leather and hollering, "Pa, holdup, there's 5 men a hiding in a shallow draw about three miles up ahead. Their not to smart as they had a small fire going and I spotted their smoke a mile away. I rode up as close as I could before getting off and walking to where I could see and count them and even could hear them talking...they know about the $200.00 gold both you and uncle Augie have, so someone was pretty loose lipped back in Missouri and I think the guy who got away this morning was one of them, by the way he talked."

"Thanks honey, now ride off to the left flank and find Augie. Tell him everything as you told me. Then the both of you high-tails it back here. See, them three cottonwoods off over yonder (pointing), that's where we'll be."

They were totally surprised to find at the base of the cotton-woods a small pool of water, actually a seep springs or from an underground river. The cottonwoods were large and would give us protection as well and much needed shade. We could almost hold off an army in a place like this. Soon the would be attack-ers, would wonder why we haven't followed the route passing their trail and come looking for us.

Charlotte and I arrived only a few minutes before Major alerted us the attackers were advancing. We could see them stopped on a small rise only about 200 yards out, obviously try-ing to figure out their next move. All of us were prepared and all had repeating rifles, even the women...Daisy and Nora were not expected to be a force but even their shooting would be a help and we already knew Charlotte was an excellent shot.

"Pard, whatcha think, what's our best defense."

"Well now Augie, not sure as we are usually on the offensive, not used to waiting to be attacked. But I do know we need to wait them out and see what their next moves be."

We made sure the women were placed in as safe of places as possible, yet still able to shoot if necessary, except for Charlie as she would be right up front with us. *It's their six men against 5 of us plus Major, and am sure Major would be a right formidable foe at close range. He was laying next to Nora, growling and seemed impatient for a fight. I figured we had the edge with our fortifications and water availability; the three large cottonwoods was extra protection as well. We actually could just wait them out, they had no natural protection from the sun, no extra water except their canteens, and probably were as impatient now as a snake on a hot rock that hadn't eaten in several days.* An hour passed and it seemed to be a standoff, but we were becoming impatient as well and wondering if somehow we could flank them, to totally surprise them and attack them from the rear."Ethan, come over here for a minute, I've got an idea, see what you think. I'm thinking I could sneak around their backside with Major, scare their horses away and hold them at gun point long enough for you to ride up, then decide what in hell to do with them."

Well now Augie, ifn' ya think you could do that, I'm all for it, we're a wasting valuable time just sitting here. Ok, when you have them covered shoot once in the air and I'll come running, and bring your horse with me." "Oh hell Ethan, stop calling me Augie, you know damn well I hate that."

Ethan told the others what Daniel had in mind and they watched Daniel and Major, take the low side of rises, sometimes crawling on their bellies and sometimes just a running hunched over till they were out of sight. About a half hour later, they heard a shot, then two more, Ethan and Charlie jumped on their horses and raced to the area, only to see one man apparently laying dead and the others at gunpoint with Major standing guard ready to attack.

"Ok Pard, what'll we do with them now?"

"Well August, they would have killed us if they'd gotten the upper hand, but I've got a better idea, it may kill them, but they deserve no better."

"Ok gents, all of you would be outlaws, strip, and I mean everything, down to your bare arses, and start with your boots and socks if your a wearing any. Do it now !

"But...but, there's a lady present...everything?" one of the outlaws whimpered.

19

"Well now," I said, "you noticed that did you? If this situation was reversed you'd probably strip her and rape her, but it's not like that is it? So get on with it, or I'll turn Major loose on whoever is a mite slow in the doing."

"You mean our underwear too Mister?" Another hellion asked.

"Mister what don't you understand what everything means?" Charlie asked laughingly.

"Now honey, ride on back to the wagons and bring um all up here. Ethan told her.

Laughing, but Charlie did as her Pa said and was astride her horse heading back to the cottonwoods and the wagons...They have lost a couple of hours of valuable travel time; but felt good that she had been able to spot those outlaws in time to avoid any real catastrophe. Thinking now her Pa and Uncle Augie would trust her even more. By the time Charlotte, Daisy and Nora's wagons were brought up, the outlaws were already walking bare-ass naked to the south, not even a canteen of water with them. The horses had been scattered north and Charlie mentioned that we should round up their horses and take them with us. Extra horses might very well be a plus on the rest of the trip. Both men thought that would be a good idea, besides the outlaws wouldn't be able to double back and possibly pick up their horses. So it was suggested to go back to the cottonwoods, only a couple of hundred yards or so and let Daisy and Nora wait there with Major while Charlotte, Ethan and I, rounded up the horses. By the time this was done, it was a couple more hours lost, so they decided to go ahead and make camp here for the night. The ladies started to make ready for the evening meal and then Nora spotted a deer grazing about a hundred yards off and thought a nice venison steak would be a reward for them all and thought it would also be quite a surprise when the men and Charlie would return. She took careful aim and brought that deer down with one shot, now both ladies would have to go bring it in.

Bye the time Ethan, Charlotte and I returned with the outlaws horses, Daisy and Nora had a fine supper waiting with a hot pot of coffee...They ate ravishingly and prided themselves on their good fortune. They unsaddled the outlaws horses, stowing all extra gear in Charlotte's wagon, as both Ethan and Charlie had nothing but personal items, amounting to very little. They refilled their water barrels, then the women wanted to take a bath in the cool springs, so the men both agreed to of course turn their backs and study their map more. Soon it was getting dusk again, they all felt refurbished, the women had dried and smoked some strips of deer meat into jerky, cut more deer meat into roasts and would cook them tomorrow evening and should last several days. Now their small wagon train had increased with the addition of the outlaws horses, they had a total of 21 horses to feed, water and care for. From a distance this would indeed appear to be a formidable caravan, and would give the Indians something more to consider, or even perhaps another outlaw band.

Morning came quickly, coffee was hot and Charlie tied the horses in a string behind her wagon and they were off before complete daylight, still bound west for Tulsa. That evening they arrived at Oologah Lake and knew they were less than a full day away from Tulsa. It was still fairly early in the evening and the ladies decided it was time to wash clothes and for the men to take a bath...or they could sleep with the horses. Well, with truth being said, Daisy and I were the only ones sleeping together whenever I wasn't pulling night guard duty, but the saying of it worked. Ethan jumped right in too. But after supper Charlie announced she was going for a midnight swim and as she neared the lake shore she heard some splashing water and someone humming. She crept a bit closer, keeping somewhat under cover to see who it was. The moon was full & bright and glistened off the water, but she could see quite clearly that it was a black man, *'oh mercy,* she thought to herself, *one of those darkies. I've never seen one up close.'* She crept closer and knelt down behind a boulder near lakes edge...she continued to watch until she noticed the man was coming out of the water and she had no way to retreat without being seen. *Well, can you imagine, that man was completely naked and I couldn't believe his body was so muscular and the size of his manhood. Why... why I was totally amazed and sent chills through my entire body and made me think thoughts I wasn't supposed to be*

21

thinking. But my legs were starting to cramp and I had to move.

Quick as a flash, he had a gun in hand and asked, "Who's there, come out, you there behind that boulder, come on out so I can see you and hands high."

As I stood up, the moon shone on me, glistened off my blonde hair and of course revealed I was indeed a woman. I said, "Don't shoot, I'm not armed."

In reply after a brief pause, he said, "oh yes you are sweet lady, you are armed better than if you'd had a shotgun at close range pointed right at me." Looking down as he said that, and noticed he was naked and standing before the most beautiful white woman he'd ever seen.

"Oh dear God Lady, please forgive me, I had forgotten myself momentarily." And tried to cover his nakedness with his his six-shooter. "Please ma'am turn around, let me put some clothes on."

"Well can I lower my arms too?" Charlotte asked, as she turned around slowly.

"Yesum ma'am, I mean yes ma'am, yes please put your arms down, and forgive this black soul. I meant no harm, yesum ma'am, no harm. Oh Lordy Lordy. But what may I ask was you a doing down here crouched behind that there boulder?"

"Well, uh well, I was coming down here to the lake to take a bath too and heard some splashing and then saw you walking this away, so I hid right here."

"So well, so did you see my altogether ma'am? I wouldn't try to hurt you ever, I promise."

"Yes I did, but not very well, and I would've looked away, but wanted to see who was coming this way. I just didn't know what to do."

"Ok ma'am, you can turn around now, I am dressed."

Charlie turned and asked, "What is your name Mister?"

"Uh, uh my name is Joseph, Joseph Freeman, and may I respectfully ask your name ma'am?"

"Yes of course, my name is Charlotte Kennedy, and our camp is but a hundred yards or so over there." nodding east with her head.

"Well Miss Charlotte, I would be glad to stand guard for you while you bathe. If you'll allow me."

"I'm not sure I should do that, your kind sir and if I stay to long my Pa will come a looking for me. I don't think he'd appreciate that." Charlie said laughingly. "I best be getting back, he might be on his way now."

"OK, but the least I can do is walk you back to your camp."

When Charlotte & Joseph walked into camp and with the light of the fire and the moonlight, you could see quite clearly. Both Daniel and Ethan stopped short, looked at Joseph, crouched as if they all were going for their guns, looking sternly, and then suddenly... burst into laughter, ran towards each other with arms outspread. Hugging and clapping each other on the back. It turned out to be nearly a reunion, so to speak...

I thought it best to explain our actions...and so I spoke, "Folks this is Joseph Freeman, we were in the war together, then we even rode together for a time on the outlaw trail. Joseph here is the youngest army corporal and youngest outlaw I ever did meet. And damn sure one of the best shots. Welcome my friend."

Ethan loudly agreed and then volunteered further information. "Ladies this man has his last name 'Freeman,' because he says he's damn sure a free man." And all laughed heartily.

Joseph, tipped his hat to the ladies and was offered to sit down and relax, then Nora offered a deer steak and potato's and carrots with wild onions with thick creamy gravy. Joseph was indeed hungry as he hadn't eaten since morning. Daisy brought him a fresh cup of coffee, and all shushed to permit him to eat his fill. The ladies served their men folk coffee too, then retired to a wagon with only one kerosene lantern burning to talk quietly for awhile and mend some torn clothing.

Morning came early but without a hitch, the women knew how to get their men in high gear and it appears Daniel & Ethan invited Joesph to spend the night. As the small wagon train started out Joseph tied his horse to the back of Nora's wagon and took his place in the drivers seat. Now with an extra man, they could spell off the scouting more often without having to worry so much. "Ma'am, I hope you don't mind, I can spell you from time to time, and I'm a much better driver than I am a pas-

senger rider. Daniel and your daddy talked me into going on to
Durango with them, I didn't have nothing else to do noways."

"No Mr. Freeman, I don't mind at all. It is a bit of a relief to
have a man handle the reins awhile and I thank you. You appear
to be a gentleman and that's all I care about."

Charlie had passed out the bacon sandwiches, some jerky and
coffee and they were again off towards Tulsa, seems such a ways
off yet. Their small caravan seems to be growing. It was still
nearly a full days ride into Tulsa and barring problems or trouble should be able to make it in the late afternoon. That would
give them time to make some additional purchases of extra water-barrels, horse feed and a few more vittles for the rest of the
trail. Daniel and Ethan had already started out ahead to scout
the best path, which was nearly a road by now, some places the
ruts of wagons wheels were deep and made for a rough ride.

They arrived in Tulsa without incident about 4PM, stopped to
do their necessary shopping, then rolled right on through town
to find a camping place on the west side of town. Joseph saddled his horse and said he'd be back later, riding back to town.
Ethan and I strolled into the 'Gilded Cage' Saloon, to have a
drink and listen to gossip, and perhaps pick-up some news of
the trail west to Cleo Springs. We had only been there a few
minutes when a half drunk bumped into us, spilling both of their
drinks...I said,

"Mister you need to sit down and stay still, your gonna end
up making some cowpoke mad as hell. Now ordinarily I'd make
you buy us another drink, but beings your about drunk I'll just
pass it on, no problem."

"Wada ya mean drunk, ya'll need to watch wherein hell ya be
a standing."

Ethan was abit quicker than me to get riled up and took offense to this, "Mister you damn sure owe us an apology and a
drink. Otherwise I might really get riled."

"Well Mister get youself riled, it don a bother me none. I
stand ready." Not at all seeming to be drunk anymore.

Just at that time Joseph entered the saloon, spread legged,
hand at the ready for his gun.

"Big John, you seem to be causing trouble again, seems to me
your picking on the wrong gents this time for sure. You'd be

dead afore you cleared your gun, but you never faced up tome that last time up in Saint Louie, and that is still in my craw. Wana try your luck now?"

"uh, uh, now Joe, I don't have a problem with you...you know that." Looking sheepish.

"Well Big John, I say fish or draw bait. You want to take me or one of those gents, no never mind to me. You'll be dead either way."

"Ok, yeah I was just a fooling anyways, my apology gents but I haven't got the dinero to buy you a drink. I'll just leave now, with a bye your leave." And sheepishly left the saloon.

"Well I'll be damned Joseph, guess you've been around Big John before...come on, have a drink with us." I said. "Barkeep pour this man a drink."

The Bartender came up to us and said, "I surely appreciate ya'll not starting a shooting inhere, but sorry, I'm not allowed to serve a drink to uh, well uh you know."

Ethan pulled out his 44 colt, quietly laid it on the bar and said, "Nope, don't know what you mean barkeep, now about that drink for the three of us?"

"No offense gents, just the owner don't let me serve to them... but I just think I'll make an exception in this case."

"Good thinking barkeep, you'll live a lot longer that way." Ethan remarked.

The three tipped their drinks and told the barkeep to give them a full bottle and walked out..Outside, they saw a milk cow tied to Joe's horse, and couldn't help but laugh. But Joe explained Nora wished she had a milk cow to take, as that way, both her and Daisy could have milk to cook with and besides Noah's a still growing and needs it, and I bought two sacks of oats for her feed along the way and her own milk pail and stool, so ok, or not?

"It's fine Joe, that was thoughtful of you and am sure the women and even Noah will be glad for it. Thanks Joe." I said.

Arriving back in camp the women were very happy with the addition of a milk cow and since it was a Guernsey, said they were going to call it Jersey. It needed milking now too, so Nora fed it a few oats and set right down and started milking. Daisy made a fresh pot of coffee poured cups for everyone, added a teaspoon of sugar and spooned some fresh heavy cream out of the pail and added it to each cup...the men were delighted.

"Well so far the trail has gone quite well," I announced. "Wonder if it'll be a hellion later on Crossing the 'Llano Estacado' and in our plain English that means 'Staked Plains,' flat as all hell, but lots of grass, days are like a fire burning and night's will freeze you to death. Prairie Dogs by the thousands and Major will probably go crazy running himself to death trying to catch one. But we must also be on the alert as there are still some old remnants of Apache still lingering in the area, but mostly Comanche and Kiowa; not to friendly yet either."

They all laughed at that and were enjoying the togetherness this camp exuded, each doing a job necessary and not complaining. So this made their job easier. But certainly didn't laugh about the Indians. In Missouri most of our Indians were what you call blanket Indians, just hanging around the towns waiting for a handout, most times drunk or wanting to get drunk. Looking for anything to steal, then sell to buy that next bottle. Well anyway, here we are miles from home with good friends. Going to make our home and mark in another part of the country. Time for bed to get an early start. Ethan made his bed under Nora's wagon and apparently sound asleep immediately. Nora just layed there above him wondering what it would be like laying in his arms... to be loved by him... to be made love too by him... oh such terrible thoughts I am having, but it has been nearly 3 years since ... yes since I've lain with a man and I do still have urges like any other woman. I just continued to lay there tossing and turning, blankets all rumpled, finally I got out of bed, slipped on my shawl and quietly got out of the wagon, and started to walk around. Suddenly a voice, soft as it was, was a warning.

"Nora, you shouldn't be out walking around alone. It may not be safe."

"Oh Ethan, sorry. I didn't mean to awaken you, I'm just unable to go to sleep tonight."

"You didn't really wake me up Nora, I'm a very light sleeper...but I'd be glad to walk with you a spell. May I also ask what is troubling you? I'd be glad to help if at all possible."

"It's very personal Ethan, just woman worries and concerns, but well, Ethan I'm a widow woman and it's very difficult to not want to be with a man, if you know what I mean."

"I think I do and certainly understand...look at me please, I was an outlaw and what chances do I have in being with a woman; no woman would want to be on the run with a man like me, so yes I understand your needs and desires Nora."

"Does it have to be this way Ethan? Your a handsome and brave man, I can't imagine any woman not desiring you; and if you'll permit me, I noticed you right off and thought about you in a desirous way. Oh please forgive me, I'm acting like such a wanton. I'm ashamed."

"You needn't be ashamed with me Nora, and honestly I've had those same thoughts about you, (reaching out to hold her hand), if you're not afraid of me."

"Afraid? No, not afraid but very apprehensive as I've never even kissed a man for such a long time now. And have urges like any other woman."Then we both laughed quietly, and I melted into his arms and we kissed, a long lingering hungry kiss.

"Stand your ground, who are you?" I asked out loud...

Still in his arms Nora answered, "Oh Daniel, it's just Ethan and I, neither of us could sleep so we're just taking a short moonlight walk." I couldn't help but giggle, oh so childish...

"Make your walk short, try to get some sleep you two, though we're staying over a day, morning still comes early." I urged and then walked off leaving them alone again.

I wasn't even a bit ashamed that Daniel caught us like that; actually I was even kind of glad as I wouldn't want to have to hide how I felt. Ethan and I walked off together arm in arm and kissed again and he lifted me into the wagon, I fell asleep almost immediately and it seemed I had no sooner closed my eyes and I had to wake up again. Morning did come early and I got up to make a couple of dozen biscuits in my dutch-oven. Daisy was frying some bacon and had bought 3 dozen eggs in town yesterday, so everyone was about to get a real treat for breakfast. Coffee was hot and Jersey was being milked by Noah, she's going to give too much milk that we won't be able to use and drink, but pancakes made with sour milk are mighty tasty too. But it would be nice if we could sell about 3 gallons today, to some

27

people here before we leave. So with the added pancakes and sweet molasses, we were a happy fulfilled family.

It turned out now that the romance between Ethan and Nora was no secret, others in the party had witnessed their walk-in-the-moonlight, and kiss. Yet no-one said a word in rebuttal, which of course was none of their business anyway. It seems that Ethan would now become a permanent fixture in Nora's life, which was a good thing as he was added protection as well. We now had four excellent shooters, plus both Daisy and Nora could also shoot if necessary, just not as fast or quite as accurate. Actually Noah had a squirrel gun too and was not a bad shot either. After a fine breakfast the men decided to walk into town, still early as it was, the saloon was either just opened or hadn't closed all night. Other shops and stores were just now opening their shutters and doors, sweeping the boardwalk and setting various wares out for potential customers to see. Though it was a brisk and cool morning it was still a nice day, though they knew by mid-morning it would be hot as blazes. They just strolled around town kinda measuring it out and just passed the saloon when a voice called out.

"Hey Nigga …. doncha hear good nigga? I'm callin ya out, tired a takin aback seat to ya."

We all three turned to see it was Big John, some people just don't have a damned lick of brains and Big John seemed to be one of them.

"Big John," I said, "You decided to die this morning? I'm Daniel August, U.S. Marshal and I'm tired of hearing you jawing at Joe Freeman here. Now come with me to the Sheriff's Office, I'm sure you probably have a few wanted posters on you. I'm putting you under arrest."

"Huh, that'll be the damned day you put Big John in jail Marshal. Look around, you might see your all 3 are already covered. I come prepared this day." Big John said with a smirky laugh.

"We've already spotted them Big John, an appears they must be ready to die also, if they stay to stand up for you. So what'll it be?"

Thing about it is Big John, it'll be me who blasts you to hell." Joe said. "My pards here will easily handle the other two. So what'll it be Big John, you want to go down or go to jail?"Just at this moment a small girl walked by on the boardwalk in front of Big John, not aware of what was going down. He grabbed the girl and held her in front of him, saying,

"Whatcha think about this now? Drop your guns, all three of you or I'll kill the girl."

"It figures you'd use a child as a shield Big John, most cowards would. But what you going to do about that gun pointed right at your head directly behind you?" Ethan asked.

"Oh yeah, ya think I'm dumb enough to fall for that one."

A soft voice then said, "you best fall for it you coward or your brains will be scattered all over the street." Charlie purred, "and I'm not a damn bit afraid to pull this trigger right now."

Big John dropped his gun and let the girl go immediately. "Don't shoot, don't shoot, I'll go."

The other two men disappeared without a word and the men advanced up to the board walk, retrieved Big John's gun, took him into custody and Joe and I led him to jail...

"Charlie honey, that was an awful dangerous chance you took sneaking up behind him like that. But we thank you and am sure the girl thanks you as well."

"No trouble Pa, he is a coward and a coward always thinks of himself first. I didn't feel at all frightened, except I was frightened for the little girl, and I was coming into town anyway."Ethan just shook his head and laughed. "Honey, I'm just a bit amazed at what you've had to learn over the years and how you know to take care of yourself. How in hell did you learn to handle a gun that a ways?"

"It's a long story Pa, maybe someday I'll tell you; but right now I wanted to go buy myself a dress or some material and have Nora teach me how to sew."

"Well don't think I'd be much help to ya there, so I'll go to the sheriff's office and see how they're doing with Big John and see if any posters are out on him. See ya back in camp."

Back at camp sometime later, I told the story of how Charlie saved the day and big John is locked up in jail. Everyone applauded Charlotte, then Nora asked,

"Who was that little girl, and where is she now? Where were her parents?"

"Oh dear," Charlie remarked, "she just so quickly disappeared, and it seems we just kind of forgot about her. I do hope she's alright. She was a cute little gal, 'bout Noah's age and appeared to be a Mexican girl, or perhaps an Indian."

"Well she most likely ran all the way home by now where ever it may be." Daisy remarked, "And I wouldn't blame her at all. Such a terrible thing to be held like that by the likes of that man. Just a shame."

They needed to take the wagons to the blacksmiths shop and get them checked over and axles greased, then Joseph remarked he had learned the trade of blacksmithing after he left the outlaw trail...didn't want to be on the run anymore, and he'd be glad to do it with a little help to save on the money as he had little money left after he bought their milk cow, it was his way of making a contribution, to help pay for his keep on the trail.

So Ethan said he'd be glad to help. They had to empty the wagons to make it easier to lift an axle and place blocks under it to take off a wheel, seemed like this might take all day as there would be 12 wheels to take off and re-grease, and check for problems. When they got to the second wagon, which was Nora's, they started to unload it and found to their surprise a little girl under some blankets eating a cold biscuit. "What the hell, hey folks look what I found, ya all gather round now." Ethan said, "It's that lil girl Big John grabbed earlier this morning."

"Well I'll be damned," I said, "Whatcha make of this?"

She appeared to be frightened, but kept on eating that biscuit. Obviously very hungry and Charlie asked her name.

"Child what is your name, and why are you hiding in the wagon? There are no bad men here."

"I am called Aponi; please do not hit me."

"No one will hit you here child and Aponi is a beautiful name, can you tell us what it means in English?"

In answer she started fluttering her arms up and down and saying, "Buu tier fly, my owner he say."

"Butterfly, oh that is a beautiful name Butterfly, but you mean someone owns you?" Charlie continued to ask.

"I tink so maybe yess, he give me faader some coins and he say go theis man. But...but he not so good, theis man, no like good fer me."

Everyone was standing around hearing this, but it was Joseph who spoke up, "No one should own another person, I think we should keep this child, take her with us, if there are no objections. I'm just a guest here also, so please forgive me, I really have no say in this."

Nora spoke up, "I will take and care for this child, she needs help, not only protection, but food and to be cleaned and most important she needs love. Being childless I am able and more than willing to do this; besides, she'll make a good friend for Noah.

"Well Nora, doesn't seem like anyone here is gona object, but she needs to stay completely out of sight until we are a good ways on the trail tomorrow. Now guess we need to all get back to work."

But Noah stepped forward, held out his hand to Butterfly and said, "My name is Noah, and I'll be your friend." Then turning to Aunt Nora he asked," Aunt Nora can you get Butterfly something more to eat than just a cold biscuit?"

"Oh Noah, of course I can, how thoughtless of me."

Butterfly took Noah's hand with a grin, "Sa' mi."

CHAPTER 3

Taloga at the Canadian

Their small wagon train seemed to be growing at nearly every stop, and little Butterfly was a welcome addition to the family, she right away took to Nora and Noah and already turning out to be a big help by gathering firewood for the women. It was good dry firewood, the size needed for a cooking campfire. With Ethan driving the wagon a half a day, Nora was able to have time to work on cutting and sewing a dress for Butterfly, to get her out of the rags she was wearing. Noah and Butterfly was becoming fast inseparable friends and was able to understand each other well, as when left alone, most kids are able to do.

Cleo Springs was basically due west of Tulsa about 5 days, that is the next lay-over if all goes well and should hopefully take only about five days or perhaps less. They had heard some word before leaving Tulsa that a few scattered, but roving bands of Indian's were on the warring trail; but they had no choice but to push on. Anyway they were forewarned, so they could be alert.

Their first day out of Tulsa was basically uneventful, they had made their 40 miles with ease and was quite satisfied. That evening after supper Ethan, Joe and I decided to go over the map again, to refresh our memories. Joseph noticed they were going a bit out of their way, by going through Cleo Springs.

"Captain Dan, I've been through that area and Cleo Springs is most time brackish, horses don't even like to drink it as it has a bad aroma and taste, but is said not to be poisoned, just not really fresh. I can suggest a better way, if ya'll will hear me out."

"Joe," I said, "Your a pardner and as important as anyone here on our this trip, if you have a better way, we want to hear it."

"Ok, well I am familiar with this particular area, some years back, and at this place we are now at, it would be much better to swing slightly south and head for the nearest place on the Canadian River, there is a small town on the south side of the Canadian called Taloga. They have a ferry there to cross the river. The waters good, and I think it would save us about a days travel time."

"Damn Joe, that sounds good to me; but is there an actual trail or road there from here, do you know Joe?"

"Don't know positive Cap'n how good the trail would be, but it is passable or was a few years back. But our wagons are sturdy, the horses are strong and I don't think we would have any trouble...years back, the Indians didn't even use that trail, but crossed it many times."

"Well Ethan, I think we should try it, damn sure can't hurt us any, especially if it's shorter and possibly no Indians to contend with."

"Ok that settles it then." Ethan said, "but I think Joe and Charlie should be the first scouts in the morning for at least half a day.

"Fine with me," Joe said, "But the main thing we need to be watchful for is Indians; but let me explain that. Ya'll remember that Oklahoma is an Indian Nation, there are many tribes that have been moved there on reservations and are not at all happy about it. There are still tribes like the Caddos and Wichita that were actually the original tribes in Oklahoma, and when the government relocated other tribes there, there have been problems and the Caddos and Wichita have mostly been run out and the main focus now is on tribes such as the Comanche and Kiowa. They refused to settle on reservations and become dirt farmers. They are proud hunters and maybe you've heard of Quanah Parker, he refused to sign the 'Medicine Lodge Treaty,' and refused to surrender to the white man. So it's particularly important to be on the lookout. Yet I've heard some good things about him as well."

Charlotte and Joe left a half hour before the others did. Joe taking the lead, as he was partly familiar with the old trail, and Charlie to his right flank. About two hours into their scouting they both came upon a lake at different points, so Charlie decided to cut up towards where Joe should be, but to her surprise, she found more than just Joe. Joe was being held in a circle of Indians, that didn't appear to be all to friendly, yet he was not tied or had weapons pointed at him.

Rebecca was contemplating what she should do, when at that moment it was decided for her; she was grabbed from behind by an Indian and forced to go towards the group where Joe was. When reaching the circle, she was shoved to the ground, and stood over so as not to be able to move. Joe attempted to come to my aid but was forced back. It appeared that Joe had been caught only minutes before I was, and was trying to talk to them, and finally one young buck stepped forward and asked in faltering English,

"What say you, why you to come to here, this be our land? Whacha you wan do?"

"We are only passing through this land to go to the river, three, maybe four days more we go to river called Canadian. We mean no harm to anyone."

"My name be Pecos, brother to Quanah, he have much heartache as white man always take what do not belong to them. We do not like land you Chief want us to be diggers, we are hunters and do not go to reservation. What say you black man, this be you woman?"

"Yes Pecos, she is my woman, and I do not blame you to not like white Chief. If you will let us pass through your land here and take some water from your lake, we will then move on and not take what you do not want us too?"

"Maybe she not be you woman, I do not think so. We have scouted you for a night and you do not go into blanket with her at night."

"Ok, yes that is true, she is not my woman, but I said yes in hopes you would not harm her, believing she is my woman."

"We talk not so important of things, we let you pass through but we need white man medicine now. Whachu think?"

"In our small wagon train we have a woman who knows some white man medicine, but is not a doctor, maybe she will be able to help." Joe was eager to add.

"Yes to you, we go to fetch your white woman medicine... she make well." Pecos gestured to his small band to let Charlotte up and not to harm either of them.

This was no small matter, this Indian believed any white man medicine would cure any ailment, and Daisy had only practiced midwifing and various ailments of her own family and small community where she lived. Now Pecos wanted to go meet our small wagon train and escort us back here to attend an ailment, disease or whatever the problem was with his, what turned out to be his daughter. Charlotte and Joe both could understand his desperation. At least we were not being threatened, he just needed help and didn't know what else to do when he spotted us on the trail, and didn't know how to approach us without us thinking we were being attacked.

Charlie suggested that he and only two of his braves go back with us so as not to alarm anyone. Pecos agreed to this but wanted one of them to stay here, to insure their own safety; and Joe was elected to stay. Charlotte would accompany them back to their small wagon train to explain what the problem was and to hurry or just let Daisy go back with them in all haste.

As Charlotte and three Indians were first seen from a distance, their first thought of course was she had been kidnapped and was being held hostage, so the Indians could easily approach in safety. Pecos told Charlotte to go on ahead while he and the two men with him stayed behind, so as to let them know no harm had been or would be made upon her. Charlie spurred her horse forward into a gallop and cheers went up and Ethan rode out to meet her. Ethan waved for the Indians to approach. At the wagon's Charlie quickly explained the situation and what was needed. This was as close to Indians the party had been and was attracted to them immediately. They did not appear to be savages and was not wearing the fearsome war paint they all expected.

Daisy exclaimed, "What can I possibly do, I am not a doctor and have no doctor medicines. I only have laudanum and a bit of cinnamon."

"Well Daisy, it certainly won't hurt for you to look at this young Indian woman, and try to diagnosis her condition the best you can. Especially under the circumstances. We're kinda in a bind."Arriving in the Indian camp at the lake about a half hour later, Daisy was led with haste directly to Pecos's sister. She was obviously in great pain and Daisy told Charlotte to fetch the laudanum, knowing that would kill most of the pain and give her a chance to further explore for her pain. In five minutes after consuming a half a glass of the tincture of opium, she stopped turning and writhing around and grabbing her lower stomach area. Daisy probed that area and suggested she had severe stomach cramping due to menstrual problems.

"Charlotte go look in the wagon and see if you can find the cinnamon, it's in a small salt shaker that I have plugged the top with a bit of cloth, also bring some sugar."

After Daisy made a solution of cinnamon and sugar, she fed this to the girl along with a small dose of the laudanum again. Half and hour later, the young woman was sitting up with no pain. Pecos was happy, actually everyone was congratulating Daisy for her quick remedy, but she cautioned them to wait for a few hours, that by morning symptoms of what she suspected was her ailment should be completely gone. If Daisy would have had the woman drink more laudanum she would have been tranquilized perhaps for several hours. Still, Pecos was happy and wanted to reward Daisy for what he thought saved his daughter, he asked what he could do for her in return.

"Mr. Pecos, is this your permanent camp or are you traveling like we are?" Daisy asked.

It took several hand signals, and more gesturing from Dan before Pecos understood fully what Daisy was asking. Finally, after a long pause Pecos said,

"I tink so maybe we go Tao's, whacha tink." His English being very rough, but was much better than our trying to speak Comanche.

"So then you will escort us to Texas, be our guide and protectors?"

"You much good healer, we pass you Tao's, eh...whacha tink. We go morrow."

So now our sojourn has grown to a respectable size with both a guide and protection from other marauders or unfriendly Indians. Daisy wanted to check up on her young patient, and was not at all surprised to see her sitting up and eating soup. It was a turkey and wild vegetable soup with a light broth, actually the aroma was very pleasing. Probably one of the best things for her. She wanted me to taste it and with a nice smile ladled me out a wooden bowl full. It was absolutely delicious with a spicy taste I was unfamiliar with.

But the main thing it seemed she had passed her menstrual problem, which of course I was very glad of. Now this was Cynthia Parker's granddaughter, so I felt honored. I think everyone both east and west of the Mississippi had heard of her, that she was captured from her Texas home by the Comanches at age 9. Can you imagine the terror she first felt and later Chief Peta Nacona married her, and gave her the name Nadua. She had sons

& daughters and the first was Quanah, 2nd son was Pecos and a daughter named Topsana (Prairie Flower) that died of an illness in 1863; and Cynthia Ann (Nadua) died in 1870.

After several attempts to actually have a conversation with her, she sent for a young boy, in his early teens, he had learned the English language quite well on the reservation. Through translation we had an interesting conversation. Her name was Aiyana, which means 'Forever Flowering,' and leave the first 'A' silent for pronunciation. Her mother Cynthia Ann (Nadua) had named her before she died. She asked my name and I of course said 'Daisy,' which was a flower also. She smiled and put her hand to her heart, gesturing we were sisters.

We continued our talk for about an hour...and learned much about each other. Then finally I ask our young translator if he would mind being our translator while on the trip...He was enthusiastic about it. So it was settled. Finally, getting back to our camp, it was time to start preparing supper, we had more to prepare for now, a total of eight. Noah and Butterfly started feeding the horses and cow, waiting to be milked. Butterfly, suggested giving what milk we didn't need to the Indians so it wouldn't be wasted. Daisy was totally delighted to see her husband Daniel so happy that things were going so smoothly and now that they had a translator, it was even better.

Pecos and Daniel was talking freely now, exchanging idea's, but what was even better, they were becoming fast and good friends. Daniel produced the hand drawn map they had and showed it to Pecos (Pecan). Pecos studied it for a time, shook his head no.

"Do not you go to Taloga, it be much bad. Better you go Camargo to be north of river. I show always best way."

"Pecos, you are our guide, I trust you, so you take us the safest way on through the Llano Estacado. Is that not your homeland anyway, that you would know best of all?"

"Yes, that be homeland and brother Quanah there he be now. But still many Kiowa, not so friendly with white-eyes or Comanches, also some Comancheros to roam in Palo Duro, which is south of where we go; but maybe so we go much more north of Palo Duro, much big canyon to get lost."

The next couple of days went smoothly other than some areas that were difficult for the wagons to proceed. It appeared the Indians were frustrated however, that the wagons could not travel faster. Yet it gave time for some of us to become friends and even close to some of the Indians. Joseph was often times seen hanging close to Aiyana with It a the boy translator then later the boy wasn't seen, but Joe and Aiyana were still riding next to each other. The bond between them appeared to develop quickly, and then even in the evenings they sought each other out; most times eating together, sharing food and actually holding hands. Aiyana was about 35 years of age, very pretty and Joe somewhere in his middle to late forties, a handsome man and they made a good looking couple. This closeness of the two obviously was not lost to Pecos either, and one evening after supper Pecos came into the camp to visit with both Daniel and Joseph, and they could see Aiyana was about ten paces behind, being very timid and sat down cross legged that same distance away. She sat there quietly, a small bundle in her hand, with head bowed downward. Pecos was offered a small cup of whiskey to sip on and pleasantries were exchanged. Finally Pecos opened the line of conversation:

"Meester Dan, you be Chief you tribe, I do come you now cause my seester Aiyana wish to couple with you Joe. Whacha tink so maabee? She say so Mister Joe want to have her too."

"Ah yes Pecos, I too have noticed how they have become one in heart, (placing his hand over his heart) and wish to be together. But it is not for me to say. Mister Joseph is his own man and I cannot speak for him or say yea or nay, to such a union. You may speak directly to Joseph."

Pecos looked over at Joseph and said, "Whacha say Meester Joseph, wan take my seester Aiyana to couple?"

"Joe looked over at Aiyana, then at Daniel and finally to Pecos, "Yes Chief Pecos, I do want Aiyana, I will care for her and give her many sons and daughters for you to be proud of and it shall bind our peoples together. Yet at present time, I have nothing to offer you in return."

I thought about this for a moment, then sad "Joe, the six outlaw horses are as much yours as anyone's so offer these to him, and I don't think Ethan or Charlotte would have a problem with it either, plus the saddles and tack...I'm sure he would accept. And, I'm thinking you need to do this right away before that little Indian girl starts a war dance."

"Well guess your right Dan, if you think it's alright with Ethan and Charlie."

Chief Pecos, may I present to you 6 fine horses and saddles for your sister? They are not worthy of Aiyana, but it's all I have."

"Ho, so we have fine dance and feast this night, we make you call marry?"

"Yes Chief, I want to marry your sister Aiyana this night." Joe asserted.

We had no preacher or any man of the cloth on this trip, except of course Ethan, but was afraid to reveal that in front of the Indians as they always thought the white-man preacher wanted to change their religion like they tried to do on the reservation; so they were married Comanche style, by the Comanche Holy man; none of us would have understood it except for our young translator Ita. The feast and dance and story telling lasted nearly all night. The singing was surprisingly done by us men, Ethan and Joseph, and yes I joined in as well with a marriage love song...But I was especially delighted to hear Charlotte sing a love ballad for the newly wed couple; we had no idea her voice was like a breath of fresh air on a beautiful spring morning. The Indians were very respectful and even did some chanting as well. The festivities lasted nearly all night and one by one people were disappearing to either go to bed or just pass out...I didn't think we'd get an early start in the morning, I'll just let the lovebirds alone and let them sleep till they wake-up on their on.

It was nearly mid-morning when we were finally able to pull out, everyone was at least partly hung over, if not by drink, at least by all the late night activities, that we were not used too. Of course the 30 or so Indians were ready in a moments notice, but we finally pulled out again by mid-morning, obviously a late start but at least a start. With Pecos, and two of his scouts as outriders, coupled with myself and Charlie and the rest of the Indians surrounding our small caravan of just 3 wagons, we felt secure, safe and comfortable. Shortly we'd be pulling into Texas land and the Llano Estacado, (The Staked Plains). Each wagon had three 30 gallon wooden barrels of water and the Indians each had their own deer or goat stomachs, that were used as water bags. Actually goats had four stomachs and a deer had four chambers to their stomachs and the Indians knew how to utilize these valuable innards to best ability. Each Indian could carry approximately 2 gallons of water in this method over his shoulder or thrown across his horse's withers, if he was riding, and often times would carry two such water bags; one especially for his horse, as the Comanches were known horsemen and cared for the horses well. Joseph was driving Nora's wagon while Nora, Aiyana and Aponi were getting well acquainted with each other. Nora was making both Aiyana and Aponi dresses out of material she had bought in Tulsa. At the same time Aiyana was making an Indian shirt and leggings for her Joe, out of soft tanned skins her brother Chief Pecos had given her. Aponi was learning from both women and would help at a given notice. They were comfortable with each other, all doing what they loved. I noticed that if you leave kids and women alone for a period of time, they could become close friends, united in everyday things or could also become embittered towards each other... I was grateful that these women and children wanted to be friends even though a barrier of different languages existed. Men on the other hand had strong objections to anything they personally was unfamiliar with; yet some were reasonable enough to listen to another side of a story. So far our trip had been relatively without serious incident, and now especially with the Comanches along with us, we should be better off, thanks to Daisy even with her limited medical skills and knowledge.

CHAPTER 4

Llano Estacado

Two days of bumpity bump and a single night we finally arrived at the eastern edge of the Llano Estacado. Even feared by the Comanches as they never knew what weather changes might occur and this was spring time and weather was very unpredictable during this time of year. Chief Pecos explained that one minute it was beautiful weather, then the next it could be snowing or even worse, the big whirling wind could evolve at any given time. Sometimes it may rain for days on end, other times then the sun could be beating down on you unmercifully, with no let up and you would pray for any change. The rolling planes looked like golden fields of unlimited and swaying tall grasses, like softly plunging waves coming ashore on a coast line. It was bitterly beautiful. Not a rise in the ground, nor a hill to be observed, just flat, but prairie dogs had made it their home, and their burrows were by the thousands, and they posted sentries at various strategic places to watch out for predators of any kind, be it desert-hawks, snakes, coyotes or wolves; of which there were plenty of all these.

So we were forewarned, and Pecos offered another way, but it would take us about three maybe four days extra. We didn't like that idea, yet Pecos was determined to tell us about it nevertheless; as he continued to say we could turn south and go through the Cap Rock and Palo Duro Canyons. He says maybe even six more days it would take; but we elected to keep going basically due west, mainly because as an after thought Pecos said it really wasn't any safer and some Kiowa or Apache could be hiding among the many dead-end canyons, plus we still have various predators to watch for. As it turned out he suggested this be-

41

cause his brother Quanah might be there and it had been many moons passed since seeing him. But staying on the high staked plains all we had to do each morning was put our lead wagons tongue pointed west; if you didn't most immigrants wouldn't know which way was which because you had few, if any land-marks to go by unless you were familiar with the stars. Further, there was very little water available, and if you did find some it could be so full of alkali that it was unfit to drink. This was no country for the weak in spirit and less in determination; this is a mean country and only the strong survive...I stopped riding, just sitting on my horse, rolled a bull-Durham, forgot to light it, but sat there thinking over everything Pecos and his scouts had told me. Was it worth putting my family, and close friends through all of this? But I had taken an oath and a man is only as good as his word, and I knew Ethan to feel the same, so be damned to hell and high-water or no water and big winds, snakes and other predators or unfriendly Indians....we damn sure would get through this. A gust of wind brought me out of my revelry, as it blew the tobacca makin's out of my lips. I looked up just in time to see a dust cloud in the distance. Who could be coming to raise that big of a dust cloud... I nudged my horse blackjack, softly in the flanks and slowly advanced towards whatever was making that dust bowl. Soon I could see a black mass swiftly coming directly at me...what the hell... and I'll be damned it's a herd of buffalo stampeding and coming straight for me and the wagons. Pecos didn't warn me about buffalo stampeding. I turned my Cayuse around and gigged her in the flanks and raced her as fast as possible to the wagons. I noticed off to my right two Comanches running their horses too. As I approached the lead wagon I yelled at Joe to turn left and get those horses mov-ing. Daisy and Nora followed closely and I motioned for all of them to stop after about a couple of hundred yards...Jumped off my horse and yelled to Joe to secure all the horses to wagons as tight as possible so they would be unable to rear-up or pull hard on the harnesses and ropes. The stampede was insight now and not far from us and hoping I got them far enough out of their di-rect path that we or our livestock would not be harmed.

I hollered, "Get your rifles out and cocked, no time for any-thing else...any of those beasts get to close, shoot to kill."

Joe hollered back, "How in hell did you manage to stampede a whole herd of buffalo, there must be a hundreds or more?"

"Well hell Joe, I don't know, just lucky I guess."

Just then a couple of buffalo swerved towards us and both Joe and I shot, and I think I heard a couple of other shots sound and two buffalo went down, and that seemed to turn them away from us, at least for now. The noise sounded like ten thousand horses pulling loaded wagons to the limits or worse. Then suddenly, they turned again and this time right at us, it seemed the hole herd would run right through us and the stock...Aponi ran out in front of them waving her arms, totally unafraid, obviously believing she could turn the tide. I jumped on Blackjack and ran towards her, needing to get ahead of her and go with the flow of the herd and get near enough to grab her up in my arms. Thank god, he must have been with me, as she clung to me in desperation as I reached for her and I headed Blackjack in another direction, hoping the heard would follow us. The herd passed and we found three more fallen buffalo, and the Indians had killed those, but in the doing that's what caused them to turn towards us; but thankfully no harm done, and we all were happy with the fresh kill. We decided to make camp here for the night, trail dress the buffalo, cut us off some steaks and roasts, cut some strips for jerky and we could dry the hides by securing them to the wagon covers. However, I was concerned why Aponi acted the way she did in running out in front of the buffalo...so after we were all settled down, had eaten well, and on my 2nd cup of coffee, sitting around the campfire I ask Aponi why she did that.

"Aponi, why did you run out in front of those stampeding buffalo? You might have been killed child."

Aponi looked at me for a moment, tears were clouding her eyes and she finally said, "I have no ever been touched by man yet in marriage way, so I be pure, no? Sauk Indian say pure child can no be hurt by buffalo...now I know no so true."

It was so sad to see the expression on her face with tears running down her cheeks, I simply could not help myself and picked this believing child up and held her close. Her little arms circled my neck tightly and held on. With her voice choking the sobs back she managed to say, "May be Sauk God no so good!"

The women all were crying out loud, such a true believing child had just been abandoned by a god she was taught to believe in. Her world crashed...Aiyana reached out and took herf rom me. If you've never seen grown men cry, then you should have seen us. She clung to Aiyana speaking in a native dialect, and we can only imagine what she was saying. With huge lumps in our throats, we all tried to hold back tears but to no avail. I wondered how long she had been holding all that back, thru supper and till finally I ask that simple question; which turned out, not to be so simple. I thought to myself that she was certainly now our child and would never abandon her and too, thinking back how we found her...she was seeking love and protection, by hiding inside one of our wagons. So now she would not have to face the world alone...Morning came early with the dawn appearing before we thought it should; but we got ourselves around, ate a fine breakfast, hitched the wagons and now faced the hazardous journey across the Llano Estacado. Chief Pecos and two of his scouts lead the way, with myself and Charlotte trailing not far behind. We all had enough buffalo to last for several days without spoiling. Dried jerky, and the Indian women told our ladies how to make pemmican, which was extremely nutritious, made of dried pounded meat, berries and nuts. Aiyana showed the women how to make this, with of course Aponi, Noah and Ita gathering the wild berries and nuts as we traveled along. We also learned of many native edible plants, that our women would never have thought of. One evening before supper Aiyana made some 'sweet pinion muffins,' and we gorged ourselves on these after supper with more coffee.

I rode up to Pecos and asked, "When do we reach the area called Tao in this Staked Plains?"

Pecos looked at me for a minute, finally saying, "We to it now Mester Dan, we be there for may be 3 may be 4 hour by sun. It be after noon time now by white-eye way."

"Will we find any water at all along the way Pecos?"

"May be so, but she no good to water drink, many such playa lake filled by rain, yet is just sit there and gets turn to black and you get (rubbing stomach) no feeling preety good, you know."

"So we should not even let our livestock drink it?"

"Sure you can do that, but horses bad for no good too. You bring much water, but be spare with it and give to horses first as you no to finish to run out of water."

So we were now actually in the feared Llano Estacado and looking out over the terrain you could see a sea of grass waving by a slight breeze like soft waves in the ocean coming ashore. It was endless beauty, the sea of grass, but hiding mystery's we have yet to learn; difficult to imagine that this sea of grass could possibly present such potentially dangerous things within it's confines. What could possibly lurk beneath the waves that we could not see. The wagon's stopped and we all gazed at this phenomenon, the beauty was beyond imagination of any poet or song. We watered the horses, and took small drinks ourselves. The Comanches doing the same, but also spreading out in a flat line, not bunched up or in single file...it seemed they were searching for something, only later to learn this was their way of scouting the terrain as it was nearly impossible to see below the tops of the buffalo grass. Yet they also had scouts far out in advance of our small wagon train and we would be warned of any and all present dangers. Except for the prairie-dog holes, we experienced no problems this first day on the Staked Plains; so this first night we camped in high spirits, and the Comanches also gathered around us...and we all shared a fine meal of buffalo hump roasts, a thick rich gravy with potatoes, camas root, and some wild carrots and onions.

Someone started singing and all gathered around...even the Comanches, then Daisy came to me and asked to dance...so how could I refuse? Soon Ethan and Nora joined in and I noticed in the background Joe was showing Aiyana the steps and soon joined with us, but then in the middle was Noah and Butterfly having a great time. Charlotte was strumming on her banjo and even though we were dancing we were also still singing. Then suddenly the banjo stopped and we saw Charlie had been swung into the dance and by one of the young braves doing a dance not so unlike our own...as the Comanche drums sounded loudly to the same beat we had been singing. No whiskey was insight and none was being drank, so we all felt comfortable that no trouble would ensue. But no sooner had that thought went through my mind and suddenly two Comanche warriors had knives drawn and were slashing at each other, the drums stopped and various forms of yelling abruptly started. Charlie was standing alone, and it turned out that one of the young braves was the one that had been dancing with her. I sought out Chief Pecos and found him with arms folded across his chest watching this fight intently. I hurried over to him and he simply made a pausing gesture, then said,

"It be no little problem, only one to get wan to be dance with pale-hair. I stop soon, no you worry."

So I just stood there and watched helplessly, hoping there would be no blood or killing. I didn't want to even try to interfere with Comanche ways.

Finally Charlie stepped in between and the two stopped momentarily, she then took both young braves by the arms, smilingly, one on each arm and started dancing with both at the same time. The drummers took up the beat and the Indians started chanting...all was again well, as other Indians joined in, so we did also. Finally it stopped, we all sat down and Joe started singing to the rhythm of Charlie's banjo as she took to the strings and a single Indian drummer kept excellent time to that rhythm. The evening ended peacefully and was now time to sleep, there was a full moon out, which we had not noticed earlier and it is said that this brings out bad behavior with some people and the Indians all believed this way. Off in the distance we could hear the wailing's of wolves and even coyotes through the stillness of the night, but carried for miles on a slight breeze. This amazed me to think about the fact there were no or at least few places with good water and how could these predators survive in this wasteland. However, fortunately this was spring time and Llano Estacado had experienced some rains so the Playa Lakes, by the hundreds were still full and supports good water, which fed not only migratory birds & animals but some that made the area their own permanent habitat. Also there were fowl such as the Road Runner, Burrowing Owls and animals like Pronghorn Antelope, and predators of Coyote and some Gray Wolves. Though sparse, there were a few Mesquite trees, Shin Oaks and Creosote bush, Prickly Pear, and also were called "Tunas, in abundance as they required very little water. So obviously Chief Pecos had not thought about it being the rainy season or perhaps he said what he did because it had not rained or at least not yet this spring. So far our luck had been good, even with the herd of buffalo nearly running us over, but even that turned out to be fortunate as we had fresh meat; milk cow was doing well, and the children finding various wild vegetables, roots and tubers, that both Aponi and Aiyana pointed out...God help us our luck to continue to be with us.

I thought about all these things, but knew it was time for all of us to turn in and get some sleep, so I told Pecos and all our group it was time to stop the festivities. Pecos said he would post the guards out tonight, so we all could get some sleep.

Along about midnight, I felt a cold breeze ruffle the blankets and looked out of the wagon to see the stars had disappeared behind heavy scattered clouds and the moonlight was being hidden from time to time...wind was picking up heavier now, the moon had completely disappeared, and off in the distance I saw a flash of light, then minutes later thunder. Seems the rain that seldom comes was coming after all, and I wasn't sure if this was a good sign or a bad sign at this time; but knew we had to bring the livestock closer to the wagons and short rope them tightly. Even Major jumped up into Nora's Wagon and as I got out of the wagon I noticed Ethan and Joe was out already. Each had the same idea in mind as I did, so we worked together. Wind was picking up very hard now, rain was heavier, lightning and thunder was much closer...horses were acting up, pulling on the ropes that we secured to the wagons. There was simply no other protection, no trees or tall bushes to get behind to help guard against the wind and pelting rain, but the animals were smart enough to turn their backsides to the storm and us men jumped back into our respective wagons. Then my thoughts turned towards the Comanches, what do they do for protection? However, nothing I could do to help them. The storm continued to get worse, the thunder and lightning appeared to be directly overhead and was impossible to sleep.

The wind rocking the wagons and trying to blow the wagon covers off, but fortunately we had secured the buffalo hides on top of the canvas coverings sufficiently; still the rain leaked in upon us a little and the howling of the wind was nearly unbearable. I can only imagine what torment our Indian friends were

going through, with no protection at all. The wind and rain
steadily pummeled us all with no seemingly let up, lightning
flashed and seemed like noon time, and the sound of thunder
rolled continuously as if we were again being stampeded by a
thousand buffalo. The women were frightened and if truth be
known, so was us men. We feared what we might see or not see
when this storm subsided and we could venture outside. What
seemed like days but was only a couple of hours, we could see
daylight trying to usher into our world and the fierce storm was
slowly fading away.

As I stepped outside of the covered wagon, dimly could I see
through the early morning dawn the ravages of the torrential
storm that invaded us. I hadn't been asleep at all and don't
think anyone else of our small cavalcade would have either. The
mud was inches deep under-neath the carpet of grass that was
lying flat instead of standing high and waving as a sea of grass.
Each step I took felt and sounded like I was sloshing in a flooded
pigpen; though I suppose I should be grateful, as our tethered
horses were still standing, even the milk cow. Major was already
out and sniffing the saturated grounds and also with his nose
high to smell what lingering scents may be in the slight breeze
coming from the west, sending a chill through the air, yet I knew
the sun would soon be out drying the wet ground and very possibly making a scorching day of it...but would be very muggy. Major barked and I looked up to see both Ethan and Joe walking
toward me, then Nora, Daisy and even Charlotte emerged from
the little protection that was offered them in the wagons; Aiyana
and even little Butterfly came out and Noah was close behind. It
seems all was accounted for of which I was very grateful. My
next concern was that of the animals, as without them, our continued journey would be extremely difficult to say the least.
Again Major barked, then turned to show me Pecos and three of
his Indian scouts were approaching.

"Ho, Meester Dan, I too see you and familee is did okayyy
with this leetlle storm."

"Yes Pecos, we did fine it seems, but how did you all do with
no cover?"

"Ah sooo, Meester Dan, we make da horse to she lay down
and throw blankets and skins over us all and we do keep preety

dry to lay down next to horses under skins. Theese she happen before some times. So whacha tink Meester Dan, canno go with wagon yet till wind & dasun she too dry the undergrass, or may bee so much trouble wid da wheel."

"Yes, I think you are right Chief Pecos, but we can stake the horses and cow out away from this mud, so they can graze and have fresh moisture from the wet grass."

So, it was obvious that we were were stuck here until the ground dried out some or we could easily get stuck in the mud-holes...The playa lakes should be full to brimming and the water good, at least for a while, but this of course brings out the preda-tors, so we had all of that to watch for now. Still it was good that this was so far the worst that has happened that we had no con-trol over. The women fixed a good breakfast and we helped dry out things that had gotten wet, re-stretched the wagon canvasses and buffalo hides and the sun came out blazing hot.

It was time to hitch the horses and pull out. The Comanches had their scouts out in front and I with Noah was doing a lead only about a mile ahead, with Joe and Aiyana taking a left flank. We came to a point on the Canadian River about evening meal time and decided to make camp for the night. Not much progress for this day, but I was thankful that everyone was safe.

After a good supper we were all in good cheer, sippin on a last cup of coffee and Joe started strumming on his guitar and sign-ing to his new wife. Well Ethan, me and the ladies joined in; then we all kinda took turns singing our own favorite songs, the campfire was burning down low to the embers and needed some of the tall buffalo grass bunched and tied into a knot, and that would be enough for now. The kids loved it when we started singing and joined in the best they could and so funny that Ma-jor would start his howling as everyone laughed and just carried on. It was good to be happy and we all thought of each other as family, looking out and helping each other where needed. Well, time to call it a night again and we knew we should post guards even though the Comanches always did; to be watchful for any-thing out of the ordinary, a strange or unfamiliar sound we were not accustomed too, a shadow that moved, the horses acting up and/or Major growling or fussing uncomfortably.

It was now morning again, just day-light and the sun is already unbearable and knowing it could even get hotter did not make our stance or frame of mind very tolerable to each other. Wagons hitched, breakfast being eaten as we were riding, but it was the women folk who made it bearable as they all had smiles and went about their duties with an agreeable attitude. Bless each and every one of our women folk. As the day progressed into mid-morning the sun was beating down upon us so fiercely we wanted it to start raining again; however, we did see from time to time a couple of clouds drifting by, some birds gorging themselves in the playa lakes, that soon would both dry up from natural evaporation and from the animals taking in all the water they possibly could. This soon after the rain there were even new grasses and flower buds emerging, and you could see bee colonies, as a dark massive cloud in the sky, only to settle down at waters edge. In places where some small very shallow playa lakes had been it was still soggy and could give us problems if we were to become mired down in any of them; so as lead scouts out in front it was our job to make sure our wagons did not get rutted in. But this also gave me time to reflect on a tune that has been rambling around inside my head ever since we left Missouri. Yet, I never could quite seem to finish it...and it was again playing in my head, taking my mind off my business when suddenly I stopped short, Major growled and Blackjack backed away.

I looked around but did not see anything suspicious to warrant Major & Blackjack's actions, I tried to urge Blackjack forward, but he refused to budge and even backed away a few more feet...but Major was slowly inching forward, so I followed his line of site and lordy, lordy about 12 feet in front of us was a nest of snakes, didn't know if they were fighting or coupling. They didn't exactly look like rattlers, but had similar markings only the markings were smaller and darker. I got off of Blackjack and lead him away a few more feet and ground haltered him, then cautiously went back so I could see the snakes more clearly. They appeared to be like some we had in Missouri, about the same size about two feet or longer and upon closer inspection, their color pattern consists of a grey or tan ground- color with a row of large brownish to black blotches or spots down the center of the back and three smaller rows of alternating spots down each side.

Aw yeah, these were desert or prairie massasauga and were extremely venomous and normally we call them pit-vipers; yet the strangest thing about them as compared to all other snakes is that they had vertical pupils. Further it has heat-sensing pits on each side of its small head, the scales are keeled and the anal scale is single...we used to catch a lot of these in Missouri as a kid. Well I backed away now not wanting to confront or disturb them as you never knew which direction they might scatter. I need to mark this area with a red flag and make a pointer to go around. As I was doing this one of Pecos's scouts came upon me and I pointed these out to him; He was thankful for the warning, but had disturbing news for me. Pecos sent word that they could no longer guide and protect us the rest of the way, that it was necessary to join his brother in the Palo Duro and the whole band was leaving immediately. It was a matter of honor. Yet he sent the word to continue to Camargo, conserve your water even though the playa lakes were brimming full, but to follow the Canadian River until it starts to go south where some quick rapids are and just go straight, do not continue to follow the river at that point. Continue due west and by and by you come to small settlement you call Sunray, that is at the north Palo Duro River, then angle just a bit north. You be okay then.

The scout gave salute then and rode off. I was anxious to get away from this area where the snakes were and would alter our course accordingly; and of course thankful for the advice from the scout. I started to head back to our small wagon train, to tell of our new situation.

CHAPTER 5

Palo Duro River

I raced back to the wagons to tell them of my news only to find out they too had a scout visit them with the same information. So then I informed them of the snake infested area and we swung the wagons a bit north to avoid that troublesome spot, not thinking of the possibility that those snakes could travel to a different location. It was spring here with rains and it was also mating time for snakes as well with other animals, so they would be more dangerous than usual. I alerted everyone to be extremely alert and cautious.

Thinking ahead, I wished I knew more about this Durango I knew they were building a railroad, that is to say, that the Rio Grand Rail and Denver Rail jointly merged to build this railroad so they could more easily ship the gold & silver ore, without thieving gangs stealing, and possibly killing innocent people in the doing. They needed a rail-head to do this and Durango was perfect for that. I knew it was a tent city and according to the Governor in Georgia, the bit of information he could pass on to me was not much at all.

They had elected a Sheriff and had a woman for a deputy, but no holding cell for whoever may be law-breakers. The railroad was the main force behind this young growing lawless town; and now it was up to me to bring law and order there. Glad I have Ethan as an under-cover deputy, and knew I could count on Joe, to help out if needed. But a thought just now occurred to me, Charlotte was an excellent shot, was street wise and seemed to be mature beyond her young years. Well, it seems I need to talk to both Ethan & Charlotte about this first off. Saloons is where you hear what people are doing, there's always bragging and some get drunk and their mouth starts flapping about their deeds. I need someone on the inside to hear all this chatter. Charlotte, as pretty as she is would be perfect for this, also as an under-cover deputy. Why, she could give a guy a few drinks and get him to talking and learn what's going on in no time. But not likely Ethan would want to approve of this, still I will talk to them.

We avoided the snakes as it turned out and now it was getting time to stop and set up camp and needed to post sentries out tonight as we no longer had the Comanches to do that. Major could help in this respect, he seemed to love working. He was one smart dog or should I say wolf and seemed to know what was needed when.

We got camp set up, the ladies were busy preparing supper, Noah and Butterfly were attending the milk cow and getting ready to milk her. Aiyana was also busy, to Joe's delight, by her knowledge of local wild vegetables that she was gathering and showing the ladies how to make flat bread.

After a fine meal and sippin on a coffee, I thought of bringing up my ideas to Ethan about using Charlotte as an undercover deputy.

"Ethan, and you too Charlotte, I have an idea to present to you I hope you'll give consideration too."

"Well Augie spit it out, we've never held anything back from each other, but how would it effect Charlie?"

"It is in a way a mite dangerous Ethan, or possibly could be. That's why I'm hesitant about it, but I think it would work and help get rid of those gangs in Durango easier and a lot quicker.""Well go ahead with the idea, but surely I still don't see how she could fit in to something like that."

"Wait a minute, if I'm included in this, why are you two talking as if I'm not here." Charlie queried.

"Your right Charlotte, my apologies. Here's what it's all about. Charlotte I want you to work as an undercover deputy, but to do this you'd have to work in the saloon. Gents half drunk want to always impress a working girl, so they'll brag about what they are doing and how much money they have or make. Often times tip off, being unawares, they'll even tell when and where the next hold-up will take place. This is what I would want you to do Charlotte and I know you can handle yourself."

"Now just a minute there Augie, we've been good friends for many years now, but to ask such a thing of my daughter is just too much. I flatly say no."

"Now you wait a minute Pa, I kind of like the idea and I'm of age now and I grew up on the street without you and the last few years even without Ma, so I certainly have a say in this. Besides I'll be getting a deputies pay, plus making tips from the drinking gents. But first I'd have to see if the saloon-keep would hire me and if I do this I'm going to need some frilly dresses and perfumes."

"Ah ah Charlie honey, you can't mean that, I don't want you having to go to the back room with those drunks and being a .50 cent girl or whatever they get now in a boom town like Durango is. That's not the kind of girl I want you to be."

"Don't worry Pa, even though I only have a bit of experience I know I can handle it and I'll never let or become a girl to take to the back rooms and I 'll let the owner know that up front before he hires me...there are girls that only serve drinks and converse with the gents so they'll buy more drinks and gamble away all their money. I'm sure they already have a bevy of girls working there already in a mining town, that do gladly go to the back rooms."

"But Charlie. I just........"

"Not another word Pa, I'm gona do it if Uncle Augie will get me a few frilly dresses and perfume."

"The least bit of trouble and I would want you to get out of it...no gun play, and both your father, Joe and me will be your back. You can count on that honey. And as we go into the New Mexico territory we will stop in Santa Fe and get you parcels of whatever you think you'll need. As we get closer to Durango we'll stop and load you on stagecoach and you can go into Durango as a working girl by yourself. I think it'll work that way as it'll show you have no connection to us. Are you really up to this honey?"

"You bet I am Uncle Augie, and thanks for putting your trust into me, I'll try to make you proud."

"Well, guess my flat no, just turned into, I have no say."
Ethan whined.

The ladies had all heard the conversation, and obviously were afraid for Charlotte, but kept their thought's to themselves and went about their business. Aiyana was finishing upon the Comanche style clothes she was making for Joe, and was very proud of it, as she showed it to the other women. Nora had also finished the dress for Butterfly, but kept it back not wanting to take away the pride Aiyana felt of her accomplishment. Later would be fine to present it to her. Aponi was learning her English quickly and was always looking for something to do, for not only the ladies but for the men as well and became fast friends with Major, and Major hung out with Noah and Butterfly whenever he was not on guard or scouting.

The next few days passed quickly and fortunately without serious incident and we finally arrived in Santa Fe. Needless to say however, we were damn glad to be out of the fearful Llano Estacado with all of it's dreaded obstacles and luckily we fell into very few of them. All of us needed a break to be sure and Santa Fe seemed to be a likely spot to lay over in. We camped on the outskirts of town, set-up a camp and the women told us men to go on into town have a drink and relax a bit if we wanted, then pick up a few supplies for the train, but that tomorrow they also would go into town to pick-up women things as needed.

So Ethan, Joe and I did just that…We walked into the first saloon we came to named the Palace Saloon & rooms, the music loud and not really very good, but drinking customers weren't really paying attention anyway. We sauntered over to the bar, kind of elbowing our way to get up next to it…"Pardon me friend just wanting to order a couple of drinks, not meaning to jostle you." I said to the man little man I had elbowed."

The little man looked up and over to me, kind of squinted and then exclaimed, "By the Jesus, if it ain't Captain Augie…what the hell Capt., what you doing down here in Santa Fe?"

I looked at this little man closely again, "Well I'll be damned, Is it really you Sarge? Damn I haven't seen you since back in sixty-six. Whata you doing in these parts?"Yup, it's me Cap, I been down here since they all's discovered gold and silver, jus a chasing the rainbow like every other damn fool, but no pot o' gold yet."

Turning to Ethan and Joe I remarked, "Hey, you guys remember Sarge Willis?

"Of course we remember him." Ethan said and Joe nodded and stuck out his hand to the Sarge.

"Been a long time Sarge, good to see ya." Joe said. "So you been chasing the rainbows and still nothing to show for it?"

"Well only enuff to keep body and soul together. Just skiffs and traces, but the bigun has a not come yet. But what you three galoots a doing down to this away?"

Ethan cut in then and answered, "We're on our way to Durango Sarge. Captain Dan here is a new appointed U.S. Marshall and I'm going to open up the Lord's Word to the sinners up there and Joe here just got himself newly married and is gona settle up there with us. We heard Durango was growing and the railroad was gona make it bigger. Maybe a good place to settle down." Making sure not to reveal that he and Joe were undercover deputies.

"Well now don't thata beat all, seems you'll have your hands full with that job Cap'n, or guess I should say Marshall, there a powerful bunch of outlaw gangs up there most betwixt Purgatory and Durango. There's Ouray, Silverton and I don't recalls how many more places just infected with them thar outlaws...It's gona take more than just one Marshall, my old friend. Maybe so you might need another hand, one who knows a bit about the ole trails upun thar. I'm available Mr. Marshall."

"Well Sarge, you just got yourself hired. I need men I'm able to trust, and you'd fit the bill just fine Sarge." Marshall August implied.

Ethan and Joe raised the glasses and exclaimed, "Here's to ya Sarge, glad to have ya join us."

August then added, "We just arrived in those three wagons you may have seen pulling through the street early today and we'll be holding over here a couple of days afore we go on to Durango, and then perhaps you can show us the easiest way to go from here Sarge."

"Aye, yes um I can do that fer shor Marshall and thankee fer the job. Yesum I did a notice them three wagons a plodding though town and might say a passel other folk saw it too, some may be the ones you might be a looking fer. After the robberies, some them outlaws likes to come down heres to Santa Fe to visit with the Ladies of the Night, ifin youse knows what I means."

"Know what you mean Sarge, and thank you for willing to join us, but you know it may be dangerous."

"Why hell Cap'n., seems as though everything you gets involved in is dangerous. Why I recalls the time when youse an..."

"Ok Sarge, we don't need to do the remember whens right now." The Marshall interrupted.

"Lets all have a round to celebrate this reunion Marshal, 'cept I'm a might low on the dinero right now. My apologies gents." Sarge concluded.

"Not a problem Sarge, I got you covered, let's drink up." August was glad to announce.

They had a few more drinks and I asserted we best get back to the women folk, besides its getting dusk now. Come along Sarge, you look like you could use a good meal."

Without argument, they all walked out and headed for the camp; only to be accosted by a ruffian that had a mad on with Sarge and he had two other men siding him with guns and holsters tied down like gunslingers.

"Hey, you there little man, we have a thing to settle we didn't get done the other night."

"Nope, seems to me we settled it afore without guns, now you got two gunslingers to side you? You want my money that you cheated to try to get, and my fists were faster than your gun. Well it was settled then, now you need two would be gunmen to get it. Not a chance."

"Well, then little man, you'll be a pushing daisies up from the bottom then."

"Let'er fly then tinhorn, I'm wearing my hog-leg this time, we'll see who's gona be pushin up daisies."

Just at that moment August saw the unfriendly glint in one of the gunmen's eyes and drew swiftly and down he went, Ethan and Joe had also drawn on the second gunman, but he held his hands high and said, "Not me gents, I'm out of this." And walked away.

Well, Mister Tinhorn, guess that leaves just you and me, as before, but this time with guns ... What you say now?"

Without saying another word, the tinhorn drew against Sarge, an' he had no sooner cleared leather and the tinhorn lay dead. "Damn now," Sarge said, "what a waste, and it was all over twenty dollars he tried to cheat me out of playing four card keno." Just now the Santa Fe Sheriff comes running up, gun drawn, and asks what's going on.

"Sheriff," Sarge interjected, "Ifin you remembers me night afore last that one gent a laying beside ta-other one there was a fighting wit me. Well he didn't like the way I finished it then, and wanted to get at me with guns this time."

"Yes, I do remember you now, but who are these gents?" pointing to me, Ethan and Joe.

"Yesum, this here's U.S. Marshall Daniel August, he caught that other one laying dead, trying to get the drop on me and dropped him dead afore he cleared leather."

"I'll be damned, so your the Marshall I heard tell about, taking over this part of the country. Glad to have you Marshall and welcome. Guess I don't need any further recommendation as to the fault of this killing. I won't even ask for a hearing. Now who are these other two?"

"Well suh, this 'n here is Ethan Kennedy, he's a preacher, sorta, and this here darkie is Joseph Freeman, best damn corporal I ever did have. They's all on their way to Durango."

"Don't guess I need any better witnesses to this killing, seems justified to me and that's the way it'll go down in the books, so you all don't need to worry about it, except for possible kinfolk and how they might take to the news."

"Say Sheriff, mind telling me just how big a territory is assigned to me. Do you know?"

"Far as I know Marshall, it stretches from here to Flagstaff, Arizona and how far north I have no idea, but it's a fair piece, I know that. You'll need several deputies for sure.""I had no idea my area of responsibility was that large, but guess I'll have to work with it. I just now hired Sergeant Willis here. But Sheriff, can you give me an estimate of how many more men I'll need?"

"Nope can't says as how I would know, especially with men that you could completely trust. So leave me out of it Marshall,

I'll continue to police Santa Fe and won't call on you unless I absolutely need your expertise. Is that a deal Marshall?"

"Deal Sheriff, but I may need your help or assistance from time to time, is that a deal as well?"

"Seems we'll be able to work together fine Marshall and soon the telegraph will be completed about the same time the railroad will be finished, so that'll be a help to us both?"

"Bye your leave Sheriff, and thank you." Walking off to camp again.

Arriving back in camp we introduced the Sarge to the lady folk and told them a little of what happened. The ladies welcomed Sarge and handed him a plate laden with a delicious stew and dutch-oven baked bread, good for sopping up the remains of the stew. Coffee was nice and hot with a slight taste and aroma of hickory blended into it, with fresh cream and a tint of sweetener to top it all off.

"Ladies, thankee, best meal I've had in years and I do mean that." Sarge volunteered

That ole tune that had been roaming around in my head for days and days now was doing it again, so I picked up my guitar and started strumming and suddenly it came to me...Charlotte joined in and soon we were all singing. Ole Sarge leaped up and rewarded us with his rendition of a dance. Actually it was pretty good...Knee slapping, high-stepping Sarge but in perfect rhythm. He was really quite a character, but was glad to have him in our little group.

Then I just had to revert back to my special tune and the words just seemed to flow with the strumming of my guitar and everyone sat back and just listened. I finally had somehow finished my song Durango. Everyone clapped and I took my bows...then Joe took his new bride Aiyana, by her hands and led her to the middle of the circle and sang a love ballad to her. She was all smiles and little embarrassed, but took it well, and Joe kissed her in front of everyone. Aiyana ran out of the circle with her hands to her face and Joe followed. Ethan and I had never seen Joe act like this before, so we knew it must truly be in love. Looking over at Charlotte through the dancing flames, it was easy to tell she was a lonely young woman, her smile faded so quickly and she tried to hide it. She was the only woman among our family that did not have a man; I felt so sorry for her, yet there was absolutely nothing I could do about it. Still she was able to keep a stiff upper lip as the saying goes and was more than capable of continuing to pull her own weight. Tomorrow, I will give her money enough to buy those frilly clothes and perfumes to make her appear to be a Lady of the Night.

Sarge spread his bedroll a few feet from the fire and Major hunkered down next to him. This was strange for Major, but apparently had his own reasons for the doing, and perhaps later we would find out his reasons. During the night I noticed Major sniffing around all the wagons and even checking on the perimeter of our wagon area, then go back to lay next to Sarge.

The rest of the night passed without incident, but Ethan must have also woken up from time to time as he mentioned this about Major to me...so we decided something must have been bothering Major. Maybe he didn't quit know what it was either, but was keeping alert. In time we felt, something would happen and Major would be the first to know and be first to stop it.

The dawn of a new day came in slowly, the rustle of early morning chores was evident to all and to not have to hurry around to hitch the team and eat a cold breakfast and drink left over coffee was a warming welcome. This morning, Nora was up making dutch oven bread, Daisy was busy making pancakes and I could see eggs in the basket waiting to be fried, potatoes were peeled, bacon slices to the ready and the large 15 inch cast -iron skillet was on the grill. Fresh coffee sent out a come and get me aroma. Aiyana was combing Aponi's hair and soon would be braided with a part in the middle; and us lazy men folk sitting around watching the ladies preparing our breakfast. Yet the ladies were smiling and going about their chores with ease.

The morning went well, mid-morning prevalent and Charlotte was ready to go shopping to make her into a Lady of the Night. Nora was asked to go with her as she was an excellent seamstress and knew fabrics and textures and would help her be that special lady. Shopping seemed to last indefinitely and finally they arrived, overloaded with parcels. Included in the parcels were some unmentionables such as lacy camisoles, bone lace up corsets, bloomers, and black silk stockings. Special step-up button shoes and even a couple of hats. The dresses barely covered the finer parts of a lady but that was as it was supposed to be; but covered just enough to make the men want that, that they could not wholly see. Charlie was indeed a gorgeous young lady, that any saloon owner would hire and probably try to make her his private mistress. She had matching luggage and had her ticket bought to Durango on tomorrow mornings stage to Durango. Coming all the way down to Santa Fe made it the long way around, but it was the only place that these things were available for Charlie and we need this to be able to complete our mission. It was still approximately two hundred miles on up to Durango, but Santa Fe was the largest town and had numerous saloons and bawdy houses for the Ladies of the Night and she needed this cover. Many other stagecoach travelers would be able to vouch that she was from Santa Fe.

Daisy, Nora and even Aiyana was fearful for her, that something terrible would be the result of this foolish cover-up. Nevertheless, it was decided upon to push ahead with this plan. Marshall August had an extremely large area to cover and be responsible for and had to take every precaution and route available to him; he hated to put Charlotte in this precarious position, yet she herself was the very one who thought she could pull off this masquerade. Next morning at dawn, the ladies were up, Nora fixing Charlie's hair as they had observed the Ladies of the Night do the night before as the men lead the ladies through that part of town and even with the ladies hanging onto the arms of their own men, they were embarrassed by how the Ladies of the Night acted, course these were the very active harlots out on the street hawking their wares. The ones working inside the saloons were not as aggressive in that manner., yet the styles were similar.

Daisy had breakfast ready, the men were just kind of fussin around and out of the wagon stepped Charlie in all her new bought finery as a Lady of the night. She was so beautiful she looked more like a rich refined lady from the East. The men gasped, the women nearly in tears as they made a place ready for her to sit down and eat.

"Oh Charlotte honey, there's still time for you to say no to Uncle Dan, we are all so afraid for you." Daisy contended.

"It's ok Daisy, I assure you I have thought about this many times since Uncle Augie brought it up. Yes I know there may be some trying times involved, but I am determined to do this and help make this a place where men and women alike can walk down the street proud and unafraid." "Well I wish we had a man available to escort you on the stage, that's a long trip on stagecoach and am sure there may be ruffians along the way." Nora quipped worriedly."Yes, well Dad gave me a belly-gun, a derringer, to carry with me in my small handbag and I have my 44 colt among my luggage and you know I am not afraid to use either one if it came down to that, so I'll be quite alright. I assure, but certainly appreciate your concern."

It was time for her to leave, having finished breakfast and saying all the byes...Augie and Ethan walked with her into town and marched her down to the stage depot, carrying her luggage. Setting her luggage down and asked the depot manager when the stage should be pulling in.

"She's a coming in now sir, just any minute." Was his answer, as the stage rounded the corner three blocks up. "The stage will have about a ten minute stop, to unload and load new passengers. Then two miles out of town, is the change over for the horses. Just no room anymore to do it here in town."

"That's fine, thankee. Please make sure this woman gets on with all her luggage." Marshall August commanded and flashed his badge, as if the woman was no longer wanted here in town."Yessum, I'll see to that Marshall." Ethan and Augie walked a short distance away and stood back to watch the proceedings...

Just before the stage pulled out, a finely dressed young man with obvious manners walked up with one suitcase in hand, tipped his hat to Charlotte and helped her board the stagecoach, then climbed in behind her. Well now, this may be Charlie's first test, as that man will obviously try to win her attention. Both Augie and of course Ethan was very concerned already about Charlie, but the wheels had already started turning and no turning back now. As they slowly plodded back to camp, down in the face, feeling lost, they looked over at each other and almost simultaneously said, "Well, it's started now."

"Say Frank, have you seen the Sarge today?"

"Can't say as I have Ethan, come to think of it, not since after breakfast, and come to think of that, his horse is gone too. Maybe he decided not to join us after-all."

"Well, in that case guess we'll just not figure on him. But I did give him a twenty dollar gold piece. Guess he's off to spend it."

CHAPTER 6

Stagecoach to Durango

The stagecoach stopped about two miles out of town, changed horses, while they waited outside in the shade of an Oak tree near a well with cool sipping well water.

"Hello Miss, it seems we'll be traveling together for a piece. My name is Glenn Hadley and I am going to Durango. I will be honored to assist you in any way possible on this journey, if you'll permit me Miss? Ah Miss?"

"Why thank you Mr. Hadley, I am Charlotte Kalee Kennedy, and I too am going to Durango. I will appreciate your assistance if necessary. Thank you sir."

"Since we will be traveling some distance together for the next few days, may I address you by your given name? Charlotte is a royal and a biblical name and very elegant, I would be most gracious to be at your service."

"Thank you again Mr. Hadley, yet don't you think it's a little early to get so personal?"

"I beg your pardon, my lady, I meant no offense, please rest assured Miss Charlotte Kalee."

With a gay laugh Charlie smiled and warmly replied, "Glenn, I was only joking, please accept my apologies and now the driver is motioning us to again board the stagecoach."

With a gracious bow and removal of his hat, Glenn smiled and held out his arm to assist me into the coach. "Ah then this will indeed be a pleasant trip, Thank you my dear Charlotte." In the coach, I looked this young man over, and he truly seemed to be every bit a gentleman. Handsome face, nice smile, neatly trimmed mustache, but otherwise clean shaven. About 6 feet tall, 185 pounds. Trim and lean, hands appeared to be working hands yet not calloused or dirty.

"Glenn, if I may ask, what do you do for a living or why on earth are you in this part of the country? You sound so refined and impressive; not someone out here to be a miner or even a cowhand as most men are here, or at least that is what I have heard."

"Ah yes, Charlotte, I own an Emporium or soon will when building material arrives in Durango, I also own part of a gold and silver mine. I am originally from Savannah, Georgia."

"Well now, that is interesting. Is the mine in Durango?"

"No ma'am, it is in Silverton, some near fifty miles farther north. We've had so many robberies these past few months that being a mine owner is not very profitable at all. That's another reason I am opening an Emporium. Now, since you know all about me, why on earth are you traveling out here. What is your business if I may be so bold to ask?"

"Oh mercy," I dropped my head embarrassed, "please sir, I do not possess the finery you have been blessed with. I am seeking work and this will be my last stop as I am soon out of funds to go farther."

"But, my lady you have such fine and appears to be new apparel and your speech is that of an educated woman. How could you be in such desperation?"

"It's a long and sad story for me and I don't care to burden you with it now. Please understand and forgive me. I am not a harlot, I assure you, yet I seek work as a hostess in a saloon. Does this surprise you really?"

"Oh my lady, forgive my boldness for asking, but perhaps I am able to be more of a service to you than before offered if you'll permit me.?"

"How could you possibly? I am not seeking charity or a handout, I am willing to work for my keep." As I cupped my gloved hands to cover my face and tears.

"Miss Charlotte, please don't be so distressed as I do have a possible solution to your needs, if you'll hear me out. I neglected to tell you I also own Hadley's Saloon. It's one of the few wooden buildings standing in Durango that is not a tent. I've invested heavily in that town as a railroad is going through it. I have a good bar manager, but not an overall manager and one to keep the books for me. Someone I can trust with the money. Is this something you'd be interested in? And frankly the investments are the last of my monies as well; so you see I am also in a bit of a spot, further, even though we've just become acquainted I feel to be able to completely trust you, and I feel comfortable with your presence."

"Why Glenn, are you sure? Why I've never had such luck. Yes, I need the job and will gladly accept, with thanks. So now all I need to do upon arrival is find a suitable place to live."

"You have more luck my dear, upstairs to the saloon is some rooms I'll gladly give to you, as I need to spend more time at the mine and managing the construction of the Emporium. I can easily board and room at the two other wooden buildings in town, the hotel. This is a boon for us both, such luck for us to meet each other like this."

The time we spent talking made this first part of our journey pass so quickly, and now we were coming to the first forty mile way-station to change the horses again. We were told the next way-station is only twenty miles as the mountainous terrain is too hard on the horses to go the forty miles as usual. We have about ten minutes to get out and stretch our legs. We actually just kind of walked around slowly stretching our legs, before again boarding and now coming from out of the way-station was two roughly dirty dressed gents to board the coach as well, so it's not just the two of us anymore and will certainly hamper our conversation. As we started to board, one of the dirtily clad men just jumped ahead of me and Glenn pulled him back and addressed him sharply. "Mister, can't you see there is a lady here and you need to be respectful."

"Well hell Mister, that ain't no lady. Can't you see she's dressed like a harlot, an uppity one at that, but still a harlot."

Without another word Glenn's fist shot out fast and downed this man like he was shot. "Mister, and I use that word loosely, this is a lady of my employee and under my protection, you will show respect while riding in this coach or I'll throw you out...and I do not want to hear another foul word out of your mouth. Do you understand?"

"Who the hell are you Mister, for you to try to do that?"

"I am Glenn Hadley and half owner of the Hadley-Clever mine in Silverton, and I will not even let you board this coach if you open your foul mouth again. Now get that straight."

"I can see this is going to be a long trip this a way, as I need to get back to Durango by day after tomorrow or I won't get in on the next bust."

"What are you talking about Mister, the next bust you just mentioned?"

"Nothing really, I was just spouting off, I'll keep my ole trap shut the rest of the way."

"See that you do, I'm tired of you already." Glenn threatened.

Then Glenn turned to me an asked if I was ok... I just nodded my head affirmative, but didn't say anything.

I thought Glenn was being a perfect gentleman and quite protective and I hated to have lied to him, but I didn't think it wise to reveal myself to him, at least not yet. I needed the job he offered and frankly the security that was also available to me through this job...puts me in the perfect spot I need to be to perform the duties required of me as a special deputy. The next few miles was bumpy as we were climbing higher in the mountains and I was glad of the quite and not having to converse continually, so I kept my handkerchief over my mouth and nose and even felt a bit sleepy. Next thing I knew we hit a hard bump and jostled me awake and found I was leaning my head on Glenn's shoulder.

"Oh, I'm sorry Glenn I must have fallen asleep for a moment."

"It was much more than a moment my dear, but it was no problem, I enjoyed your head being on my shoulder. It was more like two hours, and we are nearly to the way-station to change horses.

We bounced along for a while more and suddenly the two scoundrels across from us pulled their guns on us and took Glenn's gun strapped to his shoulder holster under his coat.

"Now don't either of you make a move or make any sounds and you might live through this."

"Ok, you got the drop on us. What's going on here?" Glenn reasoned.

"You'll find out soon enough, just keep your traps shut."

The stage pulled to a stop and a gruff voice from outside the coach told us all to get out."

"So this is a hold-up," Glenn remarked, "I might have known." As Glenn helped me out of the stage, I saw two men on horseback with two other horses on lead ropes, obviously for the dirty men in the coach with us.

"Ok now take out your wallets and empty the contents right here in my hat, and you Missy give us your money too."

We complied of course, and they somehow knew Glenn had a money-belt and forced him to take it off. All four of the outlaws chuckled about this and then the dirty rude mouthed one said. "Ok Missy whore, you and me are going out in the brush a spell, and when I gets through with you, you'll damn sure be a whore then begging for more."

I didn't move and he aimed his gun on me, Glenn couldn't do a damn thing to help me then. I was shoved off the road into the brush area and I heard laughter and all four of the men said,

"Yeah we'll be right behind you Slim, she'll soon learn what good men are all about."

He led me too a spot about 30 feet off the road, to a grassy area and told me in a loud voice to, "Take that damn dress off Missy whore unless you want me to rip it off of you."

I took my dress off watching his beady eyes follow my every move, and he was so intent on fixing his eyes on the top of my breasts sticking out over my camisole he never noticed me reaching into my small handbag. I pulled my 32 caliber derringer out and shot him right in the gut, before he could even react. I heard commotion over at the stagecoach and 2 shots, as I reached down and grabbed this outlaws pistol from his hand. Just then Glenn came running to me and saw it was all over. He looked at me curiously, then grinned and said,

"Good show Miss Charlotte, I can see you handle yourself very well...hehe, now get dressed again before I try taking advantage of you." And walked back to the coach laughing.

As it turned out, when the outlaws heard the shot it drew their attention away from Glenn and he slugged the outlaw on the ground, grabbed his gun and shot another and the coach driver shot the other mounted outlaw. They tied-up the remaining live outlaw, and short roped the four horses to the back of the coach. Their outlaw days were over and this live one would be convicted in court when ever the circuit judge came around.

The coach driver thanked Glenn and I and we climbed back into the stagecoach and proceeded on our way. In the coach Glenn asked me how I subdued that guy, so I just told him that he was more interested my breasts than he was with what I was doing with my hands. I took out my 32 caliber derringer and showed it to him and told him I always carry it.

"Your truly a wonder Miss Charlotte and I thank you myself...I was really worried what was about to happen to you and I felt so helpless; especially as I had already promised you protection."

"Well, it's over now, three dead and another will go to prison. I hate to see anyone die, but I learned to shoot a few years ago and will do so again when and if necessary.""At any rate I'm glad it's over and am very proud to know you and know you'll always be able to care for yourself when you have to. I'm also glad you'll be working for and with me."

"Thank you Glenn, but pray tell just how long is this unen-durable coach ride to Durango, and what kind of accommodations can we expect on our lay-overs?"

"Ah yes my dear, Well this first night will be at a small village named Cuba, but actually we will stay at the way-station run by a man and wife team, they have clean comfortable rooms and the wife will try to talk your head off, but is an excellent cook serving good hot meals. The coffee is a bit strong and some say will put hair on your chest...Oh, sorry there. Next stop tomorrow night will be at a nefarious little town named Bloomfield. There is a makeshift hotel there right next to an all night loud saloon, you probably won't get much sleep there unless your just completely worn out from the trip. But a saving grace to this is that down the street a few doors is an excellent little cafe run by a widow and her daughter about your age, I would guess, and they serve good home cooked meals with a smile. They are also open before the stage leaves next morning, serving good hot coffee and light fluffy biscuits with cream gravy, bacon and eggs. So if your a hearty eater, you'll certainly enjoy it there. Then finally we arrive in Durango about noon or a bit after, tired and dirty and we'll all need a hot bath to rejuvenate ourselves. But you my dear seem to withstand this traveling quite well."

"Well, so it would seem you've made this trip on many occasions. Do you often go to Santa Fe to buy your supplies?"

"Well yes, it seems to be the shipping point for various materials that Denver is unable to get because the wagons going to Denver seem to most always get held up coming from the north or west; so freighters don't even like to take that route, at least not anymore. Just to many hold-ups and killings. Even this route is not exactly safe as we have experienced."

"So is not the law doing anything about it or do you even have any form of law around here.?"

"For one thing Charlotte, the area is much to large for a Marshall to cover, and the sheriffs in these small towns are either in with the gangs or just don't care...just drawing a pay-check without doing anything, protecting their own hides. The last Marshall we had in these parts was killed about 4 months ago and the few deputies he had just vanished. I do understand however, that a new Marshall has been assigned and should be arriving in Durango in a few more days. I just hope he is honest and is capable of doing a lawful job of it, and needs to hire some deputies that are honest and capable as well."

"I should certainly hope so. So you say there is a Sheriff in Durango, and is he part of these gangs or does he try to uphold the law?"

"Yes Sheriff Allen Walker, he's a tough old coot, and does help keep the town in order, but he does have a drinking problem and continually brags about bygone years, stories he likes to tell over and over again. Likes the attention he gets from his drinking buddies and mostly hangs out at the Palace Saloon and dance hall. Has a deputy too, a woman goes by the name Mary Davis. She's quit a character herself, but can be damn tough and is an excellent shot, claims to out shoot and ride any man, chews tobacco, always spitting, says some crazy things and I think more of a comedian than anything. The two together don't get much law and order done, but both give lots of lip-service to it and the town folk just tolerate them. That, young lady is the extent of our law and order in Durango."

"Seems we are living in a very precarious town and obviously the town needs some cleaning up and some and law and order established solidly." I quipped. So with all this lawlessness, is there any medical facilities available?"

"Yes my dear, we do have a very good young lady doctor name of Doc Valerie Nichols, she trained under her own father, but went back east to further study and get her degree. She's smart, very firm and set in her ways, yet amiable in every way and is a nice person. Has a fifteen year old daughter and quite pretty. Her husband died several years ago of consumption, or at least that is the story, if there ever was a husband. That my dear lady is the extent of our medicinal facilities, just a small office, no clinic or nurses."

"Well what about the town itself, has it formed a council, who appointed the Sheriff?"

"Durango has increased it's population just in the last 6 months or so since I arrived, it's over 1,400 in numbers now, I'm sure, the Rio Grand Railroad coupled with the Denver line has brought people in quickly, all wanting to make a dollar, yes admittedly like myself, but we are still a tent city. Merchants by the many have flocked here, but I fear about half of the population is made up of despicable gangs. We have a self-appointed Mayor and 3 council members of which I am a part of, and the only thing we have done is appoint Sheriff Allen Walker, because no one else wanted the job. Obviously I'm not very proud of this so far."

"Well I feel I'm already familiar with Durango and have not ever been there...you've certainly filled me in completely. Now tell me about Hadley's Saloon, what can I expect there?"

"I have a 30 foot bar, no mirror behind the bar, seats about 60 people with about 20 tables, so total capacity is about 80 or so, but I've never had it filled completely yet, and have only two girls working the floor. I do not let them use any of the rooms upstairs which will be your quarters, as it was mine personally, but am quite sure they too are Lady's of the Night and most likely arrange their dates to be at the hotel. I just never wanted my place to have that kind of reputation. Occasionally some musicians come in and they push the tables around to clear space and have a real fandango hoe-down. You can manage the place as you see fit and hopefully it will become as popular as 'The Palace Saloon,' but they have rooms upstairs for the ladies to entertain their men. I don't know what else I can tell you about the town, it's just bustling, growing to fast to control. By the way if you think you'll need a bouncer to control riff-raff, feel free to do that."

"It seems time passes so much quicker with our conversation, and it appears we are coming into this little Cuba you mentioned. I do hope the rooms are satisfactory."

"Yes, I think you'll be comfortable under the circumstances Miss Charlotte. Yes here we are now."

As the horses pulled to a stop, the coach creaking, it's near dusk already, both the hostler and wife were outside to greet us. The woman was a large woman, not at all fat, but just huge and her voice boomed, her husband was short with a squeaky voice but competent and very friendly.

"Hello folks, come on in and rest yourselves, coffee on and supper is ready. You can wash up over there at the pump (pointing), then come on in." Neva exclaimed. "Yup folks, glad to have ya, oh, hello there Mr. Hadley, glad to see you again and heres ya are a bringing yourself a purty little thing with ya I sees. Well ya'll welcome." And disappeared inside, while we went to the wash pump and trough.

As I washed my face and hands with the scratchy lye soap, I told Glenn, "You were certainly right about her Glenn, but she is charming in here own way, I like her and am absolutely famished. I feel like I could eat a horse, as the saying goes."

Glenn just laughed, "Yes admittedly, I too am hungry, let me finish washing and we'll go in."

As we sat down to a rustic, many times used table, and wobbly chairs, Neva came out with a clean red and white checkered table cloth and spread it before us.

"I don't usually put a cloth on with just mostly men a sitting and messing the table, but with you Miss, I am glad to do it, seeing as how your a lady an all. Don't get many a coming through on the stage, matters of fact, you be the onliest one for sometime now, and guess I best get your supper now afore I go on a talking. Don't get many a folk here that's a talker though."

"Oh Glenn, she is charming and you were so right, she's a talker even if we don't talk back, I bet she sometimes even answers herself."

A delicious beef stew was brought to our table in a serving bowl, with yeast rolls and churned butter, with home made fresh huckleberry jam. The aroma of the fresh yeast rolls was heavenly. We helped ourselves and the gravy in the stew was sopping good...we smiled from across the table at each other, but both of us were so hungry, we ate our meal in silence. When we finally ate our fill of the stew, there was still a couple of rolls left and I couldn't help myself and had to take one, spooned the huckleberry jam on it liberally and sat back and marveled at the wonderfully tart yet sweet taste. Glenn looked at me and reached for the last yeast roll, and with a broad smile on his handsome face said,

"Miss Charlotte, you amaze me, I loved to see you eat so well, yet with manners and graciousness. The meal was indeed delicious and these rolls and jam are the very end. We start again in the morning right after day break, so you may want to take a short walk-in-the-moonlight with me, then off to bed with you."

"So your already courting me are you?" (laughing) "Well that sounds nice, and I'll just take you up on that walk, but are you sure there is a moon out tonight?"

"To be honest, no I'm not sure but lets go outside and see if we can find it."

"Will I need a wrap, let me go to my room and get a shawl out of my luggage and I'll meet you outside."

As I stepped outside I did feel a brisk cool wind, looking around I noticed three men talking over by the horse corrals, and some distance from them Glenn was sitting alone under a tree on a large stump, smoking a cigarette and gazing up in the sky...I just stood there awhile observing Glenn and wild thoughts went through my mind. *What if he fell in love with me or I him...oh no girl, that could never happen; I've had to tell too many lies already. So I just stood there feeling so foolish for having such crazy romantic thoughts...but still, ah forget it girl, just enjoy the now.* Glenn must have seen me standing there and came over to me right away, held out his arm and I took it and let him lead me away a short distance, then stopped.

"Look up there Miss Charlotte, there's our moon, grab ahold of it and hang on and make a wish and without telling me your wish, I'll make it come true."

I thought how silly that sounded, still I reached up and closed my hand around it and answered, "If you knew what my wish was you may not want it to come true."

Just at that moment an eerie scream sounded, breaking the silence and the moment, then another yell...Glenn grabbed me and rushed me inside, said to get into my room and do not light the lamp, and stay quiet. I rummaged around in my valise and felt my 44 colt, knew it was loaded and went to a far corner of the room about six feet from the parchment window, that was designed to permit a little light through and crouched down waiting, but didn't know what I was waiting for. I heard more shooting outside, some screams, cussing and finally silence, but I stayed where I was. Suddenly the parchment window was shattered and in came a figure of a man and as he turned to find me in the corner by the moonlight filtering in, I fired and heard a dreadful grunt, so I fired again. The door was pushed open and Glenn rushed in followed by Neva with a lighted lamp. On the floor about four feet from me lay a dead Indian, I still had gun in hand and as Glenn came to me, took my pistol and with his arms around me led me into the main room, and set me down in a chair.

"Charlotte my dear, are you alright?" He asked.

"Yes, he didn't get to touch me, I just shot without thinking, but strangely I wasn't afraid. What kind of Indians are they anyway?"

Seth, Neva's little man and hostler answered, "They be mescaleos, still a few of them around roaming the hills, they don't usually attack in this good weather, only in winter they come and attack, mostly to steal food and horses or whatever we have a laying around. Yes suh, they be Mescalero Apache, not many around anymore."

"Well it seems they were after something around here, look, they don't even have war-paint on, or is that true about what they say and a savage wears war-paint before he attacks?" Glenn asked."

Our driver then volunteered information, "No suh, it's true what they says, lookee behind his ear, or back of his neck under his hair, that where it most likey be. Lots a times they be deceiving like that."

Seth came back into the main room carrying the dead Indian over his shoulder and affirmed he had war paint on his neck.

"We shot three of them outside, an counting this one here, that's four and I noticed one riding away. So that accounts for five of them varmints." Glenn volunteered. "So what do we do with them now, bury them or what?"

I reckon to take care of um." Seth concluded.

Next morning not a word was spoken of the five Mescalero's that visited us last night, breakfast was worth being here for and plenty of it...team hitched and by dawn we were on our way. The stagecoach bumping along with all it's squeaks and rattles, the coach driver wheezing and hawing at the horses as we climbed a steeper hill. I wondered why we didn't have a shotgun rider with us and Glenn told me the coach lines couldn't afford to hire one, cause so many had been killed and the asking price to handle such a job was outrages. It's a wonder we had a driver, I surmised. So I just set there stoic like and simply accepted the bumping and jostling of the coach as it proceeded on this path. For some reason Glenn was unusually quiet and I didn't want to disturb his thoughts what ever they might be. Perhaps he was just still tired, not sleeping well after our incident with the Indians. But what ever it was, this solitude was disturbing, totally unlike the Glenn I had got to know. Another fifteen or so minutes past and my endurable patience was beginning to ebb. Then finally without warning, Glenn suddenly asked me.

"Charlotte, now really, something has been bothering me about you nearly from the start and I have hesitated in bringing it up, for fear you would get upset in thinking I doubted you."

"Glenn, I am an open book, but obviously there are a few things a girl doesn't like to divulge about herself. However, since I am now in your employee, please ask any question you will and if I feel it's too personal I will simply not answer. Is that satisfactory Glenn?"

"Obviously, I could not ask for anymore, thank you. My question is simply, where did you come from before Santa Fe and why are your clothes the obvious manner of a working girl, lastly, where and how did you learn to shoot with such accuracy and daring."

"Glenn, that is four questions total, not one; nevertheless, I am able to answer all four, and in the order you've asked me. Before Santa Fe I came from the Breaks of Missouri, my clothes was purchased for me by a gent that wanted me to join the ranks of a working girl, but we got separated and I am now on my own. I learned to shoot as a young girl growing up and living on a farm without a father and my mother died several years ago as well...so I would hunt rabbits, deer and foul to survive. And an old hostler taught me how to quick draw and shoot a handgun without actually aiming...I was anxious to learn all of this for my own survival and was a good student. Further, though you did not ask, I will answer another question, I learned my schooling myself with the help of the town doctor, teaching me how to cypher and he taught me manners of a lady of quality. He further had quality books and taught me to read and learn the basics of being a self-sufficient woman. Now I hope that satisfactorily answers your questions."

"it certainly does and I am absolutely impressed and proud to be in your company. I admire any person, man or woman that is self taught and have learned survival skills as you've had too. Now I am embarrassed for having doubted you even the slightest bit. Please forgive me, My Lady."

"Yes, thank you Glenn. By the way, do we anticipate any further trouble or problems before reaching Durango?"

"My Lady, I most certainly hope not, this trip has been very trying, but very interesting as well and having met you, please be advised, I am a single man 26 years of age, not self-educated as you, but self-reliant, if you please. My father was a rich tyrant, making his money from the slave trade of which I never did agree with or could possibly continue to put up with. I ask him for my inheritance and would leave...he did give it to me and told me not to come back. I spent most of my inheritance foolishly on the proverbial wine, women and song of which now I am ashamed and have learned a great lesson because of it...the monies I had not squandered I realized and think I grew to maturity and needed to invest the rest in an adventure to add to my small fortune, thus My Lady I have done in Durango. Now that's my sad story. I am not at all proud of it, but am trying to rectify my earlier stupidity."

I simply smiled and nodded, but remained silent. We continued on our bumpy ride for the next couple of hours in silence and I knew Glenn was wondering what I was thinking; finally we were slowing down and the driver hollered and announced we were coming into Bloomfield. I did not realize again how swiftly the time passed, but was glad we were nearing our final destination as this was our last lay-over. The creaking coach came to a halt in front of the hotel, our baggage tossed down and a young boy asked if he could carry my bags into the hotel. "Yes, please do, those two bags (pointing) are mine and give me a minute and I'll be right in. I reached into my purse and found a dime and gave it to the boy."

"Yes um Ma'am. Thank you."

I raised my eyes up only to find that the Hotel Bloomfield was not really a hotel, but appeared to be an old rooming house, converted to that of a Hotel, it was also the station-stop for the stagecoach. Glenn was apologizing for perhaps misleading me as to the accommodations of this run-down establishment.

"But My Lady, you will be able to get a hot bath, and after we'll go to that little cafe' I told you about and have a nice fulfilling meal."

I looked up at the sign again, on the front of this dilapidated structure, that proclaimed it was the Hotel Bloomfield, that was already nearly faded out and wondered what it would look like inside, and just shook my head.

"It's ok Glenn, it is what it is and certainly not your fault; but if they do accommodate with a hot bath I will be satisfied."

It took about a half hour for two men to fill my tub, and of course waited for a tip. It was hot though and fortunately I had my own perfumed soap to lather with, and I just lay there and soaked, hoping to soak away all the bruises that coach left me with. I must have nearly dozed off for a few minutes, as I opened my eyes to find Glenn standing inside the door, his back turned to me saying, "Please pardon my intrusion My Lady, your door was unlocked and I thought I heard you say enter."

"Well, Mr. Hadley, now that you've apparently seen my all-together, I assure you it will be the last time, (giggling), at least until you put a sparkler on my ring finger..."

"Ah ah, My Lady, that can certainly be arranged. Yet, if you don't mind I'll wait for you to get dressed, and I'll be in the lobby downstairs. No hurry though, please take your time."

The door closed behind Glenn and I did wonder just how much of me he did see, before I somehow realized he was in my room. The soap had apparently settled while I dozed off and did not leave many suds to cover my essentials. Yet he was gentle-man enough to turn his back, at least when he was trying to awaken me. *Well, I can't help that now, and thinking I tried to make light of it by joking about a ring. Yet, I wonder now, what it would be like to be married to Glenn. So charming and am sure he hasn't at all lied to me. Oh forget it Charlotte, you've only just met him, besides I've lied to him, well, at least not all of it was lies. But I am hungry, so outa the tub with you girl...I need to stop talking to myself, especially as I start to an-swer myself. Oh Mercy...*

Dressed hurriedly, and my hair brushed out down around my shoulders, I slowly walked down the stairs and I saw Glenn standup as I reached the downstairs level, and with a taking off his hat with a flourishing sweep, he bowed, stood and took my hand and marveled of my presence and appearance.

"My Lady, it is to my honor that you will be joining me this evening to dine, you are indeed not only a dream, rather an aspi-ration for every man. You are beyond gorgeous, you put the brilliance in every star." Held out his arm for me to take and ad-mittedly I was astounded. I certainly was not used to being ad-dressed in such a manner. *Was he really interested in me or just being exceptionally nice?* I wondered. Glenn was right about the food in this small cafe', Dora, who turned out to be the daughter was the waitress and very pretty, courteous and effi-cient. Her mother, owner and cook, was a robust Mexican woman, named Millie, or perhaps she was a half breed. What-ever, to Glenn's knowledge no one ever saw her husband, and some say she never had one. Still the food is delicious and served proudly, and as far as we should care, that's all that matters.

"Glenn I am still embarrassed the way you entered my room earlier, do you often do that? I mean like the rooms upstairs over your saloon, do they have locks on them or not? I'm not a prude, but I do have some pride and prefer my privacy, especially when taking a bath."

"Again I apologize for that, and yes they do have locks; and truth be known I only saw your head above the water. I assure you nothing else as you apparently dozed for a few minutes, though again, truth be known I did have an urge to quietly walk over and look upon you."

Glenn said this with a smile and did make me wonder if he was being honest with me. Meal finished we sat there for a few minutes finishing our coffee and a thought came to me.

Glenn, There are some things about me you don't know, but I am unable to tell you right now, perhaps later, as I do want to be totally open with you. Will you continue to trust me.?"

"Miss Charlotte, I assure you I do and will trust you. Somehow, you simply magnetize me and though you've basically educated yourself, I feel you have maintained honesty above all else. Yes I trust you my dear and I will add more responsibility to your already duties I've given you. I may be out of town when building material arrives for the Emporium, I have already assigned and staked out a plot for it to be built upon, I hope you will further accept that responsibility as it's manager as well."

"Glenn, perhaps your putting to much trust in me, I've not the experience required to carry that load."

"Well, I think you can do it and hope you'll agree to try; I really need to pay more attention to the mining operations and that would give me that extra time required.?"

"I can only try Glenn, it's just we've only known each other two days and your putting so much trust and responsibility on me, I can only hope not to let you down."

"I want you to feel as if you are a part of this, perhaps as my partner in these ventures; and come to think of it, maybe we can come to an agreeable partner relationship."

"Why... why Glenn you astound me, I just don't know what to say."

"Say yes, that's all you have to say and I'll have papers drawn up as soon as possible."

"Ah, oh Glenn, do you really think I could? I mean like I'm nearly a pauper and suddenly you are making me a princess! Yes ok, I will." I murmured.

"Good, now I know I can handle the rest and even perhaps start a freighter outfit of my own, instead of hiring thieves, that I've suspected, but couldn't do anything about it; and now you my dear shall have a completely free hand in operating and managing the two businesses in town. If you wish to change the name of the saloon, I have no problem with that either. Perhaps a different name may increase our trade. What do you think Charlotte?"

"I think I will need to reserve judgment on that Glenn, at least until I see the place. But please call me Charlie, that's my nick-name.."

We were enjoying this chit-chat, or banter back and forth, but we were informed the stage-coach would be leaving in about ten minutes. This last leg of the trip was exciting me; here I was an undercover deputy, going to pass myself off as a Lady of the Night, suddenly transformed into a legitimate business woman, with possibly becoming a business owner. This is actually apart from being a deputy. I will somehow need to tell Pa about this stroke of luck. Anyway, in just a few more hours we will arrive in Durango.

We pulled into Durango sometime after noon, and Glenn led me directly to his saloon, stood there in front of it and pointing he announced...

"There you are My Lady, your own Nest to run."

CHAPTER 7

Enter the Marshal

The rest of the trip from Santa Fe to Durango was actually uneventful for us, thank goodness, yet we were to learn of the exploits of Charlie and a man named Glenn Hadley that had passed through the way-stations just the day before on the stagecoach...it was all the talk. Some small talk had already reached Durango even before stagecoach's arrival. As we were pulling into Durango, we noticed the bustling of the town itself...people were walking up and down the main street of what appeared to be a town with growing pains. It was indeed a town made up of canvas stretched over wooden frames, and small hand-painted signs advertising their wares, someone had at least made a plot of the town and you could see some small bits of organization. I decided to stop our little caravan at a sign that proclaimed the Sheriff's office. According to the suns position it was about half past four in the afternoon, hot, but not scorching. The lady's and Joe stayed in the wagons while Ethan & I walked up to this crudely painted sign, lifted the flap and walked into the office...sitting at a table with coffee in hand was an older woman, appearing to be in her fifties, tipped back in her chair, eyes half closed and I was surprised when this figure actually spoke, pushed her hat to the back of her head and drawled.

"What's it be gents. Ya gotcha some trouble some where's?"

"No ma'am, not exactly, just looking for the sheriff. Would he be about?"

"Yeah, I'm a shore he's be about some where's er tuther, but dono tuther. Ya'll gots some business to a do wit him?"

"Well ya might say so. I'm Marshal Daniel August and this here is Preacher Ethan Kennedy, we just arrived and was told to talk to Sheriff Allen Walker, that he could tell us where the last Marshall here had his house and some other things."

The chair banged loudly as the old woman sat up strait, nearly spilling her coffee, pushed her hat back of her head again and exclaimed "Bust my britches, well suh, ya finally did arrive, been a waiting for a spell fer ya to shows up. I'm Mary Lou Davis, Allen's deputy. Let see now, it be late afta noon, he mos likee be at the Palace a mite more down a street. Might ya could a catch him thar." She quipped, as she spat her tobacco cud juice on the plank floor, narrowly missing Dan's boot.

"Much obliged deputy." I stated, turned and walked out..."Watcha think of that Ethan?"

What do I think? We certainly have our hands full and if the Sheriff is anything like his deputy we'll not get much help from the likes of either of them."

As we stepped outside the sheriff's tent, we looked up and down the street, and up the street some forty or fifty yards more and across the very wide street, we saw several horses tied to hitch-rails and saw a sign, loudly proclaiming it as "The Palace Saloon." We motioned the lady's and Joe to move the wagons up as we walked that distance. Walking along some planked side-walk and some dirt walkway where eventually a board walk would be built, we started to pass one of the few built wooden buildings. It was also a saloon, but only a few horses at the hitch-rail; obviously not a very popular place for drinking men. As we started to pass by the bat-wing doors we heard a familiar voice and looking in, there was Charlie in all her finery; Ethan kinda choked looking at his daughter, but held back, we couldn't break her cover, but we did walk in and up to the bar. Charlie turned, looked at us with a warm smile of recognition, but greeted us as strangers.

"Welcome friends, first drink on the house. Welcome to my little nest, what'll it be gents?"

"Afternoon ma'am, thank you, we just arrived in your fair bustling town. We sure could use that drink.""Sid, give these two gents a drink on me." Then turning back towards us, Charlie agrees,"Seems there's a passel of folk arriving into town daily, I'm just new here myself and took over this here place, needs some remodeling, but that'll come."

"Ma'am could we talk privately somewhere, perhaps you can tell us some things about this town before we get started?"

"Gents lets go sit at that back table and we can talk whatever your a mind too." But at this moment in time, Glenn Hadley walks in, walks up to Charlie and in a familiar way addresses her, takes her hand, implying more than just friendship. Which of course bothers Ethan.

"Good after noon Glenn, nice to see you. Please, permit me to introduce two new people to our community. Gents, this is Glenn Hadley, proprietor of this establishment, and you are?"

"Hello Mr. Hadley, I am the newly assigned Marshall Dan August and this is Preacher Ethan Kennedy, we just arrived and those three wagons you may have noticed outside are our families. We'll be needing a place to stay, until we can build our own...Any suggestions?"

Glenn and Charlie both reached out their hands, to clasp in greeting and friendship to the Preacher and Marshal; suggesting to anyone observing that they were all strangers.

"Well, this is indeed a pleasure Marshal, we've been expecting you for a time now and you've brought a preacher, now this is an unexpected pleasure. Glad to have you both and Ethan we do have a plot available to build a church and a rectory on for you if you will agree to the location, and Marshall, the late Marshall had some very small rooms he used, and the lot is large enough to make an addition on, that is just up the street a mite farther. I guess I best further introduce myself. I am a member of our town council, so I also officially welcome you and will arrange a meeting with our self-appointed Mayor and the other council members tomorrow, if that is agreeable with you both."

"Welcome again from me." Charlotte uttered, "I do hope you gents will patronize our saloon here in the future to relax and have a drink, and Preacher, though I'm a saloon-girl I do hope you'll welcome me into your church, as my leanings are that way."

"But of course Miss Charlotte, I will indeed, and will make my first sermon to the congregation, that sinners is who Jesus preached too, that he loved them also." Ethan claimed.

"Now, I need to have a few words with Miss Charlotte gentlemen, so if you'll excuse me, I'll be out momentarily to assist you both in locating your lots and rooms. I can only apologize for the inconvenience to get you settled."Thank you Mr. Hadley, we'll be outside at the wagons."Hadley just waved as Ethan and I stepped through the bat-wing doors that squeaked too loudly for the effort they employed.

"Glenn, they both acted nice, I do hope you'll show them proper courtesies and help them as much as possible. The Preacher even welcomed me and perhaps you'll escort me to his first sermon."

"Indeed I will precious, it'll be my pleasure."

"Glenn I do hope you'll not address me so familiar like that in front of customers, it may tend to drive them away, instead of drawing them here to spend their money. But go about your business now and I have something to tell you when you get back."

As Glenn walked out the door, my thoughts went to Pa and Uncle Augie, and I wanted to see

the ladies too, it's only been a couple of days since leaving them, but I missed them all

including the kids, little Noah & Aponi both.

"Marshall, thank you for being patient with me, please direct your ladies to guide the teams

strait up that small incline and your quarters, at least temporarily, is right there on the right, see those rooms there? And Preacher, we will go about ¼ mile strait on and cross that drainage ditch...it has a narrow bridge there, and your church plot is right there. We will contribute some funds to help you get started, the council members and the Mayor I mean,

but am afraid you'll you'll have to camp out until your able to build satisfactory quarters and a

church."

"Thank you Mr. Hadley, you've been most helpful. Permit us to get settled and we'll visit the town, and I do need to visit with your sheriff as well." The Marshall affirmed.

Unloading our few necessities was an easy chore, Daisy fixing Noah's bed first of all, then

turning her eye to the very small kitchen with only a flat-top Ben Franklin stove for warmth and cooking, no easy chore, but would manage. Daisy was a wonder for being able to do with things out of necessity that was available. It was still early and we wanted to see how Ethan

and Nora were doing, and how Joe and Aiyana with Aponi were handling things camped next to Ethan temporarily. Nora, Daisy and Aiyana got busy fixing supper and Daisy mentioned to

the men to go on into town and look things over as the women knew the men were anxious to see what this town appeared to be in the night.

"Go on with ya now, Augie, supper won't be ready for a spell yet, just be careful." Daisy cautioned.

As the three men walked across the little bridge and down the street, they passed the marshall's newly acquired quarters and he went in to retrieve his holster and his old Army issue Scholfeld, break-top 6 shooter.

"Augie, why didn't you invest in the new double-action Colt." It's hard to get used to but after it's much better than that ole single action Army issue. You'll notice both Joe and I did and Joe even got one of those Mexican double-loop crossdraw holsters."

"Yeah I notice you both did, guess I'm just used to this one we used during the war. It's served me damn good over the years."

We walked on down the street passing The Palace up right now, with it's loud piano blaring out music that sounded more like a fight than music, and down farther crossing the street to Charlotte's place, we all wanted to check on her to see how she was doing...there were several horses at the hitch-rail and we knew men were anxious to see the new girl in town and just what she was all about. Before we entered we could hear her singing and was glad

she was able to do this...we walked in and sitting in a corner of a makeshift stage was Charlie sitting on a chair in a revealing low-cut dress, with her guitar across her lap singing her heart out. The patrons quiet, actually listening intently to ever word, some we could see with tears in their eyes and others trying to choke them back. These hard-rock miners and cowpoke were utterly mesmerized with her singing as they were with her beauty. She presented the perfect picture of every man's dream, both young and old. When her song was finished, there was a slight pause, then loud applause, whistling and nodding of heads one to the other. Charlie got up from her chair, took a couple of bows, then raised her hand for quiet and announced:

"Gentleman, (laughingly) I am Charlotte Kennedy, the new owner and manager of Charlie's Nest, and I'm here to entertain you; not upstairs (pointing so) in rooms to be fleeced of your hard earned dollars, but right here as you've just heard...This is a place you will be able to bring your sweethearts too or if you dare, even your wives. (laughing again). Now I've just noticed some men that walked in are new to our bustling little village, and they are here to both protect and serve you. May I present your new Territorial Marshall Dan August and his good friend Preacher Ethan Kennedy. Preacher Kennedy also wears a gun and if you don't attend his services he'll come a lookin fer ya"... (everyone laughed and applauded then), "and, gentleman we do not have a church here, so if you're a mind to please go to the bar and make a contribution to the cause and for every dollar you put in, I'll match. Now gentlemen, Let's get this church built." Again, loud applause and nodding of heads, as they headed towards the bar with money in the hand.

Charlie walked over to us and shook hands, and invited us to a table in the back to sit down and talk.

"Now, we can talk for a few minutes, hopefully without interruption." Charlie stated with a smile. "I know you want to know how I suddenly came into this windfall of being a co-owner of this place. I met Glenn Hadley on the stagecoach coming here and we did hit it off quite well, there was some harrowing experiences we encountered, but I was actually lucky to have met him...he does not know I am a deputy. He offered this position to me as he does not have time to attend to proper business as a mine-owner, and he wants to start his own freighter wagon business to his current operations, but doesn't have the time. So now I am co-owner of the new "Charlie's Nest", you heard what I said about this being a legitimate business and I intend to keep it just exactly that. Oh, but it's so good to see you all again and would love to see the ladies again as well. Yet, I do need to hire a bouncer and a gambler, that can and will play a strait and honest game."

"You have done very well, much better than any of us suspected you were able to do...we are all proud of you Charlotte;
and I am very proud of how you intend to run this place." Ethan
acknowledged.

"I agree Charlotte," Uncle Dan concluded, "yet you just gave
me another idea, you can hire Joe to be your bouncer and gambler. What do you think about it Joe?"

Laughingly, Joe entered the conversation, "Well all evening
I've been holding back to see where I might fit in. Yes, I think
this would be the best place for me as I could watch over Charlie
at the same time...yes, if Charlotte agrees, I'll accept.

At this juncture in our conversation, our table was approached by several of the customers to congratulate both the
Marshal and Preacher Ethan and to welcome them to
Durango...many questions thrown at them both; but was unable
to answer any of them directly because of the overall confusion
and noise. Charlie came to the rescue.

Gents if you'll all order another round of drinks and sit down,
maybe I can talk the good Marshal here and the preacher with
Joe Freeman to sing us a couple of songs...I understand they are
also musicians...so my friends, this is "Charlie's Nest," enjoy the
rest of the evening.

Augie, Ethan and Joe looked at me with surprise, and asked,

"Charlie, we weren't expecting this... we don't have our gui-
tars with us...

"Just look behind that curtain back of the chair I was sitting
at." Charlie whispered, then loudly to her crowd of guests,
which had multiplied since her own singing, "Come on folks,
give a round of applause for these men, some ole campfire
singing at its best and if your nice...I might even join in. Come
on, LETS HEAR IT!"

applause....Charlie raised her hands..."again, AGAIN." she
hollered, and more applause sounded. "Now, that's more like
you mean it.

Glenn Hadley had just walked in a few minutes before this
and was amazed at the size of the crowd and good humored
noise, walked up to Charlie and graciously avowed that he had
made a right good choice. This is the biggest crowd he'd had in
this place since opening this saloon.

"Charlie, you never cease to amaze me, your simply a natural to handle this type of a business, this is only your second night here and have already gathered the biggest crowd I've ever had. I sincerely thank you my dear."

"Well thank you Glenn, I have a few other ideas I'll introduce as time goes on. But right now, lets listen to them sing."

The evening ended peacefully, no fights or even an argument that we were aware. They all loved the entertainment and many was saying that they just may ask their wives to join them in the festivities of Charlie's Nest, a saloon, but for all, both man and woman.

Next morning we awoke with a slight drizzle and when your high in the mountains like this, it feels quite chilling. Yet we gathered up what was necessary, re-stoked the embers in the Ben Franklin pot-belly; Daisy put on a fresh pot of coffee, and I put a wash pan of water on it also as I needed to shave. I was determined to meet with the Sheriff today, and also this Glenn Hadley would have arranged a meeting for me with the Mayor and other council members. I reflected back to last night in regards to Charlie, and hoped she would stay safe and that Glenn Hadley was true to his word. Coffee finished perking and settled and I sipped on a cup as I shaved...a few days on the road makes it difficult to sometimes do your daily personal chores. I could smell and hear the last of the bacon frying and heard Noah stirring

and mumbling to himself...quite a boy, that one, be sixteen next month and has experienced some things many other boys never will, yet other boys before him may have similarly encountered and endured like exposure to traveling across our land. Come to think of it, our whole party experienced and endured these same things of which they were not accustomed to in the past.

No eggs, but Daisy fixed a plate full of flap-jacks and still had some sweet molasses to cover them and that with the bacon made a fine breakfast...

"Augie, what are your plans for the day? This place is much to small to try to settle in and we will need a fireplace come winter."

"I've thought about that Daisy, I'll make inquires today, if there are any carpenters in town and about building supplies that may be available. I plan on making this a much larger house, one where Noah will have his own room up in the loft, and our bedroom away from the kitchen and living room., so don't fret woman." I advised good naturedly.

I stood up from the table, took the last sip of my coffee, strapped on my gun-belt and remarked, "Just do what you feel is necessary right now to be comfortable and Noah don't go running off somewhere's, stay here and help your Ma."

As I walked out of the little house, I checked off mentally the things that would be a priority, the drizzling of rain had stopped, and it appeared it would turn out to be a fine day. I walked

up the rutted road about a ¼ of a mile and noticed Ethan and Joe were about, both Nora and Aiyana were busy and Aponi, little Butterfly, was milking the cow. It appears they were a mite slower getting around than Daisy and Noah, but after all they were camped out, not in a house. As I walked up to the campfire with the usual morning greetings, Nora handed me a cup of coffee. I sat down on the wagon tongue and Ethan asked what our plans were for the day.

"Ethan, this is where we have to kind of split up, you are the preacher and need to show you are concerned about getting a church and rectory built and preparing your first sermon and I suggest you do that even before you have a church to walk into. Nora is the perfect woman for you as a preacher's wife and Butterfly is your adopted daughter. In no way can it be revealed that you are anything but the preacher. You could see Charlotte and am sure she'll give you the donations of last night, and you should be very proud of her the way she handled herself last night and what she has already been able to accomplish by setting herself up in such a way. Oh, and by the way, we both need to advise the kids and make them understand, that when they see Charlotte, she is not to be recognized as family, at least right away."

"Yeah Augie, I've already thought about those things myself. Joe and I have been discussing our roles we need to play. Joe has a much free-er hand to play with than either of us do...his work does not actually begin till customers start going into the saloons."

"Well, that's true," Joe stated, "but I think I'll stroll around town and get the feel of it; talk to Charlie and see where I maybe able to help her."

"Good thinking Joe, and I appreciate that," I admitted.

So at this point, we were all basically on our own. It was still early, so I decided to walk around town myself and get the feel of it, meet a few of the towns people that were up an' round this early morning. There was a small hubbub of activity going with a few of the tent merchants that had their building supplies and most of the talk was more about the railroad that was outside of town a several miles and would soon, hopefully, be approaching town limits. This was quite an array of people, many orientals on the railroad, plus some Mexicans and a few darkies, then the hard-rock miners and also cattlemen and merchants that all wanted a piece of the riches a new rail town usually brings. I came to a livery stable and blacksmith shop, a Mexican man and darkie was here, the two had merged, the Mexican operated the livery and the darkie was the blacksmith, but the two seemed to help each other. The Mexican livery owner was an older man named Carlos Sanchez, small in stature, spoke a smattering of English and the darkie was a huge man, in his early 30's, must have been about six-foot six, muscles apparent as there was not a bit of fat showing on him, ugly as sin...yet his demeanor was very pleasant, his name was Blackie. Now I didn't understand if that was his real name or just the name people called him. I introduced myself and we passed a few minutes of time exchanging items of interest about the town.

As I walked away, I heard "Buena suerte y que Dios lo acompane Senor Marshal." (Good luck, God be with you Mr. Marshall.)

A few other people were now out walking, and passing some ladies I tipped my hat, smiled and exchanged pleasant Good Mornings...then hearing murmuring behind me as I passed on.

I crossed the street and there was Charlotte out already, dressed in new Levis and button shirt, western hat and boots. "Good Morning Charlie, you certainly are up and around early this morning for having been up late last night."

"Good Morning Uncle Augie, and I use the familiarity only when we are not in hearing of anyone else. I have some early morning chores to attend to, need to get my new saloon sign painted today, and Mr. Hadley said a wagon load of lumber should be arriving sometime today

to get started on his new Emporium, so I need to contact the carpenters to prepare for this.

Also I just now thought you and dad will be needing materials and carpenters...I can arrange that if you like."

"Charlie, that would be nice, please do and don't forget about Joe and Aiyana, and by the way, since this is Friday, the miners will be getting off work at 5 and not long after that the railroad advance construction crews will be coming into town, so I suspect you'll be needing Joe tonight. Do you want him here at least by five?"

"Yes, so if you see him please remind him, and if he wants to come early to set up his gaming table, that is good too. Oh, and yes I have over one hundred dollars that was donated for the church from last night, and I'll put up some signs to remind people that dad, oops, Preacher Ethan that is, will have an open-air service Sunday Morning at ten. Have one of the wagons empty to come and pick up a few chairs for the service. The kids, Noah and Butterfly can help with that, besides I'd like to see them."

"Of course I will Charlie, I will pass the word along, Good day my dear, we can't appear to be to friendly yet." Tipped my hat and as I walked away, I couldn't help but think what a lovely and smart girl Ethan's daughter has grown to be and so very independent.

The rest of the morning past quickly and I think I've walked from one end of the town to the other; and passing Ethan and Joe on the street was just a nodding of heads. Finally as I was nearing The Palace Saloon I heard some very loud boisterous talking, so upon looking in I

observed an older man, near what appeared to be in his sixties, with a rode-map written on his face, standing up to the bar, with a small group of men gathered around him listening to every word of his exploits during the war. As I walked closer, his voice became clearer and looking past his beard and mustache, it was Major Allen Walker. I'll be damned, why didn't I recognize his name when I was told Allen Walker was the sheriff?

"Major, hello Major, It's been a long-time. Do you remember me?"

The sheriff stopped talking, looked at me long and hard, "Well I'll be damned, is that really you Captain August?" Yes, I do see it is... Boys meet the best damn Captain I ever had, this is Captain Daniel August, C company, 5th regiment." As he put forth his hand for me to take in a handshake, then looking at my Marshal's badge, he said, "Boys, it seems this may be our new Territorial Marshal and damn glad to have him. Been expecting a Marshal to show up, but didn't know it was you Captain."

"Well I'm not a Captain anymore, but yes I am the new Marshal and we need to talk. Come on, lets walk down to your office and you can fill me in on what we're really facing here, to get things under control or do you think that is even possible?"

As we were walking to the Sheriff's office, he ask me what I had been doing since the war.

But then must have suddenly thought of something. "Say Captain, or I mean Marshal, seems to me I recalls something about you being on the outlaw trail for a spell, and not only that, but you had been caught and sentenced to hang somewhere's in Missouri. That right Marshall?"

"As a mater of fact, that's right, but I do have a paper with me that says I got a reprieve and a pardon, I also have certified papers that states I have been dully sworn in as a U.S. Territorial Marshall. End of story, I do not want to rehash those days Major Sheriff Allen Walker! The war is over and so are my outlaw days."

"Ok Marshal, I won't bring it up again and let's hope no one else that is in these gangs around here remembers you, otherwise we may have some problems. Understand what I mean?"

"I do understand, but I'll handle that problem if and when it happens." The Marshal contended. "And by the way I see your still sporting that old single-action colt revolver, the Army issued you almost twenty years ago."

"Yup, I trust it, but them new double-action revolvers look sweet and somewhat lighter to carry around, and actually gives faster firepower, but I still like my ole trusty reliable 44 single."

As we walked into the Sheriff's Office, Mary, Allen's deputy is snoring away propped up back in the chair with her feet upon the desk. Matt knocks her feet off of his desk unceremoniously. Mary's feet hit the floor with a bang and she falls forward, gets up swearing a mile a minute, then sees who it is and says, "Well... ya needn't have done thata fool thing, I knewed ya'll were a here."

"Mary, take a walk up and down the main street here, me and the Marshall got some jawing to do." The Sheriff retorted. "Here now Captain, let me take a look at you, you haven't grown any shorter that's for sure, seems you put on a few extra pounds around the girth, but seem lanky and fit as ever, and those steely hazel eyes still could penetrate a man's soul."

"Allen, Nows not the time to be jawing over those lost war years or even the years following, you and I are here now and are the only law enforcement officers that covers a very large and from what I gather, dangerous area. I am not familiar with at all so I am asking you to fill me in?"

"Well, August first of all I'm not as young as I used to be and only walk around to keep this little town in a semblance of order, mostly just drunks, arguments, and fights that don't amount to much; I don't have the area to cover as you have, but I do hear stories, but nothing substantial I can hang on too, to arrest anyone. And a circuit judge that only comes around whenever we send for him...the telegraph or the railroad is not yet completed, so I just do the best I can with what I have available. I know that's not much help, but is all I can offer you, we don't even have a proper jail...only a shack in the back here with leg shackles, which I don't like to use at all. This town is not yet organized or unified yet, no charter and no levied taxes, to pay for a jail or even mine and Mary's wages, but a self-appointed mayor and a few self-appointed council members pay us what they can to keep body and soul together. The Mayor is a big mine-owner name a Robert Luckman from somewhere's back east, seems to be a likable fella, but also very controlling. Only one of the council members ever disputes him, that being a young fella that also owns a mine up in Silverton, name of Hadley, Glenn Hadley."

"I've met that man Allen at his saloon, and I understand he has a new co-owner manager there. What do you know about her Allen?"

"Is that a fact...well I'll be damned, I didn't ever hear about that August but I'll check into it soons I can."

"Well, me and preacher Ethan Kennedy, you recall him, and Joe Freeman, in the Army, well their here too, and we did a bit of singing at that saloon last night. Met her and Glenn Hadley, talked to them a bit...new sign going up over Hadley's, it being, Charlie's Nest, kind of a catchy name and she seems to be a charming young lady and not a Lady of the Night; seems she's gona run that saloon on the straight and narrow, and took over the rooms upstairs, while Mr. Hadley is at the hotel. By the way she hired Joe to be the in-house gambler and personal body-guard. Seems I know more'n you do of new things going on here than you do Allen."

"Seems you do August, guess I been hanging in the Palace moren I should be...the bottle has a way with me August and the boys like to hear my ole war-stories; but, when you need me I'll be ready, you can count on that, and yes Mary too. She's an old trooper, cusses moren me and chews and spits but she's a hell-raiser too and can ride an' shoot as good as any man. We'll be a hanging out at Charlie's Nest more often now too August, and I'll try finding out more about her for ya."

"That'll be fine Allen, appreciate anything you can tell me and know you'll keep your ears open for any news concerning these gangs I was told about. Two things mainly, number one, where is their hangout and number two, who is their leader?"

"Augie I've already heard about one man's name keeps a pop-pin up, ever here of a guy name a Squires, a Sam Squires, I be-lieve, but have never met or seen him face to face that I know of. Heard say he hangs mostly around Purgatory. Does that ring a bell August?"

"It damn sure does Allen, he was a part of the gang Ethan and I was a running with after the war, and in Missouri he held up a bank, and Ethan and me foiled that attempt, got the money back and I killed his brother... that was right when I got my pardon, so I had to do what I had to do then, and I didn't recognize who it was, right away. Sam got here kinda quick it seems like, must have high-tailed it here right after that."

We talked on for nearly an hour or more until I noticed the time...it was afternoon now, so thought I'd mosey down to Charlie's Nest and see what she had accomplished and what she planned for the evening's entertainment. There was a lot of hustle and bustling going on now, the main street was busy, merchants selling their wares at nearly ungodly prices and they were also trying to build the shops sturdy, wooden buildings instead of leaving them as tents. Wagon loads of lumber littered the street, and carpenters or would be carpenter helpers busy unloading, others setting out staked tracts or lots of where they planned on building. I recalled Charlie mentioning she could make arrangements for lumber, supplies and carpenters for Ethan, Joe and me. The carpenters were men mostly made up of dissatisfied or disillusioned miners trying to strike it rich, but still needed to make a living for their families, others perhaps had turned to joining the gangs to rob and terrorize. Still others were like Sam Squires, ruthless outlaws to begin with and often times not only robbed and killed at will, but raped women as well. Here I was in front of The Palace Saloon, and had not yet visited this establishment, so I walked in cautiously, not knowing what to expect at first. It was still early in the afternoon but thought I'd have a shot and see if I could strike up a conversation with someone at the bar. I was surprised to see no one standing at the bar, but there were three tables full, one group playing what appeared to be faro, another group just talking and the other group was headed by a man that was dressed in the latest eastern men's fashion, with a woman standing near. I remained at the bar and the bartender asked,

"What'll it be Marshal?" loudly, so as to be heard throughout the saloon...men looked up, but said nothing, the well dressed man, I noticed nodded at the woman to his side and she swaddled over to me and quipped,

"Well, so your the new Marshal? We heard you were in town and wondered when you'd be around to visit us here. I'm Sofia Blessing, glad to make your acquaintance, that man you eyed as you walked in is the Mayor, Mayor Robert Luckman. Here let take your drink over to the table and you two need to meet."

As I walked over to his table, the others got up and vacated, leaving me quite alone with him as even Sofia did not sit down with us, yet stayed close by. I noticed she motioned to a woman at the piano in the corner and she started playing softly. The Mayor held out his hand towards me and announced,

"Marshal Dan August, sincerely glad to meet you, I'm Bob Luckman. I've already heard your name around town, and that you've befriended one of our competitors Mr. Hadley, but he's a friend as well, further I understand your a singing Marshal and have already met Glenn's new manger at the saloon, a young pretty woman by name of Charlotte, but goes by Charlie. Sit down please. May I offer you a drink or is this to early?"

"You seem very well informed Mr. Luckman, yes I'm glad to make your acquaintance. No thanks on the drink; and I have indeed met Mr. Hadley and his new girl. Can you tell me anything about them?"

"I know only of Mr. Hadley, that he is from Savannah, Georgia come west to make his fortune grow, of the young lady, I know nothing of her first hand and have not met her yet. I did hear of some experiences she and Mr. Hadley had on the way here from Santa Fe however. She obviously is quite a remarkable young woman and very capable for being so young. Someone said he'd heard she was from Saint Louis, but I've heard nothing more. Probably just gossip. Say Sofia, come over her please, have you ever heard of our new lady at Hadley's before?"

"What's her name, perhaps if I knew her last name I may have heard of her?" As she sauntered over to our table.

I understand it is Kennedy, a Miss Charlotte Kennedy." I volunteered. "Same last name as our new Preacher Ethan Kennedy, but doubt there's any connection, as it would have been brought up when they met last night."

"Say Marshal, why don't you and I walk on down to Hadley's and you can introduce me, besides I'd like to talk to Glenn."

As the two walked those steps and crossed the street, I couldn't help but be aware that two of the gents that were in The Palace Saloon, followed us down and entered Hadley's right behind us and made their way to the bar and as they passed made no recognition of either myself or Mr. Luckman. Charlotte was near the back room directing the installation of a curtain to separate the gaming area from the noise of the saloon. She turned around as she may have heard our footsteps, and with a smile she cooed sweetly,

"Good Afternoon Marshal, I trust you are well, and you Sir are?"

"Young lady, I am Bob Luckman, at your service. I've heard so little about you yet, and certainly hope we can be friends. Your are charming my dear, what a pleasure to meet you.

I am friends with your benefactor and employer, Glenn Hadley, and If you'll permit me my dear, it's quite obvious why he has taken such a shine to you."

"Why thank you Mr. Luckman, such a pleasure to meet you as well."

At this moment Joe stepped out from behind the curtain with a new deck of cards in his hand, and interrupted, "Excuse me, don't mean to interrupt, but need to ask Miss Charlotte where the chips are?"

"Oh, this is our in-house gambler, Joseph Freeman, Mr. Luckman and you two Marshal August already know each other." I shook hands again with Joe, and noticed Mr. Luckman was reluctant to do so, but hesitatingly did.

"Pleasure I'm sure Mr. Luckman."

"Likewise, Mr. Freeman."

"Joe, the chips and other new card decks are behind the bar. Just help yourself."

"Thank you Miss Charlotte, I'll try not to be a bother to you in the future."

"Do you know that man Miss Charlotte? Do you think he can deal a straight deck?" Mr. Luckman challenged.

"Well he better or I'll fire him immediately, I want no cheating in my place at all, but just to let you know, I've also hired him as my bouncer. He seems quite capable. Now all I need is a swamper and perhaps two or three more girls to work the tables."

"Permit me to recommend a swamper for you, he is the so-called town drunk, name of Cletus Franklin, he is an x-lawman, but his past seems to haunt him, and can't seem to get over it...now everyone makes fun of him and thinks he's crazy; but I think if he had a few good meals, a bath and clean clothes and was treated better, he would at least do a good job for you, and be your errand boy. I'll send him over if you like, Miss Charlotte. As for the girls, there are a few Mexican girls that I'm sure would love to have a job, plus perhaps some of the oriental girls."

"Indeed, thank you Mr. Luckman, I'll certainly look into it and yes please send Cletus to me as well?"

"Your welcome young lady, now do you know where Glenn is?"

"Yes, he's upstairs gathering up the last of his clothes and possessions and moving to the hotel until other suitable arrangements can be found for him."

"Ah...ah you mean he's not living here with...ah, excuse me ma'am, I just assumed... ah sorry and please accept my apologies for thinking ill of your situation."

"Don't fret Mr. Luckman, no apologies necessary, but now you know I am not a Lady of Night."

Glenn Hadley was walking down the stairs, with two suitcases full of clothes and what-not. Stopped when he seen us, then continued on down the stairs, put his luggage on the floor, walked over to us.

"Good afternoon, the both of you. I see you found the Mayor, Marshal. Please gentleman let's have a drink, and tell me what you've been up to since meeting. Charlotte dear, will you please do us the honor and join us?"

"Yes Glenn, but only for a moment, I have loads of works still to be done before being ready for tonight's crowd, I hope will be. Sadie, bring us a fresh unopened bottle of Old Overholt and four glasses. Hope you gentlemen don't mind Rye, it's our best whiskey in the house right now. Oh yes Glenn, please order us some good Bourbon and even some good single-malt Scotch next time, if you will."

In unison, the three echoed, Rye is fine now." by a shake of the head and lifting their glasses to toast. "Here, here..."

Charlie lifted her glass and reminded the men she had to go check on the posters she was having made to remind people of Ethan's Church Services in the morning, and she would also send a wagon down for Glenn's luggage; and she was out the door.

"Now that is a heap of a young woman Glenn, when and how did you ever meet her?" Bob inquired good naturedly.

"She boarded the stagecoach in Santa Fe with me and we struck up a conversation which basically lasted the whole trip. She is indeed a remarkable woman, and I found out an excellent shot and not at all squeamish.

I cut in then to try to divert the conversation a little bit, but first added, "Yes, at the way-stations we were told some of the things she did, like shooting that Mescalero. But gentlemen if I may, I need to ask your assistance in locating some men to be sworn in as deputies."

"That's a tall order Marshal, as the men working are already making more money than I'm sure your able to pay them, then again finding any man honest enough to obey the law
themselves will be a task." Glenn reasoned.

"Well, I do need some deputies, guess I'll have to write to the Marshal's Headquarters in Washington and see if they are able to meet or pay more than regular wages. So please keep that in mind, meanwhile I'll just have to sniff around myself and see what I can turn up; but first I need to see that my wife and son have efficient quarters, before I go off traveling around the country-side. And I best be going to check in on them now any-way...thanks for the information gentlemen and good day to ya."

I left Glenn and Bob Luckman alone in Charlie's Nest and started walking up the street to my assigned rooms, hoping to see Noah and Daisy halfway settled at least. I knew Daisy would need some things from the Mercantile, but didn't know what for sure or I would stop and get them. Still if Daisy needed some-thing in particular, Noah was a good errand boy and would fetch anything for his mother. Damn, I surely need to spend more time with that
boy, before he's no longer a boy...manhood comes quick to a boy in these parts, soon he's doing man's work and no longer the boy you envisioned on bringing up. He was a good mannered boy though and I need to thank her for that, knew his cyphering and reading and writing, but still always asking questions.

Daisy had a good supper ready and we settled down for the night, and I simply didn't feel like going out even into town...fig-ured they could do without me for tonight, but could rest easy as

I knew Joe was out there to watch over Charlotte...and knew Aiyana was with Nora and Ethan, along with Aponi. From a distance I could hear the music, some good natured hollering and an occasional squeal. The town was alive...and growing...Monday I would visit where they were building the railroad, and try to determine how much longer it would be before they reached town; and along with that, the telegraph was coming in too. Later I would try to visit some of the mines and perhaps take a ride up to Silverton, and surrounding area, just to get an overall picture of the area in my head. Sunday was in the morning and was looking forward to relaxing and going to Ethan's first open-air services and his sermon.

Sunday Morning, no Church bells, but thanks to Charlie's posters, and the kids putting them up and handing them out to people on the street, the will-be church grounds were much fuller than I expected, with quite possibly as many as fifty to sixty souls, course some of them were here only out of curiosity of the new preacher and family.

Ethan stood up, and the talking subsided, he looked grand in his new dark blue pressed suit, and shinning black boots, yet he had his gun and holster tied down, and with the good book in hand he asked all to stand for a song that all was to know and would serve as an opening prayer.

"With a booming yet mellow voice Ethan urged the crowd to join with him and sing praise to God...

> *Amazing Grace, how sweet the sound,*
>
> *That saved a wretch like me....*
>
> *I was once lost but now am found,*
>
> *Was blind, but now I see.*
>
> *T'was Grace that taught...*
>
> *my heart to fear.*
>
> *And Grace.*

Most every one new that song and sang it as loud as they could, yet Ethan's voice sounded above all the rest.

"Folks I stand before you humbled, to be in your

102

presence, as I too was once that wretched soul, yet permit me to share with you my wife Nora, our adopted daughter Aponi, and yes she is a Sauk Indian and by god's blessing, she was given unto us. Also I have friends Joseph and his wife Aiyana that accepts the Lord as we do. Now, as I stand before you, I will say I am not up here to preach to you of hellfire, brimstone and damnation. Most of you, not living with god as your salvation, have already created your own damnation, yet, yes salvation is abundant even for you. Now some of you create harmony, togetherness and love. It's up to all of us to decided within our own hearts if we are part of the problem or part of the solution to live with your neighbor, your wife and children in peace. Drink, but in moderation,. Swear not to intimidate, but to God. Yes, swear to God, most high, to serve him in harmony and Love will follow you to the grave and unto Eternal Life. In Hebrews 12:14 it is quoted thusly: Make every effort to live in peace with everyone and to be holy; without holiness no one will see the Lord."

Now let me teach you all a new song, some of you may already know it, so help me out. It was just written earlier this year. It's "Softly and Tenderly," try to join in and we'll sing it twice.

Softly and tenderly Jesus is calling,

Calling for you and for me;

See, on the portals he's waiting and watching,

Watching for you and for me.

Refrain: Come home, come home,

You who are weary, come home;

Earnestly, tenderly, Jesus is calling,

Calling, O sinner, come home!

The song was beautiful and a lot of the women especially caught on to the words right away, and they lifted their voices to the heavens.

Why should we tarry when Jesus is pleading,

Pleading for you and for me?

At this point you could see peoples eyes flowing with tears and their voices cracking from starting to cry. Yet Ethan's voice continued to boom out...

Why should we linger and heed not His mercies,

Mercies for you and for me?

At the end, the gathered congregation was crying openly, and without shame. Yes Ethan had gathered them in.

"Folks, as you can see, we do not have a church to worship in, to protect us from the coming winter, so I ask sincerely for any donation you are able to give. On the left there you see a small table with a plate on it... please leave what ever amount you are able to give, and any able bodied men that knows carpentry that is able to volunteer is helpful. Please leave your names...God be with you!"

It was a short but meaningful service and with many peoples still wiping tears of joy from their eyes, Ethan and Nora was surrounded with well wishers, shaking his hand, leaving donations and greetings. Joe and Aiyana, who was wearing that new dress Nora had made for her while on the wagon trail and looking very much like any of the rest of them, with her new bonnet of colorful ribbons, was also greeted warmly, yet a few of them painfully turned their backs as if busy, when they came to Joe and Aiyana; overall it was a good get together. The kids were treated warmly and was making new friends or at least acquaintances. Aponi, also wearing her new dress Nora had made, but was still wearing her moccasins which betrayed her nationality, otherwise may have been taken like all the rest, but Noah stayed with her, even holding her hand to show caring and support.

I could hear Daisy, a few feet away from me, also surrounded by well wishers, some saying, so your the new Marshal's wife, we wish you well; and Daisy asking if a school was available for the kids...but all the answers were the same, that no one they knew of was qualified to teach. The open-air service was a success, the weather was conducive for outdoor activity, but as the congregation was breaking up Glenn Hadley walked over to Ethan and Nora, Joe and Aiyana who were standing together, greeted each one separately, complimented Ethan on his short but wretching sermon, and said,

"Joe, I heard you did well at the gaming table last night and not a single complaint of cheating, I compliment you and glad to have you on-board. Charlotte is a wise manager, yet I do hope you'll look out for her on a personal level as well Joe. I see you wear the new Colt double-action with a Mexican loop holster for fast draw. By the way is that a 7 inch barrel Joe?"

"Yes it is, I get greater range with it, but doesn't make my draw any faster, but it is better than the old reliable Schofield's 45, just takes a mite getting used to."

"Well, I just might look into getting one, but I just don't use a gun much, not being a gunman."

CHAPTER 8

The Railroad

Monday morning early I was riding the trail towards the rail-head, intent on evaluating their progress and when they might arrive in our township area. The proposed rails was evidently planned to go through the edge of town following the Animas River bed. It is basically what has made Durango such a fast growing frontier town; yet it was still a few months at least before it was to reach us. Still, I was to learn of the history of Durango's earliest resident's from both Allen Walker, our sheriff and his deputy Mary Davis, as told to them from earlier residents when they first arrived in this area several years ago.

The Ancestral Puebloans of over 2,500 years ago were known to be the earliest resident's of evidence found to date; these people enjoyed the rich fertile soil and abundant wildlife, before being forced to move to the mesa's southwest of Durango for reasons of self-preservation, because of invaders from the north. They carved their shelters from stone and dug pit houses right out of the side of a mountain. They mysteriously disappeared in the 1300's, some say because at the top of the mesa's they had to irrigate to grow their crops of corn, beans and wild potato's, rainfall was not sufficient and when the streams dried up, they too did also.

Hundreds of years later the Ute Indians arrived and lived in the abandoned rock cities left by the ancient Puebloans. Quite a history! In 1860 or there about a prospector discovered flakes of gold in the San Juan Mountains and people swarmed to the Animas Valley hoping of course to strike it rich. Prospectors, miners, farmers and families built homes in the valley; merchants also came to supply the mining camps with necessary supplies.

During the Civil War however, slowed the growth of the area, and it was slow to regain progress after the war.

I felt comfortable with my knowledge I had gained of Durango and surrounding area, yet I still knew nothing of the gangs, and neither the Sheriff or his deputy had any idea's either or perhaps they had just turned a deaf ear to any small talk that could have been important. I figured I was about twenty miles from Durango when suddenly a whistling of air whizzed by my ear, then I heard the shot.

I fell from my horse as if I had been hit, but grabbed my rifle out of it's boot as I did on the opposite side from where the shot seemed to have come. I was partially hidden by a log laying beside the trail, and just lay there waiting for another shot. I heard no one approaching, yet I continued to lay there for about a half hour and finally decided that whoever shot at me figured I was dead. Slowly I raised up and peered over the log I was partially hidden by. No movement at all, not even near the horizon that I could see on top of the hillside. I raised up, sat on the log and whistled for Blackjack, he came running as usual and I climbed on and headed for the top of the hill to try to find where the man had lain to ambush me, perhaps he left something behind that may identify him...that I wished to see. The only thing I found was where the grass was matted down in a suitable place to lay in wait, but just as I was about to walk away I spotted a brass cartridge casing, it was a 44/70 Winchester cartridge, popular but few of them around...it may hopefully lead me to my ambushers. I again mounted Blackjack and took to the trail again. A couple of hours later I came upon a survey crew, well two of them anyway. I ask how much farther back the track crew was and they informed me they wasn't sure, but the grading crew was about ten miles farther. So I ask how many miles of track could be laid in a day.

"Mister, that depends upon a number of things...the grading crew, the laying of ties, the weather, the terrain, and rail crews. In this mountainous terrain and if the weather holds I expect they can lay 3 to 4 miles of track a day, sometimes as much as 5, but not usual and that's working them all at about 14 hours a day. So I suspect it'll be months yet before they reach Durango."

"Well then their back there much farther than I had heard, don't see any need to go any farther. Thank you much for the information."

"Not a problem sir, ah say, by the way who might you be?"

"I'm Marshall Dan August, newly assigned to this area, that's why I'm scouting around. Say by chance did you fellas see a gent passing by here awhile back today?"

"Yup, sure did Marshall, 'bout an hour ago actually, headed due north toward Silverton. Just keep on the trail your headed on and you'll go right to it. He was a riding a spotted Mustang, but just a dallying along, not appeared to be in a hurry at all."

"Well, good day to ya, thank you for the information." The Marshal waved good bye as he turned Blackjack and headed back to Durango.

It wasn't really a wasted trip as I did find out some pertinent information. That is, I didn't think I was having any troubles from the railroad crews or anyone connected with it, at least right now; and I did find out that someone didn't want a Marshall poking around and knew I had already arrived and further knew I would be on the trail today. So, only someone at the church services that hung around after the meeting was over would know, as that is when I mentioned to only a few where and when I would be going Monday morning. Of course it could have just been idle talk to other people that may have spread the word of my where abouts for Monday, or it could have been done deliberately to have me set up... In any case I was nearly killed. That made me curious of my predecessor, how and exactly why was he killed? Perhaps he was getting to close to the truth of the whereabouts of these gangs and the leaders; but why wouldn't the Sheriff and deputy know anything about it, it seems only natural the Marshal would have shared information with the only other law-enforcement officers in the territory. This also gives me something to ponder on, I need to find out about and who the Marshall had been. I wonder now if the would-be ambusher today on the trail could have been the same one that killed the former Marshall. As I continued to mosey along, now at a leisurely pace, I surprisingly came upon Sophie Blessing, the head saloon girl at The Palace Saloon. What on earth could she be doing out here alone in this country by herself?

"Well Good Evening Sophie, what seems to be the problem, why are you about five miles out from town alone?"

"Oh Marshal, I am so glad to see you, I was simply out for a country ride and...well, well just look the axle broke or something on this carriage and I've been stranded here for several hours, hoping for someone to come by."

"Let me take a look, maybe I can help."

"Please do Marshal, it's been wretched just sitting here and I'm out of drinking water too. Do you have any left in your canteen?"

"Of course Sophie, but it's river water, not well water, so if you don't mind...here, help yourself." As I handed her my canteen.

"Oh, I don't mind at all Marshal, I'm just parched. Well what do you think, are you able to fix it or what can you do?"

"Sophie, you sure enough broke an axle...I'll unhitch your horse, you'll have to ride her and we'll leave the buggy here and send someone for it. Is it a carriage rental from the livery?"

"Yes it is, but I just hate to straddle a horse with my dress on, but guess I have no other choice."

Marshal, it seems you do look and act a bit familiar to me from sometime back, sorry, don't mean to be a busybody, but ever since meeting you that's been a nagging at me. Perhaps you may remember me if you'll give it some thought?"

"It's possible Sophie, of course as I've been out on the trail since the war was over, and I understand you've traveled some from place to place working as well."

"Ah Marshal, I know now...yes, you were on the outlaw trail with Sam Squires, at least for awhile. I recall you one night at, now let me think...it had to be in Saint Louie at the Diamond Star Saloon, you were playing Keno and the house tried cheating you, you had spread for 4 card Keno and won, but they wouldn't pay off...you killed the dealer as he drew on you and then Sam started shooting the whole place up. Yes Marshal I do recall you for sure now."

"Sophie, this is important, I do hope you'll not spread that around. I am really a U.S. Marshal, got a pardon and sworn in an all; married, well, I was married even then but running loose as if I wasn't, got a fifteen year old son and going straight."

"No one will hear it from me Marshal, you can rest assured. We all have skeletons in our closets. I have so many, they're not skeleton's anymore."

"Thanks Sophie, and here we are in town, if you want to dismount and go into the Saloon now, I'll take the horse onto the livery stable and tell him what happened and where he can find the carriage. Bye now, enjoyed our talk, but would like to talk to you some other time."

"Of course Marshal, my pleasure, and thanks for your help. Bye now."

Finally back home, it was dark now and I was bone tired. Noah came a running at me when I opened the door, Daisy looked back from the stove, smiled and said to wash up, supper was ready. I walked over to her, kissed her on the neck,

"Oh Dan, ah...not in front of Noah, now get washed up and sit."

"You know I'll have to walk into town shortly and see how things are going and hopefully hear some gossip about the gangs. It's just part of my job Daisy, and Noah, you need to understand that too."

"Yes Sir, I understand that, it's just so hard on Ma."

"Now Noah that's enough of that talk, your Pa's got to do what's necessary. We'll both be here Dan when you get back. Now sit down and eat, the both of you."

"Okay, but Pa I read about one of them telescope's to see up in the heaven's, I'd sure like to see that...have you ever Pa?"

"No son, I haven't. I suppose it would be pretty good to see farther than the eye can see. But what good do they do other than that?"

"Don't know for sure Pa, but I'd like to learn about it."

"Well, it certainly gives a person something to wonder about." Daisy chided. "Now Noah say grace and we'll eat so your Pa can do his job..no more chit-chat. Hear now?"

On my way out the door, I wondered if I'd ever see my family again. I was shot at today and only by the grace of God, I'm still alive...I decided to go back in and give each of them a loving kiss. These things I never gave a thought too when I was on the outlaw trail, but now with Daisy and young Noah depending on me, it was something to think about.

Now as I walked down the street, I paused at The Palace Saloon, music blaring from the piano and someone was trying to sing above the hub-bub and loud talking going on. I pushed open the bat-wing doors and walked in a few feet and stopped. Just at that time, all the noise stopped too, you could have heard a pin drop, and all eyes were upon me, some with slack jaw, others with their eyes nearly coming out of their heads. I was getting the impression I wasn't expected to be alive. Apparently Sophie hadn't told anyone. Finally, Bob Luckman, the Mayor and co-owner of the saloon got up from his corner table and came forward with a hand outstretched saying,

"Damn glad your okay Marshal, but we heard you had been shot today, earlier. What luck, can you tell me exactly what happened? Here first, come sit-down, have a drink."

As I followed him back to the table, I looked over at Sophie...she just winked and lowered her head. I knew then I had her on my side for sure.

"Well Marshal, how in hell did you survive that ambush? Tell us about it."

"How did you know it was an ambush Mayor, and how did you get word from anyone so soon?"

"Well, ah well, I just assumed it was. Didn't think you could have been taken any other way Marshal, and it just must have been idle talk, you know gossip travels so fast."

"Yeah I suppose so Mayor..." *and my mind was racing with this information, but I didn't let it be known it sounded suspicious.*

Sophie came over then and speculated, "Well Marshal, some cowpoke came in earlier with that tale, it was the only information given to us...so we couldn't think otherwise. But nice to see your okay."

Then the Mayor inquired, "Marshal, what's your next move? If your a hunted man, seems to me you'll need some help. I know two good men that would be your deputies...and be able to watch your back. By the way, I was talking to Glenn, you know Glenn Hadley, just this morning that we need to build a jail and a Marshal's office... What do you think Marshal? Got a lot picked out already and we have three loads of lumber that should arrive tomorrow and I have a couple of men that could start on it."

"Well Mayor sounds like your ambitious to get a respectable town built as soon as possible. Of course, but I'd like a hand in the plans of how it should be built, is that acceptable?"

"But of course Marshall, whatever you think; and I have also contributed quite handsomely to your friend the Preacher to build a church and rectory, and will lend a hand for his friend, that black feller, to get suitable quarters built as soon as possible, but tell me is that a Comanche Squaw he married?"

"I understand she is not a squaw, but is the younger sister of Chief Pecos, younger brother to Quanah Parker, who has just left the reservation again. It might be a sad day for us if something was to happen to her. By the way she is a Christian, but other than that, I found out Joseph Freeman, her husband is damn ruthless if he was to get worked up...rumor has it he used to ride with the Squires gang."

"Now that is interesting Marshal, do you think Squires has placed him here to gather information?"

"Now that I have no knowledge of Mayor, but I'm sure he'd be mighty grateful for the help with building his house and treating his wife Aiyana with respect. You know he's working at Charlie's Nest don't you? He's the In-house gambler, and doing well I heard in running a straight game."

"So I've heard Marshall. Oh, another drink?"

"No, but thanks...good talking to you, I need to move on. Keep it a bit quieter in here tonight, will you Mayor?"

Laughing the Mayor replied, "That's a near impossibility Marshal, but I'll mention it to my floor man. Have a good night now."

Across the street and a few more doors down was Charlie's Nest, several horse's tied in front, but the noise was not nearly as contentious as it was at The Palace. As I stepped inside, the good natured chatter continued, a few looked at me and even waved with a smile on their faces...this was a totally different kind of crowd that came to Charlie's Nest. These were men that just wanted a few drinks without the worry of being accosted. I observed she had hired three more girls, two Mexican girls and an Oriental girl, so now she had five girls working for her and they seemed to be handling the crowd quite well. I would guess to be about 70 to 75 men here... But how many now in the back room with Joe at the poker table?

I started walking that direction, when suddenly a bell rang and immediately Joe came out from behind the curtain with gun drawn.

"Surprise, surprise," laughed both Charlie and Joe, then others joined in. "This is just one of our security measures." Charlie quipped. "What do you think Marshal?"

Well, it damn sure surprised me, and yes I can guess why you thought of it...good thinking."

"How you doing Marshal," Joe implored, "We heard some rumors that you were dead, we just couldn't believe and now here you are to disprove those rumors."

"I think I may have disappointed a few people when I walked into The Palace before coming here. Most of them actually seemed very surprised I wasn't dead. But at least I have a foggy idea who may be behind it now, but have to wait awhile before I even bring that name up or consider it seriously."

"Ethan and I was going to go out looking for you tomorrow if you hadn't of shown up...was giving you time, we just didn't believe you had been killed. But don't suppose you'd like to give us a name of your suspicion yet, so we could keep an eye out too?"

"No, don't want to give any false impressions now, I'm going to let it grow and see where it leads; but keep your eyes and ears open, even to the ones we already know and may least expect. Now ya'll gona let me just stand here without a drink or a sit down, or just keep a jawin away at nothing?"

"Ok sit down Uncle Augie, I've got something important to say; Ti Ling, bring us all a drink.

Now sit down here, I've started running this saloon the wrong way to be able to get the type of clientele we need to hear anything about the gangs...from now on us girls are going to work as Lady's of the Night. That will attract the kind of clientele we need."

"Now wait a minute Charlotte we don't need you to do that, No way girl." August insisted.

114

"I have a plan, that it will appear I have special clients to take upstairs, but I won't really do anything, but I still need to work out the details, but I am going to convert my quarters into separate rooms for the girls here who want to do that. Yet, somehow I need to tell Glenn what I plan to do, even without telling him I'm a Special Deputy, undercover. Guess I'll just convince him I am a real Lady of the Night who accepts visitors to my rooms. In my heart, I know Glenn is not involved...so I need to level with him. Uncle Augie, what do you think? Should I tell Glenn, I am an undercover deputy or not, as I really do like him a lot?"

"Well Charlie, if you think you can pull that off, it just may work." Joe agreed.

"What do you mean act like a Lady of the Night and not really do anything?"

"Oh Uncle Augie, I could talk to some of the guys, explain my situation and give them a couple of free drinks for going up to my rooms with me and just talking, with no sexual activity involved with me at all. Just don't know who I could get right now, besides Glenn, if I could tell him the real reasons for doing this."

"Charlotte, you know your Pa isn't going to like this idea at all, even if you really are not participating, but you would get a bad reputation. And right now, even though you are a saloon girl, your reputation is good with many of the other ladies in town."

"Oh, Uncle Augie, what other solution do we have? I've tried to think of everything."

"I don't know for sure Charlotte, don't like the idea of exposing your special status to anyone yet, maybe Glenn would be okay, just not sure yet."

"Well, please don't mention this to Pa, at least not yet. The girls I have working for me now want to do this instead of going to the hotel...costs the gents extra money that way."

"Ok honey, at this point, I see no other way myself...you need the kind of clientele that may be involved with these gangs or at least in a position to hear what's going on. Those type are the very ones who want to have a time with the girls. I appreciate you willing to put your good reputation on the line to get rid of these damn gangs. But you do know a lot of gossip about you is going to be the headline here in town don't you?"

"Yes, I know…I'll just have to bear it for awhile. Later people will learn the truth why I did this."

Just then, Ti Ling was apparently having a bit of a problem with a customer at the bar, so I hurriedly walked over and inquired of the problem next to the gent she was having a problem with.

"Mister, what seems to be the problem here? Well, what the hell Sarge, what you doing here, we thought you had decided not to join us after all."

"Capn', been scoutin, problems and neeeee"…… And Sarge passed out right there at the bar.

Charlie and Joe both hurried over to see what the trouble was, thinking the ole gent was just drunk. Charlie noticed blood oozing out from under his coat.

Uncle Augie, he's been shot…Joe go get that lady Doc in town, hurry please."

"You mean that lady doctor that put her shingle on that tent frame down a few more doors?"

"Yes Joe, now hurry, he appears to be in a bad way."

Joe scurried out the door in a run, meanwhile Dan lifted ole Sarge upon top of the bar and proceeded to take his coat off. Sarge had plastered his side with mud to help stop the bleeding, but it was still oozing out. Now in came the doc with bag in hand.

"What's happened here?" She asked.

"Well, appears he's either gunshot or knifed in the side…can you do anything Doc?"

"I need to examine the wound, so need to get that mud washed off first. Can you get me some hot water and towels?"

"Ti Ling, hurry now get a pan of hot water and clean bar towels!"

In no time the doc had cleaned the wound on ole Sarge and identified it was a deep knife wound, between the ribs up high, proceeded to clean, sterilize and dress the wound in no time.

"He'll need to be bed ridden for a while till that wound heals, is there any place you can put him? My office-tent just is not set up for that right now."

"Marshal, you and Joe carry him upstairs in my room, I can look after him for a few days. I've got five girls and myself to look in on him from time to time and attend his needs."

After the Sarge was carried to Charlie's rooms and put into her bed, he was sound asleep and figured he'd be that way for awhile, so they all went back downstairs, and of course we all wanted to know just exactly who this lady doctor was.

"Doc, I'm Marshall Dan August, I didn't even know you were in town. My apologies, now who might you be?"

"I'm Doctor Nichols, Doctor Valerie Nichols, I just arrived back in town nearly a year ago. My father used to doctor here and taught me everything, then sent me to school in Boston to get my papers of certificate, I assure you I'm a qualified doctor."

"No offense ma'am, er, doctor, just curious, let me introduce you too Miss Charlotte Kennedy and owner of this establishment, and this is Joe, her gambler. You'll meet most all the others as time goes on; and welcome to this growing town."

"Glad to meet you all, but I've lived here before when it first started out a few years back with my father before he sent me back east, to get my degree."

CHAPTER 9

Ladies of the Night

C harlotte's conversion of now becoming a courtesan herself or perhaps a madam was quite a reversal for many people and was just unable to believe it, as the news spread quickly and even violently.

Charlie's Nest was quickly overrun with the so-called bad element and fights broke out as they all wanted to bed-down Charlie, but she wasn't taking any of them. She had a different plan in mind, meanwhile her girls of five were happy and clientele obviously picked-up, Charlie was busy mostly with just being the madame...and was quickly taking over from The Palace as the place to drink, gamble and bed down their favorite tart. The Mayor, and co-owner of The Palace was not happy at all. Charlie called her girls courtesans to the clientele, but many still referred to them as tart's or harlot's, or as some would just call them whore's.

Joe's roll as the house gambler kind of took on a different meaning now, as he had to be more aware of the safety of six women, which of course still included Charlotte. The one thing Joe hated most of all was taking out the chamber pot of ole Sarge, as couldn't get any of the girls to do that. No one had seen Cletus as he was supposed to be the swamper. Probably drunk. Occasionally, Sarge would come to and try to say something, but all we heard was mumbling. Nothing we could understand. Finally, after four night's and on the fifth morning, Charlie came running after me...Sarge had set up, looking pretty good and wanted desperately to talk to me. I had been walking down the street that early morning to first see the new doc and pay my respect's, then to go to Charlie's Nest to see ole Sarge anyway. As we neared Charlotte's place we saw Doc hurrying up the street towards us.

"Morning Doc, glad to see you, I suppose you were gona call on Sarge? Charlotte just informed me he set-up and wants to talk."

"Well, good morning to you both. Yes I wanted to check in on him, just hope he doesn't reopen that wound."

"Well, it's about damn time ya'll got heres...been a waiting for seems like hours." Ole Sarge acting impertinent as always. "Got sum things to tell ya, import like Cap'n."

"Just be quiet and let Doc look you over first, your still not well." I cautioned Sarge.

"Oh hogwash Cap'n, I'm fit as can be, I come ritchaway today to tell ya."

"Sarge, you been here for 5 days now, mostly sleeping and groaning, whatever you have to tell me can wait a few more minutes."

"Five days?...Well, I'll be damned." Sarge repeated

Doc Nichols checked Sarge's knife wound, cleaned and put a new dressing on and confided;

"Sarge, you old gaffer, if you weren't so damn cussedly ornery you wouldn't have lived, your wound was deep and infected, but you packing it with mud like you did stopped the blood flow, which probably saved you from bleeding out. You'll live."

"Well nows I knowed that, quit cher fussin, but I'm a might hungry, could eat a thing that don't eats me first off."

'You'll get fed, ya ole goat, now what's so damn important you wanted to tell me five days ago?"

"Suh, I been a scoutin now since you hired me on an I's found some things all mighty import... Ya recall Squires, Sam Squires, well, he's a holed up thar in the mountains somewhere's just as sure as sure and he's a headin a gang of cutthroat fer shor. But thas not the end of it tuther, rumor is that these har railroads are fussin sumtin terrible and Bat's amixed up in it on that thar oppisin side of the Topeka er what ever railaroad he's a sidin wit."

"You mean the Atchison, Topeka and Santa Fe Railway?"

"Yup, that thar's the one's alrighty."

"Sarge, and do you mean Bat Masterson, the gunslinger?"

Thas the one and onliest Cap'n, he's a backin them thar politicians fer a bunch a dinero. But he's no aroun these heh parts yet anyways."

"Sarge, I really do appreciate this information you've brought me...but how in hell did you get knifed?"

"I reckon some feller a sneak upon this ole body and a did me from the behind...left me for dead and sum ole Indian pulled me oughta the Animas jus afore them upper rapids. Pack some mud onta me, left me a smidgen a jerky and skedaddled. Don't know much else, I finalys gotched har ta ya."

"Much obliged Sarge, guess I need to head for San Juan's in a day or so, or soon as your feeling up to it again."

"I'm up to it this har minute Cap'n, shor wants to meets up with ta guy who knifed me. But Purgatory is a mite fer off."

"Doc, when do you think Sarge will be ready to ride?"

"Not for another week at least, he's lost a lot of blood and that wound needs to heal more so it doesn't open up again." Doc Nichols asserted "If you all will excuse me, I need to attend to a few other patient's, so I'll be going. Good Morning to ya'll.

"Thank you Doc, have a good day and guess that trip can be put off for awhile. Sarge, I think Sam Squires is involved in it all. Just can't figure him for the top boss though cause these gangs were busy long before he got in these parts. He couldn't have got here more than a week or two before we did."

"So that would mean he knows someone here, as Squire's is not the type of guy that is not going to be the big gun in any gang." Joe concluded.

Well, whoever is the brains behind all of this has pretty well concealed his identity, only a very few will know; it may very well be someone we least would suspect." Charlie noted. "Uncle August, didn't you say you had a suspicion of who may be behind these gangs? Why don't you tell us so we can keep our eyes and ears open about that particular person?"

"Well, I don't know. I hate to put suspicion on a person that may be totally innocent of any wrong doing. Let it just hang as is for now, I'll tell you in good time."

"Well suh, I shor do have a my spcions too." Sarge volunteered.

"Lets just keep it quite fore now Sarge. It's still early in our investigation, but wish we had an inside guy, but that's near impossible cause we just don't know who we can trust around here." I insisted.

"Oh Cap, thars another thing you oughta know. Happens thars the Stockton Gang here too, and Squires isn't wit dem. Ever did ya heard of dem Cap? Ike Stockton is the Segundo in that herd, an' don't knows how manys they's got, an thas all of it I knows 'bout."

"Sarge, you did a hell of a lot a snooping to find out all this information, and I thank you for it. But I'm going on up to The Palace and talk to Sophie, I think she's always been pretty straight, but she's in a position to hear things and in the know up there and just perhaps she can help out too. Charlie honey, how is your new idea working out?"

"Well, the girls like it cause they don't have to take their tricks to the hotel and as for me, I'm reserving myself as only the madam (laughing), at least for now. But seriously, I feel confident it will be beneficial to us in the long-run. But I have decided to tell Glenn who and what I really am. I have grown to trust him and need someone to lean on from time to time."

Yes, I see your point my dear, go ahead and tell him, but stay guarded in the doing honey. I do trust you to use proper judgment. I need to be going now myself, Sarge just stay still, let your self heal well and we'll soon be making that trip into the San Juans. Charlie, please keep Joe informed of the least little leak about any of the gangs."

"Bye Uncle August, don't worry any about me...so far all is going very well. I should have started out my business as I am now doing, I may have already heard something of importance if I had of."

"Don't worry about it now, just do what you think you can now..."

I sauntered off thinking and keeping in mind what ole Sarge told us and what Charlie had to say. As I was crossing the street, I noticed a pretty little girl having a problem with a guy, so I hastened a bit more and came up to them and ask the girl if this guy was bothering her; but the man butted in before the young girl had a chance and said, "Sorry Marshal, I thought she was someone else, I'll be moving on." And walked away.

I looked at this young lady and ask her name.

"I am Sara Jane, Sara Jane Nichols, my mother is the Doctor here, and that man was bothering me. He wanted to take me to the hotel."

"Well Sara Jane, I have met your mother, but what are you doing up and around so early?"

"Mother asked me to take this bundle to the Chinese laundry, but it's quite heavy and I ask that man to assist me...said he would if I was nice to him, so I said fine, I'll be nice, but guess he thought a different kind of nice than I did."

"I see your point Sara Jane, well to bad there are men like that, but I don't think he'll bother you again. I'll be glad to carry it for you, I haven't been to the Chinese laundry yet, so this is my chance. By the way my name is Dan August and I'm very glad to make your acquaintance Sara Jane and I am the new Marshal in these parts."

"Thank you Marshal, I appreciate that." as we walked the rest of the way in silence.

Upon entering the makeshift tent Chinese laundry, I was immediately taken back by a sweet strange smell, yet I had been associated with that aroma before. It was the embers of an opium pipe still lite...Damn, now that's all I needed to have to contend with too, along with the gangs, was an opium den here in the midst of town. Sara Jane deposited her laundry with an older woman who looked at me suspiciously and gave her a paper with a number six written on it, meaning the laundry would be ready by six this evening.

As we walked out of the laundry, Sara Jane asked what that strange smell was.

"Marshal, what was that strange smell in there, is it the detergent they use for the laundry?"

"No honey, it's a hard drug they use to smoke a pipe and is hallucinatory, makes you see things that are not there, and is very habit forming."

"Well the aroma was quite pungent, kinda sweet like, but mom has a small bottle of it in her medicine chest that she uses to kill pain in very ill and pain-racked patients. Yet I never smelled it like that before."

"Sara Jane, it's best you stay away from it...it is a dangerous medicine if not used properly; and I think what your mom has is a refined type of opium I think they call poppy tears and they make a medicine out of it called morphine, which is used now more often than the use of laudanum, and your mom might very well have some of that as well."

"Thank you Marshall guess I best go on home now. I just wish there were more kids around my age, at least just to talk to."

"I have a son that is fifteen now, name of Noah, I'll be glad to have you two meet up if you want Sara Jane. It's about 9:30 now, when was your mom expecting you home?"

"She's out making some house-calls now, then she goes back to the office by ten or so and usually there are some patients waiting that keeps her busy till at least noon, and she usually will close the office at noon, unless there is an emergency. So I think it'll be all right, besides I'm with you, the Marshal."

"Very well then Sara Jane, I'll take you there now."

As we walked in the door we could smell fresh baked bread, just out of the oven, and Daisy was humming to herself as usual.

"Look Ma, here's Pa with some company." Noah was delighted to see.

Daisy turned around, surprised to see Dan back so early and then noticed Sara Jane standing demurely beside her husband, wiping her hands on her apron, she responded with:

"Mercy sakes child do come in and please sit down, I'm Daisy that ole galoots wife, and that youngun over there is Noah. Fresh bread and have some hive honey just a waiting."

Good Morning Mrs. August, I'm Sara Jane Nichols. My mom is the doctor here and I met up with Marshal August while going to the laundry. Very glad to make your acquaintance Ma'am, and glad to meet you too Noah."

"Well mercy me, Noah go fetch the fresh milk out of the well pantry, it should be chilled now and we'll all have some bread, butter and honey with a glass of milk...Frank you sit down to for a while, and have a coffee with me. Now isn't this nice, haven't had company for a spell and sure is pleasant to get to know you Sara Jane."

Do you go to school Sara or is there a school here yet?" Noah asked

"No, Ma's been teaching me at home, no teacher here yet, but we've been expecting one to come for some time now."

"Ma's been teaching me too, but I know it takes her extra time, and no other kids, so wish there was a school."

"Dan, you need to talk to the mayor and that town council you told me of and have them get a school started. I could even teach part time till a regular teacher could get here, and think Nora would volunteer also." Daisy volunteered

The banter of chit-chat kept up till it was near lunch time and I thought it was best to escort this young girl back home so she would not again be accosted by some stranger. We passed The Palace and the Chinese laundry again and I could faintly smell the opium aroma in the air. This indeed would be a place I need to keep in check. As Sara Jane and I walked down the street, for the first time it seemed with my eyes wide-open, I noticed the ungodly amount of whore houses, girls on the street half undressed to show what they offered for a mite of gold dust or a pinch of silver. Already the noon bustle on the street was a bit degrading and to think that only a few short months ago I was a part of this unsightly parade. How could I have been so blinded by this kind of life that after the war I didn't go home to family, rather I chose the nefarious life of an outlaw, the drinking, the greed, the robberies and murders, and in my mind I was using my family as an excuse. It took a rope around my neck to make me see the life I unwittingly chose. Now here I am walking a young girl of 15 to her home, so idiots like me before, would not bother her. Yet as I looked upon this child I could see her smiling at the same things I was disgusted about. She was definitely of impressionable age, and all she could see was the glitter of gold and happy times she thought she could see before her. I feared to ask her thoughts of what she was gazing upon. Could she not see the horror of what her eyes were observing? We continued walking down this main thorough-fare and cat-calls were made to both of us...yes even to Sara Jane, boasting she could have a great time. It would do no good to stop and berate these ungodlies, as there was no law against it, so I tried to rush Sara Jane beyond this and finally we came to Doc Valerie Nichole's office-home of which the front part was tent like and back of that was a board structure of their living quarters. A sign on the front read, closed for lunch, yet inside the office on a table was a bell to be rung in case of emergency. But Sara Jane led me through the tent-office and into a clean well furnished and comfortable home, small but sufficient, obviously large enough for their needs. Doctor Nichol's father had been a frontier doctor and Valerie Nichol's, his daughter assisted his efforts and chose being a doctor as well and went to school in Boston after his death, came back out here to continue his work. She had a wild courtship while in Boston, and before they were to marry, he died by the hands of a jealous husband.

Valerie had a girl child Sara Jane and left as soon as the child was old enough to travel. Of course I found out all of this later. So Sara Jane grew up here in Durango...perhaps, just perhaps she has heard things about the robberies or gangs through the grape-vine or from other kids. I need to talk to her more, but another time may be better when she knows Noah better and could possibly trust me. Yet right now I feel she is familiar with what actually goes on behind so-called closed doors, even at her tender age. The way the old Chinese lady looked at her, and Sara Jane quickly looked away, makes a person wonder what she may be hiding, if anything...

Though, now as Doc Nichol's greeted me I found it was difficult to suspect Sara Jane being

involved with any wrong-doing. She invited me to join them for lunch, which consisted of fresh baked bread, thick cuts of ham and cheese and a spicy mustard and suggested I spread it on very lightly...wish I had paid attention, it was not hot at all, it was fire-burning to hell hot

and was glad Doc had vision enough to serve me a cool beer with lunch and I downed three large glasses before the fire cooled down to just embers...smoldering and ready to ignite again. Lesson learned to pay close attention to the little things. After Sara Jane and Doc finally quite laughing with tears streaming down their cheeks, Doc told me it was a pure mustard the Chinese made from ground mustard seed. Valerie, took my sandwich and replaced the two pieces of bread and even scraped off most of the mustard on the ham and cheese...I carefully with apprehension took another bite after she poured me another beer.

Then I found out it was very good, still spicy but had a good flavor to it with no after taste.

We had an amiable conversation and I learned there was a type of underground to Durango, that most people were not aware of...Sara Jane excused herself, saying she had to meet a friend. Doc Valerie Nichols continued with: "Marshall, I am worried about Sara Jane, for the last year or so, she just has not been herself...sometimes she disappears for 2 or 3 days at a time, then tells me she was visiting and staying over with friends, but no way to get word to me. I have told our Sheriff Allen about this, but he doesn't seem to have time to be concerned about it. But it seriously concerns me and sometimes when she is here it seems she is in another world. Would you think about this and try to include her with your overall investigation, and as nice as she acts publicly, she often times is not the same when just the two of us are together. Acts as if she's in another world, stares into space and doesn't even hear me when I talk to her. I am so worried and don't know what to do about her."

"Yes Doc, I will do what I can, but not sure what I'll be looking for, but I will keep my eyes and ears open for you. In walking with her this morning I noticed a few things I want to keep in mind about her, but you know teenagers sometimes are quite secretive. Often times we find out things to late to do anything about a problem."

"Of course I understand Marshal, and I know you cannot limit your investigations to Sara Jane; what with everything already going on in this sin-ridden tent city."

"Well Doc, I thank you for a very fine lunch and beer, but I must be going now. Good day to ya, and thanks for looking after Sarge...please give me the bill."

I strolled back out into the thoroughfare, the sun was out now from behind the clouds and was beginning to get quite hot; contemplating how I should proceed, so many loose ends and lips about the gangs seemed to be closed. I walked up the street and I saw Sara Jane enter in the Chinese laundry, and recalled their laundry would not be ready till 6 this early evening; so why is she going in there now? My mind and thoughts raced ahead maddeningly, and I wondered what she could want in there, and then again recalled the look between the old lady and Sara Jane. I decided to go into the laundry and see what was going on...

"Good afternoon, where is the girl Sara Jane"

"She no here, laundry not ready."

"Listen, I saw her come in here only a few minutes ago, so where is she now?"

"She no here, maybe go back door yard. You go now." Motioning me to leave with her hands.

What the hell is she trying to hide? So I decided to walk around the back and saw Sara Jane being handed some money or appeared to be money, but could not see who it was giving it to her. He then kissed her and walked away through the back. Sara Jane turned around but didn't see me as here eyes and fingers were counting paper money. I ducked and quickly walked to the front again and deciding not to confront her about this now, but something was up for sure. My God, what could she be into? Perhaps it was just legitimate, but left me wondering more and more and why would an older man be kissing her what appeared to be quite passionately. He was dressed in a suit with a round bowler hat, not dressed as a cowman or miner, but more like a business man.

Now Sara Jane was walking towards the livery by way of the back, trying to decide which one I should follow, I ended up following her, as it seemed she was on a mission. The livery man gave her a saddled horse and she rode out the back way heading west. My horse was at my own house to far away to get him right now as I might lose track of exactly where she is going, so I told the hostler to saddle me a horse. It just seemed strange to me, that I happened upon this, what appeared to be the making of a tryst, but why and who with? I followed her for about 3 miles and she suddenly turned off the main rode, and through a tangled unused trail and came upon an old shack partially hidden. From the outside it appeared to be just an old abandoned shack, perhaps an old miner's shack; yet from my vantage point I could see a horse & buggy tied to a hitch rail near an old water trough, and Sara Jane's horse tied there also. I wanted to see if it was possible to see in so I tied my rental horse securely to a tree and crept quietly up to a dirty window, there I could faintly see in and found much to my surprise not only Sara Jane but the Mayor Bob Luckman. I nearly fell over I was so surprised, and to see they were both partially undressed and in a tight embrace sitting on the edge of the bed. My God, was he also a pedophile? And why would Sara Jane agree to such a rendezvous, they certainly did not appear to be strangers to one another. Yet, in a weird way, this was only confirming my suspicions that he had much to hide, and I knew he may be my number one suspect. A man of about 45 or perhaps 50 that would entertain a young teenager in such a way and give her money to be his hidden mistress just didn't sit well with me. I didn't want to reveal myself to them at this time, so I silently went back to my horse, but inwardly I wanted to crash into that shack and beat the living hell out of that man and spank Sara Jane's bottom red. To me it was disgusting !

The way back to town was laborious, contemplating if or how I should tell Doc Valerie about her daughter or if or how I should approach the subject to our Bob Luckman. Yet the more I thought about it, the sicker I was getting. She seemed like a really well mannered young girl, nearly a woman by proportion, sweet but obviously had a hidden desire.

Arriving back in town, leaving the rental horse at the livery, I walked to my quarters in silence...very deep in thought.

CHAPTER 10

The Cliff Dwellings

S arge and I was on our way to the Cliff-Dwellings of the ancient Puebleons or Anasazi, and had heard so many tales regarding them, they were difficult to believe; but Sarge had also heard there might possibly be some gangs hiding out there. Yet I was hard pressed not to keep my mind off of Sara Jane and Bob Luckman, our prestigious Mayor, mine owner and business man, who normally you judge to be an upright citizen. Obviously, their relationship was not platonic in anyway, so beside him liking young girls, that let themselves become tarts or would be harlots, I wonder if there is any other.

"Say Cap'n, there's also some of dem stories 'bout ghosts still a livin in dem Kiva's in dem cliff's." Sarge interrupted my quizzical thoughts.

"Well Sarge, tell me what you heard, don't just leave me hanging."

"It's not so easy to tell Cap'n, as I don unerstan 'bout ghosts and such a ting. But I'a been scare a lot, yet I keeps agoin."

"Sarge, just how much farther are these cliff dwellings, we've been on the trail now for a couple hours or more."

"Don't rightly knows Cap'n, never been to thar afore myself, but ole Jake down at the livery says it takes a feller 'bout six maybe more'n hour to get thar, thas why Cap'n I suggested to bring us some eats and blankets."

"We've been just been rambling along easy like, so lets spur our horses and get there a bit sooner, I don't want it to be complete night fall before we arrive."

Spurring our horses to a steady gallop, I estimated we should arrive about dusk, time to set up camp, eat a few bites of Jerky and sip a coffee, get a good sleep and start out in the dwellings early morning like.

Sometime later we arrived at an area to camp, and looking east and a bit south about a mile away we could still see through a haze some high cliff's and what appeared to be carved into those caves some dwellings if that's what you'd call them. They did from this distance give an eerie mysterious feeling to me as seeing them from such a distance and through this strange haze. What kind of people would have the knowledge and fortitude to spend hundreds of laborious man hours to build living quarters into or under solid rock? And for what purpose? Obviously, protection for one I would think, and also if you looked close you could see dug into the earth at the base of the dwellings an area that had been irrigated as small ditches were still evident of farming techniques. The sun was low in the west, casting strange shadows into corners of the Cliff-Dwellings almost looking like someone moving around in them. Eating our jerky and sipping our coffee, it was actually pleasant and the panoramic scene being played out before us brought thoughts of just who or where did these Anasazi people's come from, how did they learn to build such structures and the man-hours it must have taken, only later to have abandoned their homes. A phenomenon indeed ! Now it was getting colder at night and we wished we had brought more blankets, so we stoked up the fire and added a few more pieces of the dried wooden branches we had gathered up, and the flames sent out dancing like figures from across the fire and blinded us that we could no longer see farther than just our own camp, and Sarge and I fell asleep. We awoke several times during the night, imagining we heard sounds or someone near camp, and off in the distance a wolf's howling pierced the night, with answering cries somewhat closer. The sound of a Puma growling, a Burying Owl sounding like a Rattle-snake to warn something to stand clear. Then sounds of screaming coming from the far-away dwelling's, crying through the raging night. The moon-rays casting light onto shadows into the darkest crevices of the cliff's.

We awoke just before dawn with a chill in our bones, the fire had died down to just embers, Sarge added a few more sticks of wood, stoked the fire into a small blaze and put on the coffee.

132

Rubbing the sleep from our eyes and stretching our bones out we found we were still alive, non the worse from the sounds that had penetrated before the dawn's early light.

I was very apprehensive of what we may find today, relics of a people no longer living, yet the Ute's believed their ghosts still roamed within the cliff's and it was Sacred and Holy Ground to them.

As the sun peaked over the Mesa, stark contrasts marked the peaks of the San Juan Mountains and showed a glassy mirror glance of the San Juan Rivers you could see between the cliffs in the valley. High tundra, Ponderosa Pine marked the edge of the Chuska mountains to the south. Sage brush and black brush sparsely showed on the lowlands; sparse vegetation appeared on the slickrock rims and canyons. To the west we could see cottonwoods grasping sources of perennial water and farther on were the nuded dunes of shifting sand. This landscape was not unlike a kaleidoscope of colors changing constantly with the rotation of the earth as it seems the sun is moving and shows bloodred sandstone with hidden alcoves of hanging gardens with walls dripping of water. Black volcanic cliffs hide fern growing in the recesses. Atop the mesa's appear to be solid shades of tan and pink and only streaks of water courses have been carved into solid rock. And now, as we continue to gaze the scene is constantly changing from one color to another and you think you see dancing silhouettes within the shadows of the Cliff-Dwellings. I was truly amazed at this momentous land and marveled of the ancient people's that lived, worked and played here.

"Sarge, I really hate to leave our camp and the beauty that lies before us, but we really need to get a move on into those cliff's below."

Saddling our horses, stowing our camp gear was no easy mental task as it required leaving this panoramic scene and I was reluctant to do so...yet the close inspection of the dwelling's was necessary and perhaps, if luck was on our side, we may somehow find the outlaws or at least evidence that they hang out there. Arriving at the base of the Cliff-Dwellings we were astounded at the enormous size and seemed like a Palace and or a majestic maze; and then truly marveled at the majesty of this work. We roamed from one place to another, and then finally decided to try and climb to a second or third level, which was no easy task, but there had been a few footholds carved into the sides and a few twined rope ladders that still were strong enough to support us, we managed to get to a third level. We climbed and continued to investigate what area's we could reach and coming to the conclusion that no gangs would go to this much trouble to hide, so we descended to the base of the dwellings, but we did find various artifacts such as pottery, some bones, broken knives, and gave us weird feelings, yet we did not remove or touch any of these. As we continued searching we finally came upon a slightly hidden natural cave, not appearing to have had human hands involved in the making; venturing inside we could dimly see evidence of recent habitation, ashes of a fire, some utensils scattered around, but could also see recent signs of Coyote or Wolves. Upon closer inspection, in a far corner, we found two human bodies partially devoured, obviously by the predators that also visit this area or when they smell fresh blood. Was this remains of some of the gangs or two cowboys that camped here and were somehow subdued by whoever or whatever? Were they victims of the Ute's wanting to keep these ground sacred or victims of haunting ghosts? Then predators smelling fresh blood closed in and did the rest. We found a belt and holster but no revolver, and initials on the inside of the belt read Q.T.. Perhaps someone would recognize the initials as being someone known in these parts or hopefully clear on over to Durango and area. This could possibly lead somewhere to identify other possible people he was known to run with. At any rate we would take the belt and holster back, if for no other reason than to show what we found. We searched further, but found no other evidence's of any other men or creatures in the area, but at this time it was past noon a few hours, so we moved the bodies out of the cave and dug graves for both and decided to make camp here for the night.

Off in the distance we could hear the screeching of a desert hawk as it probably caught it's prey; and other night sounds were starting to be heard as indeed the night is alive, while we sleep. Going out to the cave entrance, the setting sun to the west cast different and changing shadows giving us a totally different perspective of cliff's than did the morning sun, and you could see glimpses or vague running shadows that could be taken for rambling spirits, but were they real or just shadows jumping from place to place? I wasn't one to normally believe in ghosts or super-natural spirits, but when you are at places unfamiliar, it makes you think twice. How much do we really know about the spirits?

Sarge and I talked for awhile about the gruesome discovery we had made earlier of the half eaten corpse's and wondered if the predators would return wanting to finish their meal. No need to be concerned with that now, but obviously would remain on the lookout and be aware of noise's throughout the night, so we kept a small fire going and settled in to sleep, being much warmer inside the cave, than sleeping out last night under the stars.

Suddenly we were both awakened, but yet no weird or strange sounds did we hear, it was more of an unexplained un-canny or even a preposterous feeling. Our fire was low, just a little more than glowing embers and looking over and through the glows of embers we saw a female, nude, motioning us to fol-low and turned to walk away, and looking back, seeing we were not following, came back near the glow of embers and again mo-tioned us to follow. I arose and followed, trying to catch up to her but each time I hastened after her, her steps became quicker and I was unable to catch up, and as we neared the mouth of the cave, she seemed to disappear, to just vanish; incredible, and I pinched myself to see if I was still asleep and dreaming or what. Yet I was fully awake, and found my self trembling. She was beautiful, short in stature, but body was proportionate, long black stringy hair, deep piercing eyes and angular nose, curved sensuous lips that wanted to speak but didn't. The moon was out fully, some would call it a blood-red moon, giving her a radi-ant appearance. I looked around and saw fleeting glimpses of shapes and forms peculiar and so unimaginable, it was hard to believe, were these spirits of the dead, long ago ancient Anasazi? The girl appeared again, and again motioned for me to follow and this time I did not attempt to catch up to her but followed her to a large round structure about thirty feet in diameter, stopped, stood there and motioned me to enter the covered entryway, then again vanished. Sarge had not followed, so I was alone, trying to decide if I should do as instructed or not. Yet, my curiosity challenged my good sense and I entered a doorway into another world. I was swept away... Another world? The crazy spinning motion stopped and I found myself not Marshall Daniel August anymore, I was dressed in skins of animal, other men within this structure were dressed alike and even a few small boys were surrounding me. They were addressing me as if I was their leader, my mind is still sharp, I am thinking like I always have but unable to speak in my natural tongue of English. Is this possible, have I somehow been transported back in time, to experience another world? Would I ever be able to return to my world and time?

I later learned we were in a Kiva, a holy place where only men were allowed and some small boys as it is a holy place of the Anasazi and women were not allowed. I am being addressed as Kukulmal.

Mysteriously, I now possessed the knowledge of the Anasazi, I was Kukulmal, first brother to Manabozho, who was the dominate Chief of the Anasazi from Shipolo; we are a race of powerful humanoids superhumanly strong. We come to earth through an extra-dimensional
cosmology of worlds only a nanometer away, it is an interdimensional gateway that exists between earth and Shipolo. I have been summoned by Red Wolf to act as his mortal protege. Many of the more noble gods of the Anasazi, have had Earthly agents to interact with the mortals; because I honored the dead, and did not steal from their lodges and Kiva's, I have been singled out as one of them. I am given a pass to have long-life but not immortal or invulnerable to death. The Anasazi are much stronger physically than human beings, they are also known to manipulate mystical energies and perform feats of magic, as a strong relationship to our Mother Earth, to communicate and bridge distances, to teleport dimensional barriers and cast both evil and godly spells.

Suddenly, everything turned black, I was whisked away again, through a sea of tranquility, as being in a long dark tunnel with only a pinpoint of light guiding me through and then, there was Sarge shaking me and asking if I was alright.

I remembered everything, yet something told me not to speak of what I have learned, as no one would believe me, so cautiously I told Sarge I must have just blacked out as here I was outside the Kiva, and wondering why I was singled out and given knowledge of the Anasazi.

I was Kukulmal for a period of time, was I reborn or what do they call it, ah, yes... reincarnated. Yet again, not a lasting physical rebirth as here I am again as Marshal Dan August. Perhaps some mystical emergence to try and tell me a thing I need to know. As I continued to contemplate such phenomenon I could hear the wind blow through the Cliff-Dwellings, yes it was so strange, it was like a wild wind, and as it entered and escaped through a window or portal of the dwellings it gave off a kaleidoscope of eerie sounds, it was so wild. Yes, it was telling me the "the Wild Wild Wind," had answers. What exactly does that mean?

CHAPTER 11

The Mines

I s Purgatory or Silverton where I need to look further for answers? One thing after another has been so misleading; a potential clue here, another someplace else...Should I continue to follow Bob Luckman and Sara Jane, and where would that lead or should I follow Sarge's thinking of gangs in Purgatory, yet Purgatory is close to 300 miles away so not likely the gangs that operate here would be hiding at Purgatory, so that's out. So It seems I should I follow and Ride the Wild Wind? And where does it blow? Where would it lead? What would it uncover and what exactly am I looking for? Now I find there is a Purgatory mountain only a few miles away.

At any rate, it's time I visit the actual mining district of Ouray, Silverton, and even the Mesa's, or possibly a hole in the mountains where it's been suggested may be more than one gang that is doing the hold-ups of the silver and gold shipments to Durango for smelting, over the rough and unkempt toll road that was built three years earlier.

Also, they were surveying, and grading the Animas River valley that is 126 miles long to build a narrow gauge Rail system to Durango's smelter plant. It would be much more difficult to hold that train up. It seems that in most cases the hold-up would have to take place either where they are loaded at the mines...or at the smeltering plant in Durango. Either place would be difficult for the gangs to haul away that amount of ore, that is not yet smeltered.

Sarge and I only recently got back to Durango after spending a few days at the ancient Anasazi cliff-dwellings, with it's many mysterious, unreal, yet unforgettable images and sounds emitting from those ruins and knowing the Anasazi hunted this whole area still made a person jumpy. I'm still trying to understand if what I experienced was real or imaginary. Sarge was continually asking me about it, yet I knew he would only think I was fooling or lying. No one wants to believe in ghosts or spirits of the dead; yet people are leery of the dark, or whats behind a tree or around the corner and imagine all sorts of things. Now later we may be taking a sojourn to a place called Purgatory, the very name itself is enough to make you feel unsure of yourself. It's like somewhere between Heaven and Hell...and not knowing if you'll be chosen to go to heaven or not, and up until now you never gave it a thought one way or another. But Purgatory was 275 miles away, so not likely I'll go there soon at any rate.

Yet I had a job I swore to do, as we headed towards Silverton.

Just a few miles north of Durango is Animas City, that is actually non-existent now since Durango was established, but there was still Silverton and Ouray, and a host of smaller mining camps on the banks of the Animas River. Any one of these places could be a gang hideout.

Ethan and Joe wanted to come with Sarge and I, if for nothing else but to see the country, but used the reason of security; I nearly relented, but at this early point in my investigation I deemed it more prudent to have them stay in Durango to keep overall watch and safeguard our families from any potential dangers. It was fifty miles to Silverton and trying to track unforeseen elements that may lead to some bit of evidence, that would even take us two days, so we would camp somewhere in between on the banks of the Animas. Later in the day as we continued to go off-trail to investigate potential sites, we found no traces of hidden campsites, yet we knew the San Juan Mountains were a mystery of hidden caves, valley's and back trails that lead no where. It was the same along the banks of the Animas; finally we decided to make camp for the night, struck a small smokeless fire, put on some coffee and ate our meager meal of sandwiches Daisy had prepared for us before we started. Sarge was quiet now, of which I was thankful for, as it gave me time to think. I thought of Sara Jane and Bob Luckman, Sara was only 15 and though she was physically matured as a woman, was still a child and was already prostituting herself and very possibly hooked on opium or possibly the heroin that can be made from the opium. I thought of Noah, being the same age as Sara Jane and how well they hit it off together, yet Noah was simply totally unaware of that type of life; perhaps his mother had been over protective those many years I was away, yet so very glad Noah had not experienced the things it was apparent Sara Jane had. Now, exactly how was Bob Luckman involved except with Sara Jane? How did such an alliance develop between a 15 year old girl and a 40 plus year old man, our illustrious Mayor, businessman and mine owner. What the hell is the attraction for Sara Jane? Yet I had a strange feeling there was more to the relationship than meets the eye. Our fire was low and I added a few more dried pieces of wood. Sarge was already snoring, but knew any strange sound would awake him immediately, that's what you learn when camping out under the stars, you become aware of the sounds of nature surrounding you and any sound different than that wakes you immediately. I stared off into the night, thinking of Daisy and Noah, of Ethan, Nora and Aponi, and even Joe and Aiyana, of how we all came together, and of how we are all connected one to the other; and what actually brought us here and soon, I too was asleep.

I awoke with a start, a nagging thought running through my mind...The Chinese often times referred to the opium pipe as the wild wind, as it captures your mind and runs away with it...Where did I hear that before? It must have been when I was on the outlaw trail...but the wind whistling at the cliff-dwellings and my mysterious incident of being Kukulmal, an Anasazi,

is definitely trying to tell me something. Just need to connect the dots.

The wind started to blow harder, first it was a soft gentle breeze, then it was like trying to urge itself either around or through the mountain's to twist it's way down the Animas River Gorge.

It started to rain and I knew Sarge and I had to find shelter, the raindrops were not soft and felt more like needles hitting our skin; we quickly gathered up our camp necessities, tied to our horses, then knew we had to blind fold our horses, throwing our own parka's over their heads and leading them. The rain pelted down even harder, we were in a rogue storm that occasionally happens in this part of the country; we were leading our horses blindly and finally a short distance away we could make out a cave directly in front of us large enough for the horses to walk into, hoping it would be sufficient we entered. It was pitch-dark and knowing we couldn't go far without a torch we stopped, then lightning flashed and temporarily lit up the cave area we were in and we smelled embers of a fire, then saw the glow...I struck a match, shielding it from the wind blowing into the cave with my body. Knelt down by the embers, added a few small pieces of wood and blew softly and the wood ignited. The wind was not so fierce within the confines of the cave, yet you could hear it howling wildly and it helped to rekindle the fire to it's fullest extent. Now with the light from the fire, we could see we were in a large cave; perhaps an old mineshaft that had been abandoned and a few feet passed the fire it made a turn into another corridor and could faintly smell a strange, yet somewhat sickly-sweet aroma coming from that part of the cave. Still we hunkered down where we were hoping the storm would soon stop, but glad of this shelter, and even howling of the wild wind. Shedding our outer garments that were rain-soaked, and taking the parka's off our horses, we settled down to wait out the storm. We would investigate this cavern, cave or mine-shaft when the storm and wind died down. Yet that sweet aroma that was drifting to us from farther down that corridor was reminding me of a smell I had experienced from some where and just recently. Oh why do things like that plague me? Finally, Sarge interrupted my thoughts and asked.

"Cap'n where you think we are where 'bouts?"

"Sarge, we can't be to far away from where we camped on the banks of the river last night, so we'll find out when this storm breaks. Right now just be glad we are out of that raging storm and fierce wind."

"Well suh, I still hears the cracklin of the lightnin thunder and that damn wind is sumpin else altogether Cap'n, ye'suh, glad to be here inside this cave, but I'm a smelling sumpin like back to thar in Durango at the laundry place those china peoples have...Da ya smells it Cap'n?"

"By the damn Sarge, you nailed it...yes I know that smell now...It is opium being vaporized to smoke, what they use is an opium lamp that vaporizes opium and when smoked or inhaled you drift off into a never-never land. Thanks Sarge, I think you just helped with a large piece of the puzzle."

"Well suh, I neva did to mean to do sumpin like that, what did I say suh?"

"Sarge. Listen, I think there may be more to that china-laundry than just a washing clothes. Things are starting to come together now. Let's see if we can find something to make torches with Sarge. I want to see where that sweet aroma is coming from. I have a strong hunch there is a definite link."

"Well suh Cap'n, I hopes ya can piece it all togetha."

As we found our way through that corridor, there appeared to be a light source emitting from one corner of a large room and then I noticed 3 men laying out on the cave floor on blankets.

In the center was a large vase like contraption that was giving off that sweet-aroma and new instinctively it was an opium lamp and perhaps other paraphernalia. I wondered if the men were asleep, dead or passed out from smoking and inhaling the poppy tears. Upon closer inspection of the three men, Sarge and I determined they were simply drugged to the extent of being unconscious.

"Sarge go back to our horses and get our ropes, when these men wake up they'll be tied up, and we'll take them back to Durango, and hopefully we can get something out of them.

Then I heard a whinny, it seemed a bit farther back in this cave or old mine-shaft there was their horses, complete with hay and water and an air-shaft. So this was indeed a mine-shaft, obviously converted into a place for members of a gang to hole up, and smoke their opium.

The storm finally abated, Sarge and I tied the drugged men across the saddles on their horses and started back to Durango, satisfied that we had accomplished something and hopefully would lead to more developments of eradicating these gangs. As we left the cave we found out where we were and the only way we could have found entrance was that the wind had been blowing so fiercely that it showed an opening, as it blew heavy brush and tree leaves off to the side.

Arriving back in Durango, the tied men on their horses were trying to wake up, and I struggled to decide where to lock them up or shackle them someplace; and seemed the only place was there at the Sheriffs at that half buried log-pole with chains...We definitely needed a proper jail and that would be my next project before leaving for anyplace else. It was noon by the time we reached Durango and most of townspeople were out and about, and now watched curiously as we lead our prisoners toward Sheriff Walker's tent office. Surprisingly both the Sheriff & his deputy was there, which didn't happen very often.

"Say hey Marshall, who ya got there?"

"Was hoping you might could tell me Sheriff. Found um passed out in an ole mineshaft about a quarter mile off the Animus river. Entrance overgrown completely and if it hadn't been storming as it was last night we wouldn't have found them...also found the shaft appeared to be at least one place where whoever was using it, it is also used to smoke the opium pipe. Sure ya don't know who these gents are?"

"Well Marshall, let's gettum down off those horses, where a body can look at them straight, now just might be I've seen these gents at The Palace a few times...Mary, come on over here gal, Ever seen these jasper's hanging here abouts?"

Mary sauntered over, chewing her 'bacca, "Yessum, seen those galoots a lots of times... 'ppears they do's odd jobs fer da Mayor from time to time; but don'ts know a name to any a dem."

"Alright Mary, go on up to The Palace and fetch Mr. Luckman. Soon we should know about them and who their pals are." The Sheriff quipped.

Still standing out in the street, we saw the Mayor hurriedly walking down and across the street, with Mary straggling behind, not able to keep the fast pace as the Mayor.

"Congratulations Marshall, so you've apprehended three outlaws? Mary said they did odd jobs for me... here let me see these guys? Yes, I know them fairly well," pointing to one then the other he named the culprits as, "that's Luke, then Troy and the other one is Casey, but I have no idea what their last names are Marshal. Where and how did you catch them?"

"In an old mine-shaft, a quarter mile or so from the river below those heavy rapids as the river twists. No the place Mayor?"

"Can't say as I do Marshal; however, I do own an old mine-shaft in that area, but I closed it down several years ago and it hasn't been used to my knowledge."

"Mayor, if it is the same one it's being used as a hide-out and there is an opium lamp and other paraphernalia in it and these jasper's were passed out from smoking.

"I'll be damned," the Mayor reckoned, "I just never gave that place a thought. Well you did a damn good job of bringing in at least three. Guess we need to build that jail right away...I've got some extra material and even some iron to build the cells. I'll have a few men get started on it right away Marshal. Shouldn't take but about a week or so, maybe sooner if I can find a few more men."

"All we can do now is chain them to that post behind the Sheriff's tent-office, but when you start that jail, make it a Marshal's office and a jail and permit me to supervise the building."

"Don't see a problem with that Marshal, I'll hustle up some men this afternoon. We have many lots still available on main street here. Any place in particular you want it built."

"Yes, how about that lot right next to the Chinese laundry, seems to be kinda centralized and I like that space. Is there a problem with that Mayor?"

"No, not a problem as I own that lot. So, we'll get started right away and by the way Marshall, until then you need to keep a guard posted 24 hours, even though they'll be chained. Don't want them to have visitors that could bust them loose, understood?"

"Yep, I'm not a damn fool Mayor, I know what needs to be done."

The week pasted quickly, I supervised the building of the office and jail...and I surprised everyone by having a cellar dug, lined the walls with river-rock and mud- mortar and flat-iron of just 4 inch squares for the doors. But it did take completely 10 days before it was ready for occupancy. The office was atop the cells with a kitchen and sleeping quarters, and two cells for not so dangerous men, or just drunks; ironed off from the outside office for admittance and for the Marshal's desk and firearms. The cellar door was also made of flat iron squares to allow for ventilation, it was the most secure jail the country had ever seen.

Now the Marshal locked up his three prisoners and could now relax to a certain degree. By this time the prisoners were talking their heads off and begging for a pipe of opium, but as it turned out they knew nothing of who actually was the gang-leader, or anything else...they just followed orders. So these three particular prisoners were of no real use to them; though the Mayor was continually anxious to learn what they were waggin their tongues about. The one thing the prisoners were sure of was that there were other abandoned mine-shaft's and two, sometimes three china-men would keep them supplied with opium. Now that also brought to mind for the Marshal where in hell they were getting the opium, is there a field of poppies somewhere close by or is there some kind of an opium trade route no one knows about. Marshal August thought he knew so little about Opium, these are things you just ordinarily don't come across... to know or ask about. How could he gain information about opium or exactly how was the Chinese implicated in any of this. They were a closed-mouth bunch and would be difficult to penetrate their inner-circle.

I decided to go talk to Charlie and see if she had heard any gossip. Charlie's Nest was only a few doors down, so I decided to get out of the office and stretch my legs...and as I entered the boardwalk I immediately saw Sara Jane stumble out of the laundry. A few quick steps, reaching out I grabbed Sara Jane before she fell. She collapsed in my arms, her dress was torn in several places exposing her young breasts, one with a cut on it, and some coins fell out of her clutched hand. I rushed her to the Doc's place and luckily she was there.

"Doc, quick, Sara Jane just stumbled out of the Chinese-laundry, and this is the way I grabbed her. What the hell, she has that sweet-sour aroma of opium about her. The look of her is that she may have been attacked."

"Marshal, please carry her on back to the house, follow me, hurry now please, and get her undressed as quickly as possible..."

"Ma'am? You want me to undress her?"

"Yes Marshal, I need to start an enema immediately to pump what remains of that opium out of her, and try to keep her awake, don't let her go to sleep. I need your help Marshal, now

146

don't be squeamish about this just because she's a young girl. This is a life or death situation."

"Yes Doc...no problem, and a little prayer won't hurt either."

Noah had been out in the street when he saw his dad carry Sara Jane into the doc's office and rushed there too. He ran in to see what was going on and nearly fainted when he seen what was going on...

Turning to see his son standing behind him, the marshal implored Noah to: "Son, hurry now, go get your mom and after that get Uncle Ethan, Joe and even Charlie to get here as quickly as possible...go now!"

Without saying a word in reply, Noah turned and ran out immediately to do as he was bid. Everyone came running without a word...

"Doctor, what can I do to assist?" Daisy urged.

"Please take the Marshal's place, rinse her mouth out with water and help her breath and above all keep her awake...Does anyone know if there is any licorice root around? If it's fresh that will help."

Noah, run again to Aiyana and ask her to bring some licorice root, I saw growing behind her wagon...dig it fresh, wash it and run back here with it as fast as possible. Hurry now son."

"Yesum ma." and again left running as Noah was fleet of foot.

Within minutes the licorice root was there...along with Aiyana and Aponi.

The doc took the licorice root broke it in half and thrust it into Sara Jane's mouth...took the other piece and put it up to her nose, while Nora continued with the enema. The licorice bled as the doc wanted it to, to release the juices and vapors that would induce her respiratory system to react favorably for her breathing. Finally a brownish-green bile was released due to the working of the enema, she started breathing without help and opened her eyes to a different world...though weak and not knowing how close to death she had been. Aponi covered her with a light blanket, praying in a combination of her native Sulk language and some English she had picked up. Tears were streaming down her face unashamedly, as was everyone else, but they were undoubtedly tears of joy.

"Doc, is she out of trouble now?" I implored.

"Yes, basically she is but I am afraid she was addicted to opium, which is my fault for not paying enough attention to her and how she has been acting…As a doctor and her mom, I should have been more aware. She'll need care now to overcome the addiction."

"Well we'll leave you with her for now doc…just glad we were around to offer what help we could."

"Can I stay and watch her?" Noah begged. "Is there anything I can do to help her now or through this?"

"Of course you can stay Noah, you've already helped a lot, but yes, if she has problems catching her breath or just any sign of having trouble breathing put the licorice root up to her nose and encourage her to breath deeply.; and I thank you Noah, your a dear."

Everyone left Doc Valerie Nichol's house, leaving only the doc and Noah there to watch over Sara Jane.

"Charlotte, Joe, Ethan, please go to my new office, I need to fill you in on a few things; Ladies,

thank you very much, please go back home now."

At the office I told them everything that Sarge and I had encountered, plus some things I found out about Sara Jane, but that it all led to the Chinese Laundry, or at least through them. I also mentioned our Mayor, Bob Luckman's potential involvement and what I had seen of Sara Jane's and his rendezvous, but certainly I could not blame Sara Jane, because he was her source of obtaining opium which she somehow had become addicted. She put on a good front to her mother, and me…I had no idea she had that problem upon first meeting and anyone addicted will do anything to get it. Yes, even give her sexual favors to anyone that would give her a pipe. The Chinese keeps this quiet for obvious reasons. So now you all know as much as I do.

"Charlie, how well do you know Ti Ling? Would she know anything about this or perhaps she has heard things that we never would through the grapevine?"

"I really don't know her well at all, yet she seems to be straight as an arrow. We've become pretty close friends, so I'll try to pump her a little, hopefully not to raise any unwarranted suspicion what I am up to. I'll let you know if and when I find out anything."

"Good girl Charlie and thanks. By the way have you told Glenn yet about you being an under cover deputy?"

"No not yet, but as a matter-of-fact I was planning on doing that today as soon as he comes in. Is it still alright with you?"

Yes, I think he's in the clear completely and may even be able to be of assistance to us, so tell him whatever you decide."

"Thanks Uncle Augie, and Pa I care a lot for Glenn and he's expressed a sincere interest in me without actually using the words...Glenn is a real gentleman."

"Honey I trust your judgment completely, so do what you think is best for you."

"Well Cap'n, ah I mean Marshal, I really feel I'm not helping a lot being tied up in the bar's back room...not a soul I've been drinking with or dealing cards to has said a word about any thing that could be taken for any outlaw activity. Next time you need to go some where's I need to go with you, Ethan too, we've talked about it." Joe confided.

"Not a problem anymore Joe, and if Ethan agrees we'll leave in a couple of days for Silverton, and on the way search in the river valley for old abandoned mine-shafts like Sarge and I found. Charlie, you've had no trouble in the saloon that you haven't been able to take care of yourself, so I will be taking Joe, and perhaps Glenn can stay around a bit closer then. Is that agreeable with you?"

"No problem Uncle Augie. By the way I see another supply wagon full of wood and other supplies for the Mercantile store just arrived, so if you'll excuse me, I need to supervise that as well. Ya'll have a good day." as Charlie planted a kiss on her dad's cheek.

"Well, that's all I have, but watch Bob Luckman's movements closely, and don't be telling Sheriff Allen any of this now...we were in the Army with him, he was our commanding officer, but now the bottle's got him and he likes to get attention by telling stories. So let's keep all this hush hush for now.

As I walked out my office onto the boardwalk I saw Charlie directing the removal of the lumber and supplies to have Glen Hadley's Mercantile built. His space covered two lots so it appeared that it would be a large store. As I looked back down the street, I saw Ti Ling all dressed in her finery and enter Charlotte's Nest and that reminded me to try and become friends with her myself, well enough anyway that she may possibly trust me, but needed Charlie to break the ice for me first. Walking up to Charlie, I noticed both workers eying me closely, so I was careful with my words...

"Miss Charlotte, Good Morning to ya and I'll go in for a drink a bit later."

CHAPTER 12

Chinese Tongs

S ara Jane was having a difficult time going through withdrawal of the effects of opium, but Noah was with her day and night...feeding her cool water and hand feeding her of food her mother, Doc Valerie, laid out. Platters of fresh wild veggies and fruits that Aiyana and Aponi brought in from the mountains, as Doc said she needed lots of. An Indian goat-herder provided fresh milk and meat from his herd. Noah put up with her spasms and even yelling at him, knowing she didn't know what she was saying or meaning any of it. Kept cold compresses on her and washed her face and neck, sometimes Aiyana and Aponi came in to bath her and that was the only time he was not next to her. He had only met her once before, but became very attached to her now, there were even times when Sara Jane would ask him to hold her hand and even hug her tightly... she would up-chuck and Noah didn't shy away from wiping or washing out her mouth. Noah became her constant companion and protector; vowing to get even with the Chinese people that gave her that horrible drug, but kept that bitterness locked-up within himself.

Noah's dad, Marshal Dan August, would often check in on Sara Jane and always asked Noah if there was anything he could get for them.

Charlotte had talked to Ti Ling and told her what happened to Sara Jane. Ti Ling visited with Sara Jane one morning and when she thought Noah was not in hearing range, she told Sara Jane she thought she knew who was probably responsible...but proving it would be near impossible. Sara Jane asked her to tell the Marshal, but Ti Ling was afraid for her life.

Sara Jane nodded that she understood and dropped off to sleep...Ti Ling left and Noah stepped from behind the curtain, vowing to handle this himself.

Bob Luckman heard what happened to Sara Jane and publicly announced how terrible it was but inside he was afraid she would tell about him while she was going through withdrawal. The Mayor certainly couldn't afford to let that happen, and he was at a loss to know what to do about her. He had to do something and his scheming mind was centered on that, knowing that Sara Jane needed to be eliminated or just some how vanish. How much she really knew about the whole operation he just didn't know, but was afraid to take any chances. Something had to be done and quick.

Meanwhile, Charlie was able to get Glenn alone long enough to tell her who and what she really was.

"Oh Glenn, I just had to tell you the truth about myself, I hope you don't hate me for lying."

"Well, I recall you telling me on the stagecoach, there are somethings a girl just doesn't tell about herself, I accepted that then and now that I know what those things are, under the circumstances I accept the knowing of it now...I felt there was something you've wanted to tell me quite often, but you would hold back at certain points. Charlotte, I understand and I need to tell you I have no problem with you, you see my dear you've made me fall in love with you."

"Oh Glenn, really? I've wanted to hear those words ever since we met... I couldn't help myself, but was afraid because of the roll I took on for myself for Uncle Augie."

"Whoa, wait a minute girl, you mean to say Marshal August is your uncle?"

"Not really Glenn, no blood relation, yet he and dad had grown up together and were like brothers, so he's always been my uncle like. And before you ask the question, Yes my father is the Preacher."

"I'll be damned, somehow I thought there was a connection, but couldn't add 2 and 2...Now I understand completely what's going on; and Joe must somehow be connected, right?"

"Joe was in the army with them, they were close friends and we met accidentally on the trail here and he decided to join us, also on the way we picked up little Aponi, and met up with a small band of Comanches and that's where Joe and Aiyana met and fell in love. Now you know the complete story."

"Oh Charlie, I know there is more to it overall, but I sincerely do thank you for finally telling me and please rest assured not a word of this will come from my mouth. I'm sure you all plan to tell the truth publicly when this is all over."

"Yes Glenn, we did, but now I need to tell you just a bit more...yet don't quite know how to begin. So, I'll just come straight out and ask. Glenn I need you to move back into your rooms with me, as if your my personal lover. I need to be your woman so our guest's won't expect me to service them as the other girls do. Now, please do not get the wrong idea here, we will not really be lovers physically until you put that sparkler on my ring-finger...with sincere intent to make our relationship a life-long partnership in marriage. Ah, that is if you really have those intentions toward me."

"Charlotte, since first meeting you my dear, that has been my intentions, make no mistake about it. And by the way, my lady, I shall move back into the rooms with you today, and be damned what people think, and above all I will respect you now about not being lover's, but will give that impression to everyone eye's. Is that how you want it my lady?"

"Yes Glenn and I shall love you all the more...and thanks for your forgiveness of my lies I had to tell you initially. No more lies from here on out Glenn. But now, I need you to stay here with me as I want to question Ti Ling about some things. OK Glenn?"

"Yes, of course Charlie, but tell me first, give me a quick summation of what about."

Glenn, It's about Sara Jane, Bob Luckman, opium, prostitution and what not. Is that enough?"

"Well I'll be damned, I think I know what you are getting at and I've often had suspicions along those same lines, but didn't know how to pursue it.

"Alright, let me call Ti Ling and get that Mexican girl Sonja behind the bar for awhile?"

"Ti Ling, I have a few questions to ask you and its very important you answer truthfully... Will you do that?"

"Yes Miss Charlie, if I am able I will."

"Ti Ling, what can you tell me about the opium here in town and do you know how Sara Jane got mixed up in it and about Bob Luckman our Mayor?"

"Oh Miss Charlie, yes I do so understand your concern. About the opium is run by a very strong Tong; and is usually delivered from somewhere in the south with various supplies that we get daily...He is a very strong Tong leader from Shanghai. I only know his name be Ba' Da Yung Lin. He be master to all Chinese here and we do all he wishes. I only be able to work here cause he say permission; and I give all my money to him and then he give my family a bit to live with. Please I beg, do not say I tell you this."

"It's alright Ti Ling, no one will ever learn this from Glenn or me. Now, do you know any of the relationship our Mayor has been having with Sara Jane?"

"Miss Charlie, everyone she know Mr. Lucky has special thing for younger girl...someway he gets the very young Mexican and China girls on opium then he uses them..when he get through with them then they be like me here to sleep with someone who pays silver and gold.

That's all I know Miss Charlie, please do not to tell."

"Glenn, do you have any questions of Ti Ling?"

"Yes, but only one... Ti Ling, is Mr. Lucky connected to your master Ba' Da Yung Lin?"

"I tink so maybe... sometimes the master he to tell Mr. Lucky what he to do, and asks things when the ore come down from mountains and he give him some of the opium, and sometimes new girl who just turned woman from girl because she now let blood like woman, but also sometimes even before that. Sometime she be only 10 years by you age. Then Mr. Lucky go to the mountains for a few days. I know no more really Mister Glenn."

"Thank you Ti Ling, what you've told us is safe with us...now go back to work and tell the girls Mr. Glenn is moving back here with me."

"I still have work with you here Miss Charlie?"

"Oh, yes of course Ti Ling, and keep our conversation private...do not share any of this with the other girls or any of your men customers. Now go on back to work."

"Thank you Miss Charlie... I say to nothin.

"Well Glenn what do you think of that, we certainly need to share this with the Marshal, as soon as possible."

"Charlie I will look him up as I go to the boarding-house to pick up my things. Yes this is very important. I'm on my way."

As Glenn stepped out onto the boardwalk, he was faced by a stranger that demanded what he called satisfaction...

"What in hell are you talking about Mister? I don't even know you."

"You got my lady there in saloon...I don't want her in there."

"Well now Stranger, there are several women that work in Charlie's Nest, which one would you be referring too?"

"My Sonja, she say she work for Charlie, so I come to see Charlie."

"Now Mister, that is funny, I'm not Charlie, Charlie is also a lady and yes I have met your Sonja, but if she is your lady, why did she come to work here?"

"Charlie cannot be lady, Charlie is man's name."

Just at that moment Charlotte stepped out as she heard the talk from inside... "Mister, I am Charlie, what's your grief about Sonja and if you want satisfaction of any kind you need to get it from me. Hear me now?"

The stranger turned quickly, eyes on Charlie... "But, but no lady have name Charlie. I just want my lady Sonja."

"You must be the guy Sonja told me about that you paid for her one time at the hotel and now you think you own her...Mister, Sonja is doing what she wants and needs to do to keep food on the table for her sick granpa and feed her children...she belongs to no one, especially you. Now go on about your business and leave Mr. Hadley alone...you've got no quarrel with him."

Charlotte planted her legs apart, faced the man, her hand near the gun handle on her hip and

continued with, "Mister, now if you've got a beef, take it up with me, or get the hell out of here and don't come back. You've got no claim on Sonja, and Sonja wants nothing more to do with you."

By this time, the ruckus had drawn a crowd and Charlie wouldn't let up on him. "Mister, what you gona do? You keep pushing and you'll soon be stoking a fire in hell."

Joe stepped out of the saloon and told the stranger, "Mr. this lady will draw and quarter you afore you get that hog-leg out of your holster, best do as she says, you started this party and you can end it here...just walk away."

Sheepishly the stranger, looked down, slowly turned and started to walk away, then abruptly turned and drew his pistol. Two shots rang out and the stranger laid dead in the middle of the street. Charlie just stood there, the strangers shot was high over her head.

"Damn Glenn I didn't want to do that, but to have such jealousy over a woman, that was just simple stupid. Get Sonja out here and ask if she knows what this guy's name is, will you Joe?"

"Miss Charlie I only know his first name as Luke, and I was only with him that one time."

"Thanks Sonja, what a waste, well Joe go get Marshal August and who around here takes care of the dead for burying?"

"Charlie, I'll take care of that after the Marshal gets here... I know Cletus must be somewhere around."

Murmuring throughout the crowd that had gathered, *fastest draw I ever did see...my god Charlie did that?...now that's woman to ride the trail with...well, I'll be down right damned...*

Charlie turned and walked back into the saloon, and a big part of the crowd followed her in, bellying up to the bar, and Ti Ling and Sonja served them with a smile and the talk about Charlie continued... *need to watch out for that woman... damn, I just blinked my eyes and it was over...I saw that Luke draw first, but Charlie nailed him good...now that's one hell of a woman, did you hear her tell him to stop pushing or he'd be stoking a fire in hell? Jesus be.*

Marshal August walked in, "No need to explain anything Charlotte, Glenn already told me and there's talk spreading all over town. To bad you had to shoot him, but that's the way of it here."

"Marshal we need to go somewhere private like as I have some important information to tell you. It's about our illustrious Mayor and a few things I think you may be completely surprised about."

Glenn came back, having found Cletus to clean up and bury Luke, whatever is name was; so we went upstairs in my rooms and Glenn and I related exactly what Ti Ling had told us about Mr. Lucky and Ba' Da Yung Lin, the Ba' meaning master, even by force...

"So well, somethings I believe was getting to me, but now it seems that the real boss is that Tong leader we never even thought about. And that opium business is his tool to get people to do his bidding...quite a set-up." The Marshal concluded, then continued with, "But we need to somehow catch Luckman in the act of either giving money or opium to a young girl or a girl that is not afraid to testify against him. Perhaps after Sara Jane is well, we can convince her to do that."

"My thoughts exactly marshal; yet we also need to somehow make a plan to know what, when, or how that Chinese Tong Leader Ba' Da Yung Lin operates. Also, who's actually doing the robberies." Glenn reckoned.

"I'm going to need more than just the few deputies I have now. Glenn, would you be willing to join us, if so that would give me six deputies I can trust and count on, that being, Charlie, Joe, Sarge, Ethan, you and myself...not sure we can count on Sheriff Alan or his deputy Mary.

They may be more trouble than we need. Perhaps you know of a couple of trustworthy men, it may be dangerous obviously."

"Honestly marshal, I know of no one here in Durango, but I do have two men that works the mines for me that I would trust completely and am sure they would be glad to join in, that being both of my foreman's, those two being Alonzo Garcia and his cousin Pablo...both good men."

A knock on the door, Charlie answered it. "Ti Ling, what do you want?

"Miss Charlie, sheriff Alan be downstairs, he want to talk to you."

"Have him come up Ti Ling and thanks."

"Sheriff, glad you came...come on in. I suppose you came about the shooting?"

"Well for a fact yes, but I suppose it'll not really be necessary from the talk I been hearing."

"Settle down for a spell Sheriff, got a few things to run past you, see what you think?"

Marshal August related only some of the things Charlie and Glenn had related to him from Ti Ling's talk they had had earlier, without telling him who told them.

"Sheriff I need to know if you or Mary your deputy, would be willing to go up to Silverton with us, we plan to scour the mountains for old abandoned mine's from here to Silverton...It's kind of a posse like...if we find any outlaws along the way."

"I don't believe anything would hold Mary back, hell she's a damn good tracker, rides well and shoots well, just buy her a couple chewing plugs of tabacca and she'll go; that'll leave me here to keep things in order. That suit ya Cap'n?"

That'll be fine Sheriff, tell her to pack rations for about 3 or 4 days of anything special she wants and I'll have a couple of pack horses and even take extra riding horse's for us. I know those mountains to be treacherous. We'll be leaving the day after tomorrow, sunup, from my office. By the way Major, need you to keep an eye out for Sara Jane at doc's place, plus checking here at Charlie's Nest often...will ya do that Major?"

"Sure nuff Cap'n, yeah I heard about Sara Jane, to bad she's a mix-up in it, bet Doc is beside herself. Guess I'll be paying them a visit, to let'um know I'm around and a watching out fer'um."

"Let's adjourn this little meeting and get on with the day, and as they went downstairs, there was still talk about Charlie shooting that Luke fella, and as Charlie descended the stairway, an applause went up, all congratulating Charlie on getting rid of a bum.

"Gentlemen please, shooting someone is not pleasant but he left me no choice...now please forget about it. Sonja, Ti Ling, give everyone a drink on the house. By and by Gentlemen, I'll be taking off for a few days, day after tomorrow, so mind your manners and watch out for the girls for me, (laughing), or I'll come a gunning for ya."

A joyous yell from the crowd and more applause, they turned and downed their drinks, and it started to quiet down, but still the talk about Charlie wouldn't stop.

"Damn Charlie, you know just how to control them, you are an amazing lady, my dear." Glenn boasted.

Preacher Ethan stepped into the saloon, looking of course for Charlotte. "You alright Charlie? I just heard what happened?"

"Yes Preacher Ethan, I'm quite alright... I've learned that the doing what a girl has to do, you just have to do it and not fret about it later. But it was a senseless killing, no need for it, but that Luke just wouldn't let up."

"Let's not talk about it anymore." Suggested Glenn. "But of course, I'm thinking some big guns are going to be hearing about this, and come looking for Charlie here in Durango, only to find out Charlie is a woman and then some of them won't care if she's a woman or not and want to try their skills and or luck. Best be aware of this possibility and be constantly on the look-out."

"That's a real possibility alright," Marshal Dan agreed. "and we all need to be on guard, things around here will really start poppin soon."

"Damn, it's been pretty quite overall for a spell here, but any-time there's a shooting, word spreads quickly, especially a shooting like this here one. After awhile there'll be ten different stories of how and why this shooting happened." Sheriff Alan speculated.

"Alright, enough of this banter...the sooner we quite talking about it, the sooner it'll quiet down." Preacher Ethan urged. "We've got work cut out ahead of us, let's be thinking about that."

It was very evident that everyone in town had either seen the duel or had heard about it by now, more people came into Charlie's Nest, wanting to get a look at Miss Charlotte, with tongues still waggin a mile a minute. *It would be near impossible to stop this kind of talk the Marshal thought.*

The day to leave on their trip to Silverton arrived with a bit of light sprinkles and it was totally overcast, nevertheless the marshal was determined to continue, they needn't delay this venture, so Mary, the Sheriff's deputy, Sarge, Preacher Ethan, Joe Freeman, Charlotte, Glenn and myself, the seven of us with 2 pack horses and an extra horse each started up the Animas River gorge.

Daisy, Nora, Aiyana, Aponi, and Noah stood out in the chilling rain watching them go, hearts heavy because of the potential danger this trip they were undertaking represented. When the small cavalcade was out of site, Noah turned to his ma and said,

"Ma, I should be going too, I'll be 16 in only a couple of days and I'm man enough to handle these things."

"Yes son you are indeed, but guess your pa thought you needed to stay to keep an eye out for us women and the fact that you need to keep watch over Sara Jane."

"Ya, maybe your right ma, and if you'll fix my breakfast, I'll get over to her now. Last night is the first night I didn't stay over with her and I've been concerned about her. She's improving though, but slowly; and Doc Mitchell counts on me now so she can tend to her appointments."

On Noah's way and nearly to the Doc's place, he noticed a man come out of the Chinese laundry and go into Doc's office, so hurrying a bit more, he went in also, but saw no one in the outer tent-office, so quietly he entered the door to go into first room where Sara Jane was, and saw that man bending over her with a knife in hand. Without even thinking Noah threw himself at the man and they both went down on the plank floor, and an unexpected grunt from the man as the knife pierced the throat of the attacker and he lay there twitching and gurgling...Sara Jane woke up, screamed and her mother came bursting through the back room door.

"What's going on?" she demanded. Noah, who is that man?"

"Ma'am, ah Mrs. Doc Mitchell, I saw this man ready to attack and cut Sara Jane so I just jumped on him and I guess the knife in his own hand somehow cut his own throat. I don't know how that happened, but it did."

"Well, thank you Noah, I had no idea Sara Jane's life would be in danger like this. Please go get Sheriff Alan, as I know your dad and others have already left this morning. Sara Jane are you alright, he didn't hurt you did he?"

Noah was out the door immediately, running at top speed for the Sheriff...when Sheriff Alan arrived Noah and Doc Mitchell had to repeat everything they knew what and how it happened.

Sara Jane fortunately had not been touched, and Sheriff Alan noted the man was a Chinaman.

"Son, that was a lucky thing you noticed a man come in here and good that you reacted so quick to save Sara Jane. I'm proud of you young man." The Sheriff was quick to acknowledge.

"Oh Noah, you saved my life, thank you Noah, I love you."

Noah beamed with pride but also knew that the way it all happened was kinda accidental. *Still, perhaps if he had stayed over here last night as he previously had been doing, he might still be asleep himself, on the floor next to Sara Jane, and she would have been murdered ... perhaps without him even waking up...strange how things work out. Noah thought.*

"Doc, I'll have a couple of men over to get this body and take it to the laundry and I'll have many questions for them there. Sorry, but you'll have to clean up the blood yourself."

"I'm used to blood Sheriff, that part is no problem, but please do get some men over here right away to get this dead man out of here."

"That I'll do right away Doc."

"Ma'am, if you'll permit me, I know how to use a pistol a little, and I'm thinking maybe for some reason someone will try this again on Sara Jane. I need a firearm to guard Sara Jane and you, and I know you can't stay here all the time yourself... so I'll run home and get one of my Pa's guns."

"Noah, no need to go home, I have a 44 colt double action here, it was my dad's and yes your welcome to use it, and I thank you for being so protective, and thinking of us as you do."

"Oh yes ma, Noah has been so good, and I'm scared, I have a lot of things to tell you both I am so ashamed of doing and hope you will forgive me."

"Whatever it is I'll still love you and forgive you even before the telling!" Her mom exclaimed.

Doc Valerie Mitchell left to go get the 44 she promised to give Noah, just in case someone would try such a thing again....*but why?*

"Here Noah, please be careful. I hope it's alright, I have never used it since my Pa passed on to leave it for me."

"Yes Ma'am, I see it needs cleaning and that'll only take a few minutes, but it'll work out fine and yes the extra cartridges are good but hope not necessary. Thank you ma'am."

"I'm gona fix us some breakfast, I'm sure we all could use that."

"Ma'am, thankee but I've already eaten, but would surely use a cup of coffee, if'n ya don't mind."

"Oh Noah, I'm so ashamed of what I have done and become...I see myself now, so selfish and was so easily led, and never would have done such terrible lewd things that I did. I just don't know how to tell anyone about it, especially you and mom, or for that matter just anyone."

"Sara Jane, it doesn't matter what you done, I'll stand by you. But if you care not to tell me, I'll understand that too."

"I've been such a fool and was led so easily into doing ugly things. I hate myself now, just hope I can in some way make up for all the things I've done and become. I'm such a harlot doing things like the girls that take to bed with strange men for a few pieces of gold or coin. Can you ever forgive me Noah?"

"Sara Jane, you don't have to tell me anything, Pa told me what that opium can do to a person and make them do such things. I see no fault in you."

"But Noah, I really need to tell someone what happened and what I continued to do for awhile, yet at the same time, it didn't seem to bother me, it didn't feel like I was doing anything wrong. Most times it seemed like I was a different person, that it really wasn't me doing those awful things."

"If you really feel like you need to tell me, I'll listen Sara Jane."

"I want to tell mom too Noah, so when she comes back in, I'll tell you both. Just please understand how ashamed I am."

"I think I understand, it must have really been bad, you just being a girl an all, not yet grown."

Doc enters with a bed tray of scrambled eggs and small piece of ham and a biscuit, with a glass of chilled milk for her daughter and coffee for both herself and Noah. Sat down and calmly told Sara that she felt herself to blame and could not help but to over-hear some of the things she told to Noah.

"Sara Jane, please honey, you must not be ashamed of something you actually were not aware of yourself doing...opium can and will make a person do what they normally would not do without it. It is my fault for not recognizing what was happening to you, I should have been more aware."

Thanks mom, still at first I knew what I was doing, or thought I did... I was angry at you and most everything around me, and thought I was getting even. Now look at me, a spoiled brat."

"Honey, you were just misled by people who wanted to take advantage of you; yet I also think I know how you feel, but you need not take all the blame on to yourself."

"But Ma, now I am ruined for any man. What man would take me for his wife now?"

Quite involuntarily, Noah quickly spoke up. "I would Sara Jane, if you'd have me too. Ah, sorry Mrs. Mitchell, I didn't, well yes, but well I mean..."

"It's alright Noah, I know what your trying to say. Your a nice young man Noah and you feel strongly about Sara Jane."

"Noah, do you really love me? Oh Noah, I'm sorry I'm just not worth it... I, I, well thank you.

Anyway, I cannot change what I have done to myself, but I am sincere in my regrets and am able to recount nearly everything of what I have heard about the Tong and the master Ba' Da Yung Lin; even he took advantage of me on several occasions."

"I know this is painful to you honey but I can sense a need for you to tell it, and that is good as it should help you to recover and think better of yourself; so please just tell it like it actually happened, without embarrassment." her Ma whispered.

CHAPTER 13

The Sojourn

The Animas River Gorge was frequently treacherous, especially when storming, you never knew when a landslide or rockslide may occur or the river rising to flood certain low-land crossing area's, not to mention the slippery footing for the horses. Yet the seven outlaw hunters were a determined lot to end the hold-ups and murdering of innocent people simply trying to earn a living, working in the dangerous mines. Then there were the freighters, teamsters and suppliers that were also at risk. The railroad construction gangs, the lumberers to cut and form railroad ties for the narrow gauge railroad in progress. Normally you would think the trek would be dotted with these workers preforming their various necessary skills; however, this rain coming down seemed to be getting worse and may possibly turn into a full fledged storm. Perhaps this was not such a good idea to have started this particular trip on this morning, yet again, this type of day may be what is needed to find and catch the gangs unawares.

They had to be holed up somewhere in these San Juan moun-tains...with their many hidden canyons and mine-shafts that had been dug since first discovering the color of gold and silver back in 61, nearly twenty years now and somewhere men like Ike Stockton and Sam Squires were holed-up and waiting to take what honest men worked and died for. The Chinese were also somehow involved and who exactly was their leader and how did they operate? Yet the addiction of opium was a powerful stimu-late and imprisoned a man without them knowing it...they would do anything for the pipe and a few coins to spend on drink and the women of the night, and their lives being forfeited to the use.

My thoughts turned to Sara Jane and how she may have been led into such temptations of opium and sex. It's going to be very difficult for her to recover and...

Lightning suddenly flashed and struck only feet away from us ahead as we could feel the heat of it and the horses reared up and it caused pandemonium among everyone, then seconds later thunder rolled through the mountains...rain pelting down harder and harder. Needed to find shelter again. Then I heard shouting...

"Cap'n, were only a short distance from that mine-shaft we holed up in ta other night, can you hears me Cap?"

"Lead the way Sarge we'll head for that and hole up awhile till this storm lets up."

Another flash of lightning, horses acting up worse...thunder rolling as if it was on wheels, wind picking up stronger and it re-minded me of the way the wind blew at the Anasazi Cliff-Dwellings blowing wildly ever which way through these moun-tains.

What seemed like ages, Sarge finally lead us into the old abandoned mine-shaft, but you could still hear the wild wild wind and occasionally feel strong gusts blow into this shaft.

As we continued to go further back into the mine, I wondered if there would be enough room for all 16 horses and us... Sarge struck a torch, and we followed him into the area of the mine that we had been in a few days ago...our horses making noises they couldn't help and suddenly we were confronted with,

"Hold up there, that's far enough. Who the hell are you?"

"Might could ask you the same Mister, who the hell are you and how many of you are there?"

Marshal August returned.

"Mister, were not looking for trouble, just holed up here to get out of the storm. There's just the three of us."

"So have you three got names? Names your not ashamed of?" The Marshal retorted.

"Mister, really, you'd not get any trouble from us, I'm Mike Evans, I work for Mr. Glenn Hadley up in the mines."

"Mike, is that you Mike? Glenn blurted out. "What are you doing here?"

"Glenn I can recognize your voice...but can't see you. Damn glad it's you and not some of the gang that's taken over your mine, and not just your mine. Come on back, we've got a fire burning and set a spell and I'll tell you all about it."

"Mike there's 7 of us with 16 horses, is there room for us all."

"That many might get a bit crowded but there's room, damn glad it's you Glenn"

Horses squared away, we all gathered around the small fire Mike had burning, the Marshal introduced himself and others, and were introduced to the two other men with Mike, they were Charlie Burns and Dave Kingsley.

"Such luck ya'll turned up Marshal, we were afraid it might have been men from the gangs still chasing us." Dave suggested.

"Well. What the hell happened?" Glenn demanded

"Not sure Mr. Hadley, but I think your partner Josh Clever is mixed up in this and a feller by the name of Squires, Sam Squires I believe I heard him called...he and about ten more men ran us out and we headed south to find you in Durango and the storm hit us, so here we are?"

"Josh? Are you sure Josh Clever is mixed up in this Mike? Hell of a note...did you recognized any others?"

"No sir Mr. Hadley, actually we didn't see Mr. Clever, but heard his voice clear as a bell, not many sounds like him."

"I know Sam Squires Glenn, he's a rough no-good sucker, and mean as hell. Just as soon shoot you as look at you, has no scruples what-so-ever. I shot his brother during a bank hold-up in Missouri before coming out here."

"Glenn has told us about you Marshal August, glad your here...but how'd ya'll come to be on the trail today"

"Would have been sooner, but we had no leads or any idea where to start looking for the gangs...til just lately and that's why we're on the outlaw trail now. We were on the way to Silverton, but thought to look for hide-outs here in the San Juan's when the storm hit us as it did you."

"Damn lucky for us it was you a come into this old mine-shaft." Charlie interjected.

"Say, anyone got's a cup of coffee?" Sarge wanted to know... "Keeps a body warm an'a moving, an' from time to time I feels that ole wind a whipping through this shaft to make a body chilled."

"Ah hell Sarge, I'll put some on, quitcher bitchin. Jus hep me to digs it outa da pack, ya ole gopher." Mary quickly chided good naturedly, as she spat out a stream of tabacca juice.

Their talk lasted till the storm let up and now the Marshal and all basically knew who was responsible, but one thing they didn't know enough about was the Chines Tongs or the leader Ba' Da Yung Lin, but they had heard his name several times; but was unaware of how he could fit in.

"Mike, Charlie and Dave, do you want to join us, and do you know what may have happened to Alonzo and Pablo?"

"I'm pretty sure Pablo was killed, but don't know about Alonzo." Mike claimed. "But yes, I'll be glad to join with you."

Affirmative nods from both Charlie and Dave and they were on their way; ground was muddy and slushy; horses were slower than we would have liked, but at least we were again on our way and with three extra men.

Not bothering to look for any more hid-outs in the San Juan's, we headed directly for Silverton with as much haste as possible. Along the way we came across a construction crew grading a low-crossing area, water about a foot deep and mud even deeper made going near impossible...Yet, they were determined to get the narrow-gauge railroad built. They still were some 35 miles to go and working in one of the worst area's. Probably would take weeks just for this one mile stretch only a few feet above the river itself and whenever it rained even just a little this area became flooded. Then there were other area's they had to tunnel through solid rock as there was only one way to go around, taking them several hours out of their way.

Finally, they had to make camp and estimating they were only about 10 to15 miles out of Silverton, made a cold-camp so as not to attract attention from any possible gangs that could surprise them with an ambush. Posting three guards at a time, east, west and north and giving the horses extra rations to help keep them quiet we tied them to a secure high-line, made sure the rings were spaced out to give each horse room to move around abit and not get tangled with the other horses...actually we had to rig 2 high-lines, one with 9 horses, the other for 10 horses... we were now a formidable small troop. Before securing our horses to the high-line Sarge, Mary and Dave made sure each horse had been watered good at the rivers edge. Now each person securing their own small space to layout their saddles and tack...throw down their blankets for sleeping and was given cold biscuits and beef jerky. Thanks to both Nora and Daisy, it was quite palatable and certainly unlike the old hardtack you could break your teeth on.

Morning came quickly as dawn was turning to day...the guards had been changed during the night and seemed their cold camp was secure. A small fire started under a thick branched pine tree after clearing dried pine needles from under it, so smoke would be filtered up through the pine needles, so as not to attract attention...coffee was put on, and all was given another biscuit and a sizable pemmican...extremely nutritious.

Glenn had only heard of pemmican but had never eaten any and asked, "What is this pemmican anyway? I've only heard it is the Indians staple when they go on a war or hunting party."

"Glenn, it's made from dried and pounded meat, usually buffalo, deer or elk, ground nuts and various dried berries, sometimes the ladies would add dried ground corn and it's held together with grease, go ahead bite into it, I think you'll find it delicious and filling along with your biscuit." Charlotte volunteered. "And here I'll pour you the first cup of coffee."

"Now, this is damn good, I salute the Indians for their ingenuity, knowledge and skills to survive in the wilderness."

"Yes Glenn, much can be learned from our Indian brethren." Preacher Ethan concluded.

And all ate in silence, breaking camp and quietly saddling their horses, leading the horses to water and ready to head out again, thankful for a good nights sleep; they were ready to tackle the riggers of the day and hopefully pursue and catch the outlaws. Sarge and Mary led the way as scouts, both good trackers, reading sign as if a book was being read.

Horses found a good gait at about 6 miles per hour as average, not to wear them down but could go at this rate indefinitely. About an hour into their trek, Sarge came galloping back to report seeing some riders heading this way...but didn't know who they may be.

"Men, oh yes, ladies too, lets find a place we can hide-in to surprise these riders and find out who they are...Mike be sure and tell us if you recognize any of them." Marshal Dan urged.

Fortunately, there were plenty of places in these mountains to set up a type of ambush, and Marshal Dan told them all, not to shoot unless shot at as he wanted them alive if possible, so he could gather more information and possibly for them to tell us for certain who their leader was. Soon, riders could be heard in the distance fast approaching our hidden spot, but suddenly the pounding of hoofs stopped, all was quiet and thoughtfully I guessed we may have been spotted, and rightly so, but we remained hunkered down, waiting impatiently for something to break this silence.

Now a voice rang out, "You all behind those rocks, who you be and what ya doing here?"

"I'm Marshal Dan August and if yere all not outlaws, we got no problem with ya, come on in. lets do a bit of palavering."

"Don't think that's possible Dan, I recognize your voice...Sam Squires here. You don't recognize my voice Dan? We have a special score to settle or have you forgotten you killed my brother?"

"I figured you'd somehow show up around here Sam, and I don't mind settling our quarrel right now either. What do you say, just you and me Sam, here, right now?"

"Not a chance now Danny boy, I'll pick my own time; right now I have other things to attend to. Got a few chores and scores to settle other than you first off. I've got another thing in mind for you."

"Well now, if'n you thought to go through us to do your chores, you best figure on a fight here and now. Hoping you don't mean to dry gulch me, I want to face you man to man. And I got ten men that surely wants to change your way a thinking."

"Another time, another place Danny boy and you and me will dance to a jig, count on it Danny boy. We're headin out now, but am leaving a couple of sharpshooters behind to slow you down and whittle that 10 number down, if'n you dares to take the chance of following us."

"Chances are you'll not be seeing your hard cases after this day, they'll will be resting in the bone orchard Sam, but hell you never cared about anyone's life anyway; protecting yourself with someone else."

"Well adios old buddy, take your chances, cause we're a go-ing."

"Damn, Sarge, you and Glenn circle wide around to the west there and Ethan, take Joe with you, circle east, I'll take Charlotte and go straight on. If he did leave a couple of dry gulchers, maybe we can catch them by surprise or at least in a cross fire."

After about a half an hour, no sign of any sharpshooters so it was a good bluff that Sam did pull-off, but you just never know, so it's best to be cautious. We lost time but didn't lose a life... they pondered to either trail after the outlaw gang or go onto the mines and see what's left and just what kind and how much damage has been done by the marauders. Sam Squires and his gang will be around later on that, the marshal felt sure but wondered just what he was up to now, where exactly was he headed for now.

"Sarge, trail after them and take Mike with you, keep a close eye on their every move and Mike when ya all think it's important enough, come running after us as quick as your able. After we see what's going on at the mines we'll be heading back down towards Tacoma and maybe Needleton and maybe off west into old Purgatory or even that Durango mountain area. Grab some rations and get high-tailing it, we've already wasted valuable time."

Without saying a word, both Sarge and Mike gathered a few rations and were off...but staying alert for any dry-gulchers along the trail.

Having a lot of ground to cover, the marshal and the seven with him was a determined lot, somehow and someway things seem to be coming to a head. What the hell happened that I missed along the way... Going back over, in my mind, the events that have happened these past days I must have missed some important facts. *Let's see now...first off the gun-holster and belt left at the cliff dwellings with the initials Q.T., a body muti-lated beyond all recognition,*

Sara Jane's rendezvous with Bob Luckman, Chinese-laun-dry and opium, the ole mine-shaft with an opium lamp and 3 drugged outlaws, Sara Jane's overdose on opium and why & how did she become involved in all of this. And now these gangs being on the outlaw trail openly and even attacked the mines in Silverton. "Hell of a mess! I couldn't help but say out-loud. *Hmmm, seems to be a definite take over, but who's be-hind all of this, ah yes, not Bob Luckman, or even Ike Stockton and certainly not Sam Squires. Who am I forgetting? Well, hell yes, it's got to be that Chinese feller, what's his name...oh yeah, the master Ba' Da Yung Lin, but how exactly does he fit in besides just having a ready supply of opium? Is he capable of having such a straggle hold on all the robberies and killing going on around here?*

"Augie, whatcha been a thinking on so hard, you seem to be lost completely in thought." Preacher Ethan implied.

"Preach, I've been trying to piece this puzzle together. All the pieces just don't seem to fit together, at least not yet. Why in hell are the gangs on the move now, what's going on we don't know about?"

"Well, lets put the spurs to these cayuse's and get to Silver-ton, perhaps we can find part of the answer there Augie."

Arriving in Silverton, Glenn pointed out his two mines and office shack, of which has been burned down. The mine-shaft's openings blown shut; but as it is easy to see, several other mines have been attacked the same way, a few men about, trying to help other men who have been wounded and picking up, to re-move debris hopeful to find other men not dead. It was obvious to anyone, the gangs started a full scale war.

"Dave, where were you and the others when all this hap-pened?"

"Marshal, Mike, Charlie and me are mine working gang-lead-ers, we were all in the office here with Mr. Hadley's two fore-man's working on a schedule to start three shifts to work the mines on a 24 hours bases...and all of a sudden hell broke loose. First the mine blew up, we ran outside to see what was going on, then the office was set a fire, I think Alonzo or Pablo got caught in it, probably was trying to save some papers. Then we took off cause the gangs started shooting at us."

"Seems you did right Dave, at that point ya'll couldn't fight them off.

Just then, standing not far from the burned down office, they heard a moan and observed a slight movement under some burned debris; quickly then ran to the spot and pulled away the mess atop this man, thankful, that at least he was still alive.

"Well I'll be damned!" Glenn boomed. "It's Alonzo, Alonzo are you hurt, how are you? Quick someone get some water." as Glenn cradled his foreman's head in his arms and Charlotte rushed to him as well with canteen in hand.

Alonzo guzzled the water, had a few slight burns, but otherwise seemed to be alright, except for him being groggy.

"Senor Glenn, gracias a Dios es usted...nos atacaron, quieren toman posesion de las operaciones de las minas y matarmos a tados. Alonzo confided in a near whisper. "Josh is with them." He finished in English.

"What was that?" the marshal asked.

"Ah, sorry Marshall, sometimes Alonzo speaks his native language, he basically said, thank God it's you...we've been attacked, they want to completely take over all mining operations, they mean to kill us." It's as close as I can do with translation; and Josh Clever is my mining partner, this is hard to believe he's somehow mixed up in this business. I trusted him completely."

Alonzo was drinking more water and finally stood up, covered with ashes saying, "Pablo died in the fire, he must be under all that that burned lumber, he pushed me out the back window, I must have hit my head hard as I didn't come too until you all arrived...but Mr. Hadley there must be about 12 men either dead or trapped in the mine. We've got to get them out somehow."

"With the manpower we have available Alonzo, that may be quite a task as the Marshall here

is on the path of the very ones that have done this...I'll stay and do what I can, if your feeling up to it Alonzo, find what men you can and we'll start clearing the shaft. Marshall, I've got to stay here, and I'll need Charlie Burns and Dave Kingsley to stay here too."

"Of course Glenn, and I'll leave you a couple of horses to harness up to help you pull the rubble out of the way. Good luck Glenn, hope you find your men alive and well."

Glenn grabbed Charlotte, drew her tight to him and kissed her longingly, then whispered in her ear, "Darling be careful, I love and need you so much, but go with God. I know your place is with your father and uncle Augie right now."

"Glenn, I love you too, you know that, be careful." As she endearingly embraced Glenn in response.

The five left in the Marshall's posse, but Charlie couldn't help but to look back as the distance grew beyond sight, yet knowing Glenn was following her as well.

They put their horses at a fast gait trying to make up time they have lost. Going straight back to Durango as it appears the gangs were no longer in hiding and Marshall Dan August figured that's where they would be headed, in force... *Fifty miles to go in treacherous terrain, putting the horses at risk. Not something I liked doing but felt I was left no choice. Still it would be impossible to reach Durango till well after dark or perhaps even early morning...I made note to change horses somewhere along the way and glad we had thought to bring extra horses. The horses can run about 20 to 25 miles an hour for an hour or so, but that's very grueling and if they've been fed, watered and rested, these horses, even the extra ones have been mostly on the move for two days already. If this was not a time to warrant an emergency, I don't know what is, so we put the spurs to our horses and raced as fast as possible.*

It was dark by the time we reached Durango, I figured sometime around midnight, not only The Palace Saloon and Charlie's Nest had lights streaming out their open bat-wing doors and a couple of dirty windows, but it was a Friday night and the cowboy's, miner's and a few town-folk were still out milling around. Gambling and drinking was the name of the game, and some just wanted to see the sights; red light's appeared along the boardwalk so we knew the Ladies of the Night were busy and even the Chinese-laundry had a faint soft orange light emitting from within. A typical Friday night in a mining and cow-town and a few railroad construction crew

*men were still just not yet drunk enough to pass out in an alley
or some right on main street.*

The Marshall looked around as they slowly rode down main
street and tied their horses to the hitch-rail in front of the Marshall's new office & Jail, a single solitary soft light was showing
through the one window next to the door. The posse was tired,
totally worn out from the exertions of the past couple of days,
especially with the long hazardous forced ride from Silverton.
Yet all were cautiously alert because they expected the gangs to
be rampaging here, and it was suspiciously quite. As Charlie
dismounted from her horse, she saw a shadowy movement to
her right not far from the doc's office. *Maybe somethings going
on there, she thought.* So she cautiously walked in that direction, the Marshall noticed her movements and followed along
behind. Reaching the corner of the building leading into an alley, she peered around and found to her surprise the Mayor, Bob
Luckman, laying on the ground...she whispered to the Marshall
and he stepped forward leading the way. Our Mayor was lying
face down, unmoving. *What the hell was he doing out this
night and who in the hell killed him for no apparent reason or
at least no reason that we knew of...but obviously someone
wanted him dead and they accomplished their mission.* "Charlotte, his neck is cut nearly into...Did you see who it was that left
this place just minutes ago?"

"No I only noticed a shadowy figure leaving, dressed all in
black or at least it appeared that way. He just seemed to vanish
in the shadows and darkness, but he could only have disappeared into the Chinese-laundry, I'm sure, otherwise I would
have seen him in the street."

"Charlie, go on down this alley here and then up the back way
to the laundry, I'll go in the front-way and let's see who we
might flush out, or catch in between."

It was dark in the alley and with the wind blowing as it was,
the swaying of bushes and trees made the moonlight shinning
through them dance and play tricks on a persons eyes. Every
move of the bushes could be someone hiding behind and then a
twig snaps and you suddenly find yourself frozen in place, completely alert, waiting for the next sound, but it didn't come.
Then a voice rings out in the night.

"WHO'S THERE, STEP INTO THE MOONLIGHT AND SHOW YOURSELF." A hidden voice boomed out.

Charlotte stays where she is but answer's, "I'm Charlotte Kennedy, but not moving from this spot until I know who you are."

"You the gal that took over Hadley's Saloon, partners with Glenn Hadley?"

"That I am stranger, now you step out and identify yourself."

"OK lady, don't shoot, I'm Josh Clever, Glenn's partner in the mine's and I'm not armed."

Charlies mind flashed suddenly to a conversation she had heard up in Silverton; *Josh Clever was suspected of being in with theses gangs, maybe even one of the gang leaders...I'll just play a game with him, letting him believe we know nothing of his possible deceit.*

"Alright Mr. Clever, I'm stepping out, and you do the same, but hands high and no tricks, Glenn is in the saloon bending an elbow right now, after a long ride and we'll see if he knows you...You good with that?"

"Yes, sure nuff young lady, no problem at all."

As Charlotte stepped into the moonlight, the voice said, "Lady, hands high, your covered, not a movement or your a goner."

Charlie raised her hands and as she did so, another voice sounded, "Mister, it's you that are covered and will be a goner and buried in boot hill, I hate a four-flusher and you just proved that to me. Now drop your gun, turn to face me and down on your knees."

Charlie immediately drew her gun at the ready. "Damn four-flusher, thanks, you just taught me a valuable lesson I'll not ever forget...Thanks for covering me Marshall. Let's take this hooligan to your new jail."

"Now, now, now wait just a minute, I was just a fooling...I really am Josh Clever, Glenn's partner and close friend. I, I well..."

"Shut your face Mister, you are going to jail, then we'll worry about who you really are...You threatened the life of a deputy Marshall, and that's against the law." Marshall August accused.

"Charlie, go tell Glenn we have his partner in jail and bring him here. I'm curious just who exactly this guy really is...and ya know he may have been the one that killed Bob Luckman."

When Glenn arrived, they went down into the jail's cellar and as Glenn walked up to the cell, he said.

"Hello Josh, so it is you, got yourself caught did ya? So you are also a bunko artist, among other things?"

"No Glenn, ya all got me mixed up...you know I've always been honest with you."

Just then one of the other jail inmates they had dragged out of that mine-shaft all drugged out of his head, spoke up...

"Wait a minute, what did you call him? That's not any Josh whatever...his name is Quinton Taggert, murdering son-a-bitch, he's the one been telling us what and when to hit you guys. If there was good grade filtered dust, we would hit ya all up at the mines or on the trail, if it was heavy ore, we'd hit ya all after it had been smeltered."

SILENCE, all around...

My mind reverted back to the Cliff-Dwellings, the mutilated body and the holster & belt with initials Q.T., it's making sense now. *So very possibly he murdered that man wanting anyone that found him to believe Quinton Taggert was dead; and started a new life as Josh Clever.*

"Well I'll be damned, so you been hood-winking me from the start...I had my suspicions a few times, but well you did cover up pretty good. But now I know who and what you are, your nailed to the counter and I'll see you hang."

"Quinton Taggert, well now, don't that beat all." Marshall Dan quipped. "I have a belt and holster upstairs in a draw with your initials I found way over in those Cliff-Dwellings and been wondering who they may lead to. Who did you murder there, and I feel certain your the one who just killed Bob Luckman in the alley. Oh Glenn, that reminds me, can you get a couple of men to take our mayors body over to the doc's, and we need to find someone to bury him."

"Well, I'm through here Marshall, yes I'll do that right away. But it's late, after one in the morning, hate to wake her up now."

"Ah hell, your right Glenn, have him brought in here."

"Doc, can't do anything for him anyway Uncle Augie, but sure would like to learn how Bob Luckman and Josh, damn, I mean Quinton Taggert figure in this together." Charlie puzzled.

"Well, he took the long ride home Charlie, but his jig was up. Scoundrels usually end up this way, and it's a damn shame he bamboozled so many along the way."

They decided to call it a night, apparently the gangs did not yet have orders to try to stampede Durango during the night and its nearly 2 in the marrow, so off to bed and get some sleep and see what happens as the sun rises.

CHAPTER 14

Revelations

N oah awoke quickly hearing a strange clicking or tapping sound on the window above his head...he searched for and found under the covers the pistol Sara Jane's mother gave him. His hand gripped the handle and his finger found the trigger as he eased himself against the wall under that window. Click, click again and a bit of a squeak and the window started to slowly open... Moonlight was filtering through the widow and Sara Jane's bed was right next to it and he saw a hand with a knife in it reaching towards Sara Jane. Quick as the eye can see Noah lifted the revolver and squeezed the trigger blindly and jumped up immediately to see who it was, but apparently he did not hit his mark. Yet he heard a grunt and wheezing and heard running faultering footsteps.

Sara Jane awoke frightened and Doctor Nichols came running in the room..."What is it Noah? Sara Jane, are you all right?"

Yes Ma, just scared is all...I don't know what it was either."

"Ma'am please excuse me, but someone was trying to cut Sara by opening the window just enough to reach in and I heard it just in time."

By this time Doc Valerie had lite a kerosene lamp giving off an eerie spectrum of colors as that light clashed with the moonlight still streaming through the partially open window. Upon close examination of the window sill blood, stains were still fresh and you could see the bullet hole clearly. Suddenly a continuous knocking sounded on the outside door and voices shouting to open the door and are you alright, is anyone hurt. Valerie opened the door and first in was Charlie and then Glenn.

"Charlie looked quickly around and found no one hurt, she asked, "So what happened, why the shot?"

Both Glenn and Charlotte was appraised of what happened and inspected the window sill and hole in the window...sure enough fresh blood on the sill.

"Glenn, take a lamp and go outside, there must be footprints to follow or maybe a trail of blood, Noah go get your Pa quickly as you can...I'll stay in here presently in case someone tries to come back and finish the job...Sara Jane your life is in danger, I hate to tell you, but it is. From now on we need to take every precaution."

"Charlotte," Glenn tapping on the window, "there is not only footprints but a trail of blood leading to the back...strange sort of footprints too.

"Wait for the Marshall, Glenn, then you both can follow the footprints or blood trail."

Marshall Dan arrived within minutes, appraised of the situation, found no one was hurt and went outside with Glenn to view the footprints and blood trail.

"Marshall, there's something odd, but familiar with those footprints. I've been around here for several months now and have learned those prints are Chinese type footwear, called hanxue, you see the toe is slightly turned upwards and is blunt, not pointed, no definite heel marks, so our would be assassin is obviously Chinese."

"Well Glenn, as I piece this together, it doesn't surprise me. Did you follow those prints any distance?"

"Yes, they lead directly to the wash area of the Chinese-laundry, then both the blood and prints vanish."

"Seems as though that's were we need to investigate, but knowing we'll not get any cooperation from anyone there."

"Well, perhaps we do have someone that would be willing Marshall. But need to approach the subject delicately. But under the overall circumstances, just maybe she'll be a help. I'm referring to Ti Ling, but I think it would be best of Charlotte talk's to her about it."

"Ah yes of course, she has been reluctantly helpful before, so perhaps she can be persuaded again."

"Let's go appraise Charlie of the situation, I'm sure she can convince her."

"It's a good thing Noah insisted on staying with Sara Jane, he's been sleeping on a pallet next to her bed ever since she was found sick. I think I also need to ask Charlie if she'll teach Noah to shoot; I normally would have, but since I was a way all his growing years, well, I can't do anything about that now, just glad he was not afraid to shoot."

"It's still early Marshall what you say we all have breakfast, it's just getting dawn, then we can start our investigation, besides Ti Ling won't be up and around for a few more hours anyway."

"Good idea Glenn, let's get Charlie and go to my house, Daisy has probably been awake for sometime now anyway, and most likely has fresh biscuits already in the oven. Besides, I need to wake Ethan and Joe and tell them what happened."

Going back into the Doc's place, we told them what we had in mind.

"No problem Marshall, I'll start breakfast here for Noah and Sara right away, ya'll go on and do what you have to do. I know Sara Jane don't want to let Noah out of her site and perhaps it's also the other way around too. We'll be alright."

Charlie, grabbed both Glenn and Uncle Augie's arms and marched them outside and up the street to the Marshall's house, knowing Daisy would welcome the company, and would appreciate hearing the news of what's going on and knowing Daniel, her husband, returned safely from their trek.

Ethan and Nora, Joe and Aiyana with Aponi all gathered around the table, breakfast nearly finished Glenn surprised everyone with his intentions towards Charlotte.

"Excuse me folks, I have something very important to announce or ask. Ethan, with your kind permission, I hope you will grant me permission to marry Charlotte? That is, if she'll have me." And produced a ring from out of his pocket, it glistened brightly, as Charlotte's eyes took in the beauty of that ring, knowing the full meaning of what Glenn was asking both her and her Pa. A tear trickled down her cheek and it made here eyes sparkle as brilliantly as the diamond.

"OH, oh Glenn, it's so beautiful," as her eyes flooded completely with tears and couldn't help the audible sobs that emitted from her throat...*and remembered the day at a stage stop she had told Glenn he needed to put a sparkler on her finger to see more of her.*

"Well now folks, this may seem like a very inopportune time to ask such a thing, but I've been holding onto this little ring for over week now and am afraid of losing it, just thought it would be safer on her finger." Glenn admittedly confided with a chuckle.

"For crying-out-loud then Glenn, ask her, Ethan jested. "You indeed have my permission, though we all knew it was coming sooner or later.

On his knees still at the table, Glenn looked up at Charlotte adoringly and asked: "My Darling Charlotte, will you marry this unworthy, so in love with you, man you see kneeling before you?"

Charlie could not contain herself then, and broke down crying profusely, and through sobs she finally was able to say..."Glenn, oh yes, well hell yes I will and it's about time you asked, I was beginning to think I would be an old maid. But what will people think of a married woman running a saloon and the men are going to hoot as loud as they do in a whorehouse on nickel night?" Charlie couldn't help but to laugh at herself...

Everyone, even Nora and Daisy laughed out loud, knowing Charlotte basically raised herself and was outspoken like that, but in a good way.

Glenn slipped the ring on her finger, and it was now official, Charlotte was a betrothed woman.

"Wish we could have a celebration of sorts," Uncle Augie piped, "but we really need to finish our business before we celebrate now. When this business is finished I promise to give you both the biggest wedding and celebration this country has ever seen.

They thanked Daisy for a great breakfast and departed together. The town was beginning to wake up, storekeepers setting up some of their wares on the boardwalk, unawares of what transpired during the night, just another night for them. However, Sophie Blessing, co-owner of The Palace was already up and about and meeting them face to face on the board-walk, she confronted the Marshall.

"Marshall, I've just been informed my partner Bob Luckman is dead...is that right?"

"Yes Sophie it is, he's at the jail now, we didn't want to leave him laying in the alley; and also someone tried to murder little Sara Jane Nichols last night as well. Now Sophie, you hear a lot being in The Palace like you are. Did you hear anything about that?"

"Now I am sorry to hear about Sara Jane, is she alright?"

"Yes, she's quite alright, but was shook up some last night of course...but why would anyone want to have Sara killed, by the Jesus, she's only 15 years old?"

"Seems that's a puzzle for sure Marshall, my regards to her, though I never knew her personally, I'd seen here walking around from time to time and never heard nothing bad about her. Now please take me to your new jail and show me Bob, seems it's up to me to have him buried."

As they were walking towards the Marshall's Office, Sophie continued with, "You got any idea's who the killer was Marshall?"

"No, not a clue Sophie." but made a gesture to Charlotte, Glenn, Ethan and Joe not to say anything about the footprints and blood trail the attacker left behind at the doc's place.

"Ya'll excuse me please," Charlie declared, "Glenn and me are going to check in on Sara Jane, we'll be along shortly."

At the Marshall's new Office/jail, Sophie was surprised to see it and exclaimed, "Marshall this is damn sure quite a hoosegow you have here, but where is the jail cells?"

"First off, over here in the corner is you partner on the floor, throats cut, nearly took his head clean off. Need you to run down some men to pick him up and bury him Sophie, I'm sure you'll want to do that."

"Yes Marshall I'll have that done, though truth be known, me and him never did get along well. Now show me the rest of your jail here."

The Marshall seemed surprised that Sophie was so interested in the jail and especially where the cells were, but he lead the way to the cellars and showed her...

"I'll be damned Marshall, sure as hell no-one can bust these critters out. Well hello Quinton or should I say Josh, seems you finally got your tail caught in the door."

"Marshall, when in hell do we get fed in this hell-hole?" One of the prisoners barked.

"You'll get fed shortly, your not going anywhere noways, so just shut-up. With ya all in here your the least of my concerns. Let's go back up-stairs Sophie."

But something else clicked in the Marshall's thought's, *why would Sophie be so little concerned over her partner being killed, yet wanted to see the jail cells...and how did she know of Quinton Taggert?*

Back upstairs, Sophie excused herself by saying, "Marshall, need to get back to The Palace and get some boys to come get this unlucky soul and I've got lots of work to take papers over to our only lawyer in town...Seems The Palace is all mine now, plus the mine he had."

"Thanks Sophie, hope your day will be better than the way it's started out. Good morning to ya now."

Ethan and Joe had also witnessed the way Sophie seemed to be interested in the jail-cells and was also surprised she showed no emotion to her partner being killed. Yet perhaps because she just inherited The Palace and a working gold mine, she was thinking only of that and simply not showing grief for Bob Luck-man.

Shortly four men arrived and carried Luckman's body away and the Marshall announced he needed to check on Sara Jane and Noah, and also talk to Charlotte. Both Ethan and Joe went along also.

At the doc's place, they found Sara Jane up and dressed feeling much better, Noah sitting beside her on the bed and Doc in the back room.

"Glad to see you looking better Sara Jane," the Marshall greeted. "But do you feel up to talking some?"

"Yes sir, I'm fine now, thanks to Noah."

"Well good Sara Jane, but I'll have Charlotte teach Noah how to shoot better, if she will, but that's not what I wanted to talk to you about. Some questions are pretty delicate in nature and I suspect you should have your mom present," and as the Marshall said that the door opened and Doc Valerie walked in.

"Good Morning to ya again doc...I was just asking Sara Jane how she was and was also thinking she'd want you present when I ask her questions. Some are gona sound rude or perhaps you'll think they are none of my business, but it's very important that you know why and know the answers as well. Also if you prefer I can ask everyone else to step outside."

"Well Marshall, I think Sara Jane hopes to get everything out in the open, but I'll leave it to her how many people she wants to have privy of her private life. Sara Jane, what do you think?"

"Ma, at this point it doesn't matter, and perhaps if I just make a clean breast of everything it'll be much better."

"Now Sara, some questions will be of a very private nature, you still want to do this with everyone present including Noah?"

"Yes, Noah most of all cause he not only saved my life this morning, but has stayed with me when I've been so sick. Noah deserves to know."

"Good girl Sara Jane, often times it's best as confession is good for the soul." Preacher Ethan interjected.

Now Sara, my first question is how you became involved and smoking of the opium pipe?"

Sara Jane took a deep breath, looked around the room at everyone, sighed and clasped her hands together and first said, "May God and you Ma, forgive me.

Murmurs and nodding of heads through out the room, all was quiet.

"Last year when I was only 14, I was walking the board-walk and Mr. Luckman was also on the board-walk, he stopped me and introduced himself as our Mayor and said he knew I was the doctor's daughter and how pretty I was and made some other fancy talk I wasn't used to hearing, but it made me giggle and guess I acted silly to him, but I met him the same way several morning's like that, one day he asked if I'd like to have some sweetbread and goats milk, that the Chinese-laundry had some for sale. I nodded yes and went with him to the laundry. I think I was impressed with him cause he was not only our Mayor, but a handsome gentleman as well. Very polite. Then one day he took me down in the cellars or a cave like beneath the laundry and told me he had a surprise for me...said it would make me feel happy and that I could have it anytime I wanted too. We smoked the opium pipe and I drifted off to sleep, I remembered Mr. Luckman next to me pawing at me and taking my dress off, but I had no will to stop him. Then a big Chinese guy was hoovering over me and I think he was naked too, but I don't remember anything from that point on, I must have blacked out but I do recall waking up completely naked with Mr. Luckman next to me. Ma, can I have a glass of water please?"

"yes honey, are you sure you want to go on with this."

"Ma, I need to get this out of my head and hoping ya'll can forgive me...yes I want to continue.

"Very well honey, I know it's difficult, but go ahead." Doc Valerie urged with tears in her eyes.

"Well that opium pipe really got to me and I asked Mr. Luckman several times to let me have it quite often and each time I did, at some point I would end up naked; and didn't realize right away what was being done to me when I fell asleep...I guess I turned out to be an easy girl for that big Chinese guy and Mr. Luckman having their way with me...after that it was easy, I met them often even out at an old abandoned line-shack out of town, even without smoking the pipe...they said I was their favorite tart, also told me I better do it or they would tell you, Ma. I am so sorry."

"It's alright honey, I forgive you, but I feel a lot of it was my fault...forgive me child."

"Who is this Chinese guy Sara Jane and how is he involved?"

"I don't really know much about him, he only came around to do it to me whenever he told Mr. Luckman to have me ready...but I do know his name. His name is Da Yung Lin, and everyone calls him master, even Mr. Luckman. I've also heard him tell Mr. Lucky, everyone calls him that, to tell his people he had a job for them to do. That's really all I know about him and there were times when Mr. Lucky was gone and just Da Yung

Lin was with me that I would hear a woman's voice and some-times they were arguing, but I never could tell what they were talking about."

"Well, you do know Mr. Luckman is dead don't you honey?" Glenn asked, "So he won't be bothering you anymore."

"Yes Sir, Ma told me earlier this morning. I'm not sorry, he made me a whore and I'm not even finished growing yet...I'll just be a Lady of the Night the rest of my life, not fit to be a wife. I think I'd rather be dead."

"I'll take you to wife Sara Jane!" Noah blurted out... "Just give me some time to grow up to take care of you."

"Oh Noah, you truly are a man now I think, look how you saved my life. I'd promise to be a good wife to you too." Sara Jane avowed, crying her eyes out.

Despite the fact of her crying profusely, everyone in the room burst out laughing. "It's alright Sara Jane, you'd make a good wife and Noah would be a good husband and you both would be lucky to have each other. You'll do fine." Charlotte agreed. "Now, look here Sara Jane, look at my finger, Glenn and I just became engaged."

"Seems, we are getting off the subject, but I have no more questions for you anyway Sara, and I thank you for being so can-did with us. It shows you have strong character, you were just lead down the wrong path by a selfish dirty ole man." Marshall Dan concluded.

"Oh Miss Charlotte, I'm so happy for you!" Sara Jane piped.

A Big grin from both Charlotte and Glenn, nodding thanks was noted.

"Well Doc and Sara Jane, it's still morning but the town is waking up and I thank you again Miss Nichols for being so straight forward and truthful and that has helped us a lot. Good day to ya both and Noah you take care too and soon Charlotte will teach you how to shoot with skill, as she does."

Getting back to the office, the Marshall noted both Mary Davis and Sheriff Allen was sitting there waiting. "Well now Marshall I hears from my deputy here that ya'll had a hell of a time of it. But your back safe now...and now our Mayor is dead and he was also a part of all the robberies...Don't really surprise me none, but he covered it up pretty well it seems."

"Yeah Sheriff, but it's not yet been proven for a fact, but it still bothers me as to why he was killed. Haven't yet figured out what part he actually had in all of this."

"Well suh, it'll come out sooner or later, you can rest assured."

"Say Sheriff, surely you've heard of a china-man around here goes by the name of Da Yung Lin? He's supposed to be some kind of master of all Chinese people living here."

"Can't rightly say as I have Cap'n, course you know a I don't get around much these days. Ever hear of that name Mary?"

"Sure have, but he don't stay around here much anymore...he bosses the railroad gangs too and runs a supply wagon from the south, somewhere's round Tucson I think they say. But I have seen him a few times talking to the Mayor."

"Just keep you eyes and ears open 'bout him, but don't spread the word I'm looking for him; but sure would like to ask him a few questions." The Marshal shot back. Yet, my mind was sorting out the information I have received and was now putting it all together. *If Da Yung Lin has been having his way with Sara Jane, of which I do not doubt, and Bob Luckman was killed, attempted murder of Sara Jane and footprints from a Chinese-styled land boot adds up to a definite cover-up. So now I figure to know what I'm up against...someone who will kill even a young girl to keep from being caught and he thinks Sara Jane may know more than she actually does. Yes another attempt will surely be made on young Miss Nichols. Noah is just simply not ready or yet equipped to handle that real possibility, so this puts both of their lives at risk.*

The Marshall's thoughts were interrupted by Sarge coming in with the prisoners breakfast, yes a bit late now, but we all had been busy.

"Marshall, Ma Teel wants to know who's agona pay for theses meals she makes up for them prisoners?"

"I'll go talk to her soons as I can Sarge, tell her to put your meals on the ticket too. That suit you Sarge?"

"Yep, course I'm no a bother, don't take much for me." Sarge snickered, as he opens the back room cellar-door bars to go down and feed the prisoners.

"Seems I best contact the other members of the council and tell them our illustrious mayor is no longer available and need to vote in at least one more council member and elect a new Mayor. By the way Ethan, would you be willing to being a council member." and by that, Glenn excused himself as Ethan nodded affirmatively.

"Charlie, we need to figure out a way for you to teach Noah to use a gun properly without exposing either one of them to danger...got an ideas?"

"Only thing I can think of without leaving Sara Jane alone is to take both of them with me out in the country, but it would also be necessary to have a rifleman stand guard as I wouldn't be able to devote my attention to teaching without that. And, it would need to be in the mornings as my afternoons are full as you know."

"Good idea Charlie and I'll have Sarge be your look-out, best man I can think of for that."

"That'll be fine then Uncle Augie, we can start in the morning if it's alright and Doc Valerie approves too."

After about 10 to 15 minutes, Sarge is hollering his lungs out, "Cap'n, Cap, ya best hurry on to down hea, sumtuns all mighty wrong. Cap'n, ya best to hurry now I tells ya."

It took both the Marshall and Charlie less than a minute to get to the cells in the cellar. "What the hell is going on Sarge?"

"Don't know Cap'n, but looka thar," pointing to the prisoners, "theys be sumtun wrong hea.

Two of the prisoners were vomiting and into convulsions, the other two including Quinton Taggert were not even moving. Don't know if they were dead, passed out or what. Thinking it may be a trick of sorts, Marshal Dan was very cautious..."Charlie, run get the Doc, don't know what's the problem. Just get her here fast as you can."

Within a very few short minutes Charlie was back with the doc. "What's the emergency here

Marshall...what? What's going on?"

"Well now doc, seems we don't really need you now, all four of my prisoners are dead, but what the hell killed them."

The Doc goes into the cells and examines the bodies, of which indeed are dead, but still warm. "It seems your prisoners have been poisoned Marshall, but don't know how, yet their symptoms appear to be one of three types. Rattlesnake, Heroin or perhaps even a lethal dose of Strychnine, all of which has similar reactions and usually death occurs within minutes, if not treated immediately and if enough has been given to them. Who has been with them or what have they eaten?"

"Sarge just brought down their breakfast maybe twenty to thirty minutes ago, could their food have been poisoned?"

"If they've had no other visitors, that's quite likely Marshall. Did you get the food from Ma Teel's?"

"Yes, but surely she wouldn't do that, but perhaps one of her cooks would. Who knows who Ma Teel has working for her?"

"Marshall, I can only give you an educated guess as to how they were poisoned, but by what poison, I would need to do some testing, and I can suggest it was put into their coffee. That's all the information I can give you now."

"Sarge, go back to Ma Teel's and find out who actually served the food and coffee for you to bring back, but be careful, don't tell anyone what happened."

"Right-away Cap'n."

"Well Doc, do you need the bodies to make tests or what?"

"No Dan, er... Marshall, I'll only take some coffee with me, as that is the logical means of poisoning in this case. Is there still some left in the coffee pot?"

The rest of the day went smoothly, the prisoners bodies were removed and taken to a would be mortician, that was new in town and no one new anything about, but they just needed to be put into a pine box and buried...with markers, in case any possible relatives should inquire of them.

The next morning Charlie had both Noah and Sara Jane out of town a couple of miles and set up targets to practice with; however, the targets were not used, instead Charlie instructed Noah to take the gun apart and put it back together, not just once, but several times and Sara Jane watched carefully as well.

"Noah, knowing your gun and how to take care of it is nearly more important than anything else...anyone can pull a trigger, but by knowing your gun, it's weight and feel of it, it becomes a tool, an extension of yourself. Do you understand what I mean Noah?"

"Yes ma'am, ah I mean aunt Charlie. I do understand, it's like I just pulled the trigger on that guy, I was in a hurry and didn't aim properly and was kinda frightened myself, afraid I would miss and nearly did."

That's right Noah, it's alright to be scared, but to be able control you fright is important, you just need to react before the fright sets in when faced with another gun or someone trying to harm you."

When do I get to shoot?"

"Noah, there are still some other things you need to learn before shooting. Here again, do not be in a hurry...the more you learn about the tool in your hand and how to maintain it, the better you will be; one thing I will stress to you, never pull your gun on someone unless your ready to use it right then and there, without hesitation."

"I think I am really beginning to understand what you mean Aunt Charlie, it's much more than just aiming and pulling the trigger."

"Yes and it's also necessary to know as much about who your up against as well, the way he stands to face you, straight on or standing sideways, or even in a crouch position, and trying to take advantage by positioning of the sun or obstacles that may throw you off. What and how he may talk to you, trying to distract you and yes, so many other things. If you give me complete attention Noah, I will teach you these things. Not for you to be a gun-fighter, but for self protection and to be able to protect you loved ones."

"Miss Charlie, will you teach me also? I don't think Ma would mind." Sara Jane asked imploringly.

"If your Ma agrees, I will teach you both, since it's necessary your both out here with me."

Getting back to town and then to Doc Valerie's place, Charlie, Sara Jane and Noah found the Marshall and Preacher Ethan there also...Doc was starting to tell them of her testing the coffee for poison and sure enough, enough poison in it to kill ten people with just a half a cup.

"What kind of poison is it Ma?"

"It's called strychnine, farmers and ranchers use it to control various pesky rodents and even snakes and wolves. It comes from a genus of trees and climbing shrubs of the gentian order...sorry about getting so scientific. But both the seeds and bark contain this powerful poison...It usually takes 1 to 2 hours to kill a person, but the amount in the coffee was exorbitant and obviously killed them within minutes. I at first thought it may be heroin, that's a derivative of opium and given how things are taking shape, and the symptoms are closely aligned with strychnine, but that we have a source of opium here and that would have made it easy to get and use."

"So, the poison could basically be bought by anyone claiming they had pesky rodents or varmints on their place."

"That's correct Marshall, but usually it's sold only through or by apothecaries, but in some cases a mercantile will carry it."

"Thank you Doc, I appreciate your time you've taken with this. Well hello Noah and yes, you two Sara Jane, hope your practice went well."

"Not like I expected Pa, but then I didn't know what to expect, but Aunt Charlie is a good teacher and I have learned a lot just this morning alone. I had no idea learning about guns would be so exacting."

"Ma, I want to learn about guns too...I watched and listened to Miss Charlotte too and it is very educational, interesting and I think necessary, especially after what nearly happened to me."

"Well, we do live in very precarious times and area, I think it would be appropriate, just your grandpa would not have approved. But he is no longer with us, yet he did often times carry a firearm, though he tried to hide it from me."

CHAPTER 15

The Ambush

S trange how the mines were attacked the way they were and then nothing else happening. *Even Sam Squires said he had other things to attend to first. But what could it have possibly been? Things are just not all making sense.*

"Well Glenn, seems your fellow council members think quite abit of you, appointing you Mayor and also accepting your appointment of Ethan to the council. Do you plan on having a regular election soon?"

"Well our town has to be incorporated first, and an accurate as possible census taken, and yes that will come later."

What's the talk about our former Mayor Bob Luckman?"

"The least said the better I think; yet the news is, that he was a wanted man back East somewhere's, changed his name like most of them do…and actually started out to be an honest reliable citizen. Yet unfortunately just couldn't keep from putting his fingers in the cookie jar when he saw the opportunity; but his big problem was his yearning for young girls and that's most likely why he was a wanted man. But enough about him, much more important things now to attend too.

"Well now Glenn, perhaps it's time to set the record straight about myself, so there'll be no surprises later on. Ethan and I both were running with gangs after the war, we were eventually caught and nearly hanged, but making a long story short, we were given pardons if I agreed to become a Marshall and Ethan here an undercover deputy. Charlotte is Ethan's daughter, and raised herself mostly and is also an undercover deputy. Joe Freeman is a man just kinda running loose who we were with in the Army and decided to run with us, same as ole Sarge. I'm telling you all this Glenn because I tag you as an honest man, your the new Mayor and your in love with Charlotte, you could never find a better girl than her...so just thought I'd best wipe the bowl clean."

"Doesn't surprise me a bit Daniel, I did suspect something nearly from the start, but could never put my finger on it. I have no problem with you or any of your deputies," Glenn insisted, "especially Charlotte, though she was the first I suspected dressed as a harlot on the stagecoach, yet I knew she wasn't one and that in itself was interesting to me and yes I fell in love with her. But now Marshall, we still have the gangs running loose and don't know where for sure they are hiding out now and what they'll be planning next. What the hell can we do?"

"Glenn, I have several idea's now, which gives me an edge and it seems everything is now leading to the Chinaman, Da Yung Lin. Look how Bob Luckman was killed, throat cut, then the attempt on little Sara Jane, also with a knife and obviously by a Chinaman as well. In both cases a knife was used and footprints that match a Chinese made land-boot with toe turned up, then my four prisoners in jail-cells that were poisoned and Sarge reported to me that Ma Teel had two Chinese men working for her and one of them was responsible for making up the breakfast's that were served, but one of them just vanished, never showed up again after that happened. But still a small part of the puzzle is missing and I can't seem to put my finger on it."

"It seems to me there are two things that we need to find out," Ethan interjected, "first we need to find out what Sam Squires is up to and where he is, and secondly we need to talk to Da Yung Lin. Don't know what that'll accomplish but just putting him on the hot seat may rush things up abit as there just seems no doubt he is definitely involved up to his eyebrows."

"Right you are Ethan, I think perhaps we need to talk to Ti Ling again. But we need to do this through Charlie, so as not to arouse suspicion, and not get Ti Ling killed.

"I'll make a point of talking to Charlie and not Ti Ling, I'll take Charlie up to her rooms and tell her everything we suspicion and need to try to find out some things from her. Charlie can do this without arousing any suspicion I'm sure." Glenn surmised.

"Oh Miss Charlie, please to forgive to me, I can no a say a thing...if ever Ba Da Yung Lin were to ever find me out, my head, she no longer be mine."

"It's okay Ti Ling, yet I assure you anything you tell me to help get rid of him will never be found out from me...and I'll protect you myself as well, and of course Jim is here also."

"I can say only Miss Charlie, he will be here tomorrow to collect his protection money and taxes we all have to pay. But he has found a deep attraction for Miss Sara Jane and will be expecting her to service him, as I'm sure he knows an attempt on her life was made but failed.

But further, he would have ordered her killed and now I think maybe he would want her to bed and then kill her himself. He thinks that way and he's so strong he gets away with whatever he wants."

"Ti Ling, thank you, that gives me a great idea. Go on back to work now and don't mention to anyone what you've told me."

"Yes Miss Charlie...maybe so things to get much better, I hope soon."

"Glenn listen, from what Ti-Ling has told me we can easily set a trap for Da Yung Lin; if Sara Jane will not be afraid to be used as bait...and she'll be guarded at every moment."

Gathering Sara Jane, her mother Doc Valerie and Preacher Ethan, at the Marshall's office Charlie informed them all of what Ti-Ling told her and also what her plan was.

Everyone agreed to this, even Sara Jane, well all except Ethan of course.

"Listen to me now," Ethan argued, "Isn't it enough what Sara Jane has already been put through, now putting her life on the line just doesn't set well with me.

"Well, I'm for it Preacher, sorry to say, yes I'm scared but if it'll help stop what's been happening I want to do it." Sara Jane interjected.

The next day, about 10 AM they started to put their plan into action...

Sara Jane staggered into the Chinese-laundry acting like she needed the pipe, the woman told her No...but Sara Jane started crying and screaming, a Chinese man came from the back and whispered to the woman and took Sara Jane out back and put her into a buggy and drove off out of town in the direction I knew they would be taking to the old abandoned line-shack out of town. Charlie, Ethan, Glenn and Sarge were already in place at the shack in hiding. I followed far enough away not to be noticed, but about a mile before the turn-off, I took another trail, so as not to be spotted...Sara Jane was still acting like she needed the pipe badly. She was doing her part perfectly.

Sara Jane was put into the line-shack and told to get undressed before she could have a pipe...she did this, got into bed and pulled a sheet up around her, just letting enough breast show to arouse anyone coming in. we waited about an hour and knew Sara Jane actually drifted off to sleep, and it was around noon time that another buggy pulled up to the shack with two people in it. One of them wore a cloak and baggy pants and we could not tell who it was as that person also kept his face covered at all times...we could not hear what was being said, but each pointed to Sara Jane several times...finally, the cloaked one left, getting into the buggy and driving off. We stayed in our places until the buggy was out of sight and hearing range then surrounded the shack and burst in as the naked person was crawling into bed with Sara Jane. Da Yung Lin was so surprised that he literally jumped out of bed naked, but had grabbed Sara Jane as a shield, and was spouting what we believed to be his Chinese language, expecting someone to burst through the door to turn the tables on his captors, but we had silently taken care of that problem. Yet he still held Sara Jane Captive and exposing her nakedness to everyone in the room.

"Are you alright Sara Jane?" Charlie worried.

Sara could only nod her head affirmatively, but obviously distressed because of her naked and helpless condition.

"Da Yung Lin, there is no way you are walking out of this shack alive if you don't let that young lady go and unhurt...and I mean now!"

"I don't think so, this girl she is willing, she want me to, she has told me this many times."

"That may or may not be true Da Yung Lin, but that girl is under the age of 17 and when she has been under the influence of your drug opium, she was incapable of making a sound decision. So you are under arrest. Our new Mayor with council has made it a law, that what you have done is against the law."

Suddenly Da Yung Lin viciously threw Sara Jane down on the bed and jumped out of the window, obviously cutting himself quite badly... but was stopped short outside by Charlie with gun drawn and ready. Da Yung Lin stopped and cowered at the site of her standing stead-fast; then remembered his nakedness and tried to cover himself with his hands.

"I see why you have to rely on drugs to get young girls in your bed...your not man enough and your manhood size is like a young boy that never grew up. Your a laughing stock Ba' (master) Da Yung Lin. HEY, inside someone, bring out this little boys clothes before I laugh myself to death."

"Thanks for stopping this child rapist Charlie." As I tossed his clothes on the ground in front of him. "Put them on and by the way I removed your knives and belly gun from them so no need to search for them. Your going in our new jail-house."

With Da Yung Lin securely tied to the surrey, so there was no way for him to jump off, they rode back into town, believing that perhaps with the Chinese master, Tong leader caught the gangs would be seriously hampered in continuing with the robberies.

Since it was well into the afternoon now, the streets of Durango were busy and all people turned to look upon the Tong leader tied to the surrey and wondered what was going on. Stopping at the newly constructed jail and office, the Tong leader tried to hid his face, but a small crowd had already gathered at the jail as they had followed the surrey down the street.

Leading the master Tong leader into the jail was no problem as he wanted to get out of the lime-light of the towns people or at least his own people, so he submitted quietly. After being put in the cellar cell he burst out with,

"This is be no jail, we are in cave-like, can no breath like this."

"To bad Mr. Lin, this will be your home for a while, unless you wish to be poisoned as you had done with my last prisoners. There is no escape from my jail unless it's by death."

"My men will kill all of you, you wait and see, it happen soon."

I slammed the cell door and made sure it was locked securely, went up the 12 steps to the ground level and closed and locked the floor door bars. Below the cell was nearly dark and you could faintly hear the great Tong master hollering, but I paid no-mind to this. The only dim light that the cells had came from the single barred door leading up to the upper floor and single jail cell and the jailers rooms. I had remembered reading in a book about some Count, I think it was the Count of Monte Cristo being locked in a dungeon and in building this jail, I had that in mind. Though I do also recall this Count did escape after a number of years. *Oh well, that's another story, but now it seems we still have to find out what Sam Squires and Ike Thornton may do and where in hell are they; and will Da Young Lin's Tong try to break him out? I'll have to ask Ti Ling or have Charlie ask her what kind of weapons I retrieved from Da Yung Lin's clothing, very mysterious, six small star like pieces of metal with extremely sharp edges with a hole in the middle and a short curved bladed knife with no actual handle. The belly gun was a small 32 caliber single shot, no problem with that one.*

"August, what are you so deep in thought about?" Ethan implored his friend.

"Ethan, I was just going over in my mind, what we have learned, it seems we have done a lot but still no closer to actually catching the gang's that are doing all the robbing and killing. Further, we have no proof of the Chinaman's involvement other than raping young girls by use of a powerful drug. So with him in jail, we need to concern ourselves with Sam Squires. Where in hell did he go with his band and what exactly is he up to?"

"August, did you know ole Sarge took off right after we captured the China-man? What do you think he may be up to...he does that without tell us anything."

"You remember he used to do things like that in the army, and yet always seems to come up with information needed badly. Perhaps he's doing that again."

"yeah, very possibly, guess we'll just wait him out. But now how are we going to feed this China-man? I don't think we should get his food from Ma Teel's and don't think we should allow any Chinese to be allowed close to him or bring him food, no telling what could be hidden somewhere's, or perhaps taking a chance on him being poisoned."

"Good thought Ethan, guess I'll just have to ask Daisy to prepare his meals, and he'll either eat it or go hungry. But who can we trust being a jailer and taking the food down to him, I don't want Daisy doing that."

"I've got a suggestion if you'll go for it. You have Noah, give him a shot-gun and have him stay behind the locked area here in the office...Sara Jane can stay with him, there's a bed, stove to cook on and some of the other women like Daisy, Nora and even Doc can check on them from time to time, here in this outer office. He'll be 16 in a few more days, let him be a man August."

"I don't like the idea at all Ethan, but maybe your right, he's wanting to do things on his own now and needs to realize responsibility, of which, granted, he did do by staying with and protecting Sara Jane. There's a definite bond between them."

"Ethan, I need you to stay here fore now while I go to the Doc's place and talk to Noah, Sara Jane and Doc.. To see if we're able to put that plan into action."

"Marshall, I sent the kids to the Laundry together, my linens needed cleaning badly and they have a sterile type detergent to do that."

"Come with me Doc, lets go there, something important has come up that I need to discuss with all three of you together, and I want to make sure they are safe."

Arriving at the Chinese-laundry, as we step in it was very quiet and we noticed three people bowing in front of Ti Ling and Noah and Sara Jane standing back.

"Ti Ling, what is this about, what is going on?"

But one of the Chinese men spoke up saying, "Mr. Marshall, we cannot dishonor the Princess, she is our "Wo ya'o gia'ngjian ni, it is proper we show her great respect that she so deserves."

"What does that mean, are you able to translate?"

"Perhaps the translation will be lost in your language, the best I can say is, it means Princess of the Land of the Sun. Ti Ling is most Mei lide gong zhu, which is Beautiful Princess; she is daughter to his most Royal Highness in Shanghai. Princess Ti Ling was kidnapped by Da Yung Lin about two years ago...there are factions that wish her to be dead, but there are also many of us who worship and respect her and will protect her at any cost...she wishes me not to say to you all of this, so I must not say another word."

"Ti Ling, you said Da Yung Lin was your master, so please explain.

"No sir, with respect, I said he claimed to be master, not my master however, yet I have no way of protecting myself from his demands."

"You do now Ti Ling, he is in my jail and no way of escape... Would these people be able to tell you anything else about Da Yung Lin or the gangs out of respect for you?"

"Yes, I think so Marshall."

"Oh, I just can't believe we have a real princess among us." Sara Jane boasted. "That is so wonderful, like in a storybook."

"Sara Jane, hush now, it has not been pleasant for this young misplaced Princess. Look what she has been forced to do, just like Da Yung Lin did to you." Her mother corrected.

"Mr. Marshall, I am Chen Lee Haung, I was Ti Ling's chosen before she was kidnapped, yet now she has been dishonored and made into less than a commoner, she is ashamed, but I am not ashamed of her... I have learned the English good for me cause we now live in your country. If you shall permit me I will be glad to tell you what I can with the Princess's permission."

"Very well, let's go to my office so we can discuss all of it." I suggested. "Come on kids and you to Doc and Ti Ling. There seems to be a lot to talk about."

At the jail, I explained my plan of having Noah and Sara Jane staying at the jail and in a way guarding Da Yung Lin, basically not permitting anyone from seeing him at all. It's like he is in total isolation from the outside world...however, it could be dangerous...and I went on to further explain that. Doc was apprehensive about letting Sara Jane being farther involved in these things, but there were so few they could trust, outside of their own. Reluctantly Doc Valerie agreed as Sara Jane and Noah both were shaking their heads affirmatively.

Everyone departed then, to go about their duties as needed. Charlie took Noah and Sara Jane out of town again and started their practice...Sara Jane surprisingly was able to disassemble and reassemble her S & W .38 double action, with 5 inch barrel with top break, her mother had only recently purchased and was one of the newest models Smith & Wesson manufactured. Noah was still using one of his father's old .44 Schofield's, but Glenn gave him a new 12 gauge shotgun break over double side by side. This day, Charlotte set up targets and let them try on their own; but it just wasn't good so she not only instructed them but showed them how to draw and shoot, not a fast draw, simply to get a feel for it...speed would come later after accuracy. Noah especially loved the shotgun and Sara Jane could handle her .38 quite well and felt comfortable...Charlotte explained how different it was when shooting at another person that sometimes it's difficult to pull the trigger. But in split seconds you have to think it's kill or be killed and must act accordingly.

Sarge was not with them this day, as chances were he was off to who knew where doing his thing of snooping and somehow had a knack for it; however, this is perhaps a day he should have been with them as Charlotte detected the sound of a hammer being pulled back, whirled and shot twice in the direction of the sound and out staggered one of the late Bob Luckman's men from behind a bush no more than thirty yards away and fell dead. But it wasn't over, apparently someone had sent out at least to ambushers to kill Sara Jane or perhaps all three of them. A bullet whizzed past Noah's head and he grabbed Sara Jane and ran her to cover with him behind a large rock outcrop. Charlie had also found cover opposite them behind some downed trees. They did not have time to be scared, they simply reacted in a way Charlie has instructed them. Peering cautiously over and around the outcropping Noah saw

two men about 50 yards away and then looked for Charlotte. They were basically out of range for their small firearms but with the right elevation that old .44 Army Schofield and even Charlies .44 Colt with six inch barrel should be able to shoot quite accurately, at least Charlie could with her experience. Charlie signaled them not to shoot and keep undercover, let the ambushers worry by not showing ourselves and they will try to get closer...to flush us out into the open.

The waiting is always agonizing, especially for inexperienced Noah and Sara Jane, but they did as Charlie instructed and stayed undercover...

"Noah, why do they want to kill me? I've done no wrong to any of them."

"Sara Jane, I think they are desperate outlaws and their leader has probably told them to kill you, they are desperate because they are afraid you know more about their operation than you really do know."

"But, but just look, they have already disgraced and humiliated me. Oh why was I so dumb to allow myself to do what I did?"

"Sara Jane, It's not you fault, look how they have already treated a princess, they don't care about people, they are just greedy and want power. Besides you are not ruined for me, I love you no matter what! Please don't ever forget that Sara Jane."

"Oh Noah, you are to good to me. I love you too, and I really do pray you will someday take me to wife."

"That's a promise Sara Jane, you can count on."

A shot rang out and ricocheted only a foot about their heads. Sara Jane grabbed tightly to Noah and she reached up and kissed his cheek as another shot rang out, and they hunkered lower behind the large outcropping.

"HEY, you men, seems you have us cornered and there are only kids with me...how about a little bit of fair play? Give me a chance, I'm only a woman against you two...wana step-out and tangle? Unless you want it known you backed down from a woman, or you just gona do us all three by hook or crook."

"Don't know about that Miss, we heard a lot about you."

"Just lucky I guess and now there's two of you...an ya'll are supposed to be hard cases?"

"Well alright, let's do it then Miss, lets all step out easy like, hands away from guns. We'll deal you some fair play."

Both men, ragged looking stepped out and faced Charlie, legs spraddled, hands at the ready, stood there facing each other.

"Noah, come out and count loudly to three, that will be our cue gentleman to draw...Are you good with that?"

With an affirmative nod from both outlaws Noah said "1, 2"... the outlaw closest to Noah drew and Noah killed him instinctively, just up and fired that old Schofield and down went that one...

"I hadn't counted 3, want me to start over or is 3 still good?"

"But, but you wasn't supposed to shoot, you... you weren't included," the one outlaw still standing kinda stuttered.

"He started to cheat." Charlie said, "Noah only did what was right...Now you want to go ahead with this or are you backing down? If your backing down, I'm gona take you to the Marshall's."

"Yes I'll go peacefully, I ain't no gunny noways an I didn't ever cotton to the ambush order to begins with."

"Throw down you gun and back away." Charlie demanded.

Riding into town openly, people could easily see he was tied securely and no gun so they knew he was a prisoner being taken to the Marshall's office...some of the girls on the street jeering and hootin at him, knowing him to be a four-flusher. Some of the girls that had been cheated by him yelled out some very unpleasant cat-calls.

Just as they pulled up to the Marshall's office, a single shot rang out and the outlaw fell off his horse, shot through the neck...blood spurting everywhere. Quickly looking around Charlie spurred her horse forward heading for the livery down the street.; and the Marshall took off running in the same direction. With her horse still running Charlie jumped off her horse as they neared the livery, gun drawn, crouching low and headed for the back door and the Marshall close behind, but went straight in the double doors in front.

"All right, come on out, we've got you covered front and back." I yelled. No answer and I knew this to be another gunfight.

Suddenly a horse broke loose from the stalls and ran headlong at Charlotte at the back door, Charlotte only had seconds to try to get out of the way and the horse clipped her shoulder and sent her went sprawling. But the would be escapee suddenly fell off his horse as a shot from Noah's shotgun sounded through the livery-stable and he lay headlong in the dirt unmoving.

Running up to Charlotte, Noah lifted her up, just as I arrived. She seemed to be alright, just dazed, so I walked over to the man on the ground, he was definitely dead as Noah's shotgun blast completely obliterated his face, beyond recognition.

"Well that's that, just wish we could have seen his face, but you did good Noah, I'm proud of you that you did what was necessary."

"Very good Noah, you really followed some things I taught you, I too thank you." Charlie added.

"Now we have three assassins dead and no answers, but with the Chinaman in jail, I think I need to find out what Sam Squires is up to; cause I know Da Yung Lin would sooner cut out his on tongue as say anything."

"I think your right about that Uncle Augie, but I've got a hunch. Some things just coming to me." Charlie speculated.

"Care to share them with me Charlie?"

"Not now, I need to think more on them and do a little digging first...hope that's fine with you?"

By the time Noah, Charlie and the Marshall had finished, other townsfolk had arrived at the livery and was speculating who that dead guy was.

"Well I recall that geezers clothes, he's a regular at The Palace, can't mistake him, what with that black and white cowhide vest, with those silver Mexican conchos. That's Zeb, was one of the Mayors right hand men for mostly dirty work." A man of the crowd claimed.

"Yeah, I've seen him many a time going into a back room with the Mayor from time to time." another man of the crowd claimed. "No mistake about it Marshall."

"Thanks and some of you men pick this guy and the one in front of the jail up and take them to the undertakers...See if you can find out their names to put on the markers."

As the crowd begin to disperse I mentioned to Charlie with Noah in hearing distance, "I need to go to talk to Sophia at The Palace, perhaps she can shed some light on what's what or at least give me a name for those two owl-hoots. Charlie talk to Ti Ling some more or to Chen Lee, see if either of them can tell us anything more; Noah don't let Sara Jane out of your site, keep a sharp eye out for her and I'd prefer both of you stayed inside now at the jail."

There was a blood trail now, needing to see where it leads, yet the trail seems to have no definite beginning, so where exactly do I start...talk to Sophie, but what can she offer? I still need to trace down Sam Squires as he's a shifting one. He had his chance at me back on the trail, so what could have been so important to leave that go for another time? Well Sophia, hope you can give me a few answers.

Entering The Palace, it suddenly became quiet, the piano stopped banging, everyone turned to look at me as I walked straight up to Sophia's table, pulled out a chair and set myself down, reached for the bottle and poured myself a drink.

"Hello Sophia, been awhile since we have had a talk."

"Afternoon Marshall, yes it has been, I hear your onto something big... Say, by the way, I know you've got that Chinaman in jail, out of curiosity, I'd like to see that new jail you have."

"That can be arranged Sophia, but now your sole owner of The Palace here and own the Lucky mine, but I need to ask you a few questions...should we do it here or in your quarters?"

"Follow me Marshall, to many eyes and ears down here."

In her lavish made-up apartments, we sat down and she poured me a drink of her finest single malt scotch.

"Now Marshall, what can I do for you?"

"Sophia, I know you must be familiar, at least to some extent, of Bob's dealing's, and the men who worked for him. Ah, just recently someone is trying to kill Sara Jane and sent out ambushers to do that, but the tables were turned, and just minutes ago one of those men was shot dead in front of my jail, but we caught up with the bushwhacker and he's also dead. Now since our illustrious Mayor is also no longer with us, who could be giving the orders?"

"That my dear Marshall, I have no idea. Do you have any leads, anything at all to go on?"

"No Sophia, nothing at all. I know Sam Squires just is not all that smart and was a come lately part of the gangs anyway. Yet, I do have to deal with him. But someone is still giving orders and since Bob is dead and I have the Chinaman in jail, there's obviously someone in charge that is over them as being the man that actually calls the shots. Was hoping you could give me some idea."

"Wish I could Marshall, it might could end this lawlessness, but I'm as mystified as you are."

"Thanks for your help anyway Sophia and for that good scotch. Have a good day."

"I do wish you luck Marshall and watch your back, ya hear?"

As the Marshall walked downstairs and out of the saloon, something kept nagging at him, something he was missing. *I still need to find Squires, what the hell is he up to and where is he?*

Back at the jail he found Daisy waiting for him along with Noah and Sara Jane. Daisy ran up to him and hugged him tightly.

"Oh Daniel, I've been so worried and now from what I've heard, rightly so. When is this terror going to end?"

"Daisy, wish I could answer that and it seems to be coming to a head, but still the answers are avoiding me. But tomorrow I'm going to take Ethan and Charlie with me, and maybe Joe to check on a few things. Can you pack us some lunches?"

"Of course Daniel, just promise me you'll be careful, don't take any unnecessary risks."

CHAPTER 16

What Railroad ?

Sarge burst into the room after being gone again for a few days, we just never knew what he was up. "Cap'n suh, oh I means Marshall, got some news fer ya. That thar three railroads I before tols ya 'bout, well suh, they's a comin with a payroll thas not been paid a for bouts three months. Thinkin sumpin ups thar fer shor Cap'n."

"You mean the Atchison Topeka and Santa Fe Railroads Sarge?"

"Thas the one's suh...loaded with gold and script. Though, can't imagine why's it takes all three of them thar railroads. Beats me to hell and back, but ya's got dem right."

"Ah Sarge it's not three, well never mind. Do you know their stopping point or how far they are along now?"

"No suh's but theys be to comin."

"Thanks Sarge and yes that does give me an idea, I think that's what Squires had in mind right along and since they've been gone for several days now, they most likely are holed up somewhere along the way for an ambush of the train. Somewhere where there is easy hiding and least expected. Glenn might very well know the railroads route...lets go to Charlie's Nest and have a talk with him."

Charlies Nest was just filling up, only about twenty customers that Sid and Ti Ling had to contend with, the other girls would come in later. Glenn sitting at a back table, absent mindlessly shuffling cards.

"Gentlemen, to what do I owe this pleasure? Thought you'd all would be by gone now."

"Glenn, plans have been changed and we need your help again. I've heard your familiar with the route of the Atchison Topeka & Santa Fe. Right?"

"To some degree yes, but what exactly are you looking for?"

"Where would it be now or where would be the best place to ambush it?"

"Now that is a curious question Dan," *laughing,* "Do you plan on robbing it now?"

"Glenn, seriously I believe Sam Squires may very well have that in mind now, I've just learned that a three month back pay in gold and script is coming for the railroad crews. So are you able to help us?"

"Perhaps I can Dan, sorry for laughing, there is a spur stops in Pueblo, but there are also several other spurs, yet the mainline will go down to Santa Fe by way of Trinidad. There are many places where the train has to slow down because the uphill grades it has to take in the mountains, many of those places are quite hidden by curves and trees and tunnels it has to go through."

"Both places are to far for us to reach either one in time and still not knowing exactly along the tracks they'd do it...but perhaps we can meet them on their way back here to Durango; but which trails do we take?"

"The most likely trail they would take from Trinidad is on up to Alamosa and then to Monte Vista, and cut through the Rio Grande Pass and over the San Juans down to Pagosa Springs then nearly due west here to Durango. That's only about sixty miles from here."

"Well, seems we have no other choice but to take that chance your right Glenn, yet if they are caring about their horses it'll take them three days cause all that gold is going to take awhile and possibly they'll be using a wagon, so that'll make it a mite slower." Glenn concluded.

"Appreciate you help Glenn, care to come along with us?"

"You bet Dan, wouldn't miss this for anything. Let me know when ya'll be leaving?"

How about we'll leave tomorrow, that should give us time to take 2 days and set ourselves up in a convenient area some place along the trail to surprise and overtake Squires and his gang?"

"That'll work for me Dan. Be glad to do what I can. Will Charlie be going with us?"

"Yes, I plan on taking her Glenn, she's possibly the best shot among all of us, at least with a handgun and I've seen her shoot my 44/40 Henry with damn good accuracy too."

"She's a handful alright and I'm a damn lucky guy for her to take a shine to me like she has."

"Yes you are Glenn, but you have a few good qualities too." *laughing as I walked away.* "See you at sunup Glenn."

Next morning as dawn was breaking, I was surprised to see my small army waiting for me, there was Ethan, Charlotte, Glenn, Sarge and Mary Lou and then as we were getting ready to ride out Chen Lee Huang showed up on horseback ready to ride.

"Chen Lee, are you sure you want to do this?"

"Yes Sir Marshall, I think Ti Ling and myself have a stake in this...I wish to go, I have my horse, food and weapons."

"Very well Chen Lee. Let's ride!"

So I started us out at a slow lope, about 8 to 12 miles an hour and our horse's are able to maintain this cantor nearly indefinitely, without tiring much; yet after about 2 hours we stopped at a small trickling stream and watered our horses and refreshed ourselves for a ten minute break.

"Everyone alright, any problems? I figure we can go another 3 hours, that'll put us about 50 miles from Durango, but more importantly only 10 or so miles from Pagosa Springs and that gives us sufficient time to find our hiding place to surprise Squires and gang. But as I look around and recall when we crossed the Little Piedra River it is actually a very good place to spring our trap. It's only about 1 or 2 miles back and gives us fresh water and upstream a ways I'm sure we can find a good camp area that cannot be seen from the crossing...and we'll post look-outs up trail, so we won't miss them."

"Good Idea Marshall, I think it'll work, mainly as we have no idea how long we'll have to wait, yet I suggest we make only a cold camp, and string a high-line for the horses" Glenn suggested.

So we all rode back to the Little Piedra and sure enough we found an excellent place about a quarter mile upstream from the crossing to make camp.

"Well lets make a large pot a coffee now, and drink it sparingly, a dry fire under a pine tree filters the smoke and will keep the coffee warm." Ethan argued.

"Sounds good to me Ethan, let's do it." I urged.

"Sarge you and Chen string a high-line and make sure the horses have plenty of room spaced out so as not to get tangled. Mary Lou, and I will gather some dry wood along the River bed, that's been washed out...Charlie and Glenn, how about finding a pine-tree and clear the needles and some fallen boughs away, make sure we have 4 to 5 feet space under the trees limbs. There shouldn't be any smoke to speak of except when we first start it, and you can be sure the fire will be small as only thumb size wood or dried wood pellets we'll gather. Ethan, I'm asking you to go back up trail some and find a high place if possible to watch the trail, but be able to get to us in time to warn of their coming."

"Well, I be damned," Ethan laughed out loud, "that's more talking you've done all at once in a coon's age Augie."

Everyone laughed at that but went about their chores and soon a cold camp was set-up and a dry fire with a pot of coffee was boiling. Settling down to eat cold sandwiches, the camp became silent, each with their own thoughts and as dusk settled in you could hear natures nights sounds both near and far...the howling of a wolf in the distance, the hoot of a night owl, the yipping of a coyote not to far away, then a hissing of a big cat...but these men were seasoned to the night and nature was a part of them; and as the moon slid in and out of the clouds, they one by one drifted off to sleep.

Dawn ushered in with a sprinkling of rain, the air was crisp, but clean and the smell of coffee was a pleasant aroma to them as they each arose to do necessary chores and ready for a new day, not knowing for sure where it may lead. Yet ready to face any adversary that dares to upset their plans of stopping the viciousness of the killing gangs.

Gathered around the dry-fire, sipping on our coffee and chewing jerky with a cold biscuit, I thought this may be a good time to express my thanks for putting their lives on the line to stop the lawlessness that prevailed. The greed, the power hungry men that wanted control over others and didn't care how they accomplished this and to think only awhile back I was among this element...God forgive me please.

"Men, and yes ladies too, we all know what we are faced with this coming day. If we have surmised correctly that Sam Squires and his gang have already robbed the train, and that we believe them to be headed on this trail, they may very well be along about noon or after...I can only say, Thank you one and all and may God be with each of us that we may prevail. I know that may sound rather trite, but well, I do thank you."

The sky suddenly darkened, thunder boomed and lightning flashed through the clouds giving off an eerie spectrum, dazzling, dancing flashes of light played havoc with the clouds, thunder crashed and rolled in a continuous roar as lightning continued to dance from place to place. We barely had time to break camp and saddle our horses and stow our gear, as the rain pelleted down like stinging needles. Needing to find the shelter, out in the open away from trees and rocks that could bring death by lightning in an instant.

A voice was heard through the thunder, "Lay your horses down and lay across their necks, so they cannot spook and run. Cover their head and eyes, and talk to them soothingly."

I knew that to be the voice of Ethan, as we had experienced a like circumstance while crossing the Llano Estacado, and that's the way the Indians did it. Laying across a horses neck prevents them from raising up.

The storm was continuous, lasting through noon and we started to see the clouds part and the rain was dissipating; yet the wind started howling fiercely, perhaps to bring more rain, the wind whipped wildly through us, leaving us shivering and cold. We could no longer keep the horses down, but letting them up we kept a tight rein on them. Yet through all of this we knew the Squires gang to be even in worst shape, trying to pull a loaded wagon through this rain and mud-soaked trail. So we settled ourselves down and took cover under the pine trees that took the force of the wind, shielding us to a degree. Again we wait, Chen Lee was on look-out duty now up the trail and I hoped he has been able to find sufficient cover and still keep his eyes peeled for any movement, that could be the outlaws. The waiting is what is agonizing, the not knowing for sure if we were doing the right thing, and hoping we made sufficient plans to capture them to avoid anymore killing.

"Sarge, go see if Chen Lee is alright, and relieve him. Keep your eyes peeled now, first sign of movement you see coming down the trail, hightail it back here pronto."

"Yes suh Cap'n, I's on da ways."

"No, wait a minute Sarge, I just had another idea, Mary Lou go with him and tell Chen Lee to stay put until you see them coming, then send Chen back, but you and Mary Lou trail behind and when they reach the crossing, we'll attack, and you do the same, we'll catch them in a crossfire if we have to shoot...but stay to the side so we don't shoot each other. Go now."

An hour or more passed, the wind had completely stopped and the sun beat down like the devil opened up the furnace and heat waves shimmered, it became unbearably hot and muggy, sweat rolled off us as if we were still being rained upon, yet we held our ground knowing our adversaries must be feeling the same. Then finally far up the trail, there appeared movement, yet still to far away to determine who it was... two horses were pulling a wagon, and by count there were 9 horsemen, and the one driving the wagon made 10.

"By damn Sarge, I believe it's who we've been waiting for. Chen Lee, go back, keeping out of sight and tell the Marshall they's a coming about a mile passed our look-out."

The time has come, we didn't have to wait long, the outlaw cavalcade was nearing the Piedra where we hoped our trap was set tight. The lead horseman, raised his hand some 50 yards before the stream and they stopped...several of the outlaws conversing and two finally galloped their horses up to the stream, looked around, everything quiet and natural, then walked their horses about half way across, stopped and let their horses drink, all the while looking around; finally they rode out of the stream and waved to the other outlaws and they started towards us again, as we had hoped for. Just as the wagon entered the river I shot a warning shot high overhead, they stopped, but suddenly started shooting, someone shot the driver on the wagon and he fell headlong into the water, one of the lead wagon horses fell, so the wagon was halted. Firing broke out everywhere, some obviously misplaced as the horses were bucking and twirling and the riders were unable to shoot accurately. I counted four down as the shooting continued, yet the owl-hoots would not give up, it was a do or die situation for them. Through all of this I spotted Sam Squires trying to bring his horse under control so he would be able to get a shot off to hit his mark. Chen Lee did not have a gun but his special throwing knives he called Hira Shuriken's, *meaning sword hidden in the hand,* were hitting their mark and another man went down. I could not see or tell if any of my men were hit, yet I heard no cries of despair or death chortles, so the fight continued. I saw two more men go down and then Squires, along with 2 remaining men lite out for parts unknown, just to get the hell away and leaving the wagon with the gold and script in the middle of the Piedra. All shooting stopped, it had gone as planned, and I called out to all my men if they were alright. Mary Lou had a flesh wound on the calf of her leg and Chen Lee had a bullet graze across his cheek, but no other casualties.

"Glenn, you and Charlie follow those ones who rode away for a ways to make sure they don't double back and back shoot us, Ethan, will you tend the wounds of Mary and Chen? Sarge and myself will unhitch that downed horse and pull it out of the way, and see if we can pull the wagon out of the stream."

Struggling with a downed horse in the river is no easy task, but we finally managed and pulled the horse out onto the river bank, now to harness another horse to the three remaining and pull the wagon on across. Now the task of burying the dead men or should we load them in the wagon with the gold and take them back to Durango? Also, we had six extra horses to trail back, I just didn't like the idea of leaving them out here to fend for themselves, though there were wild horses roaming these mountains; these horses were domesticated and needed care.

Arriving back in Durango two days later, we seemed to attract a lot of attention with our small cavalcade slowly slogging down the street, with dead bodies in the wagon and all those extra horses, we pulled up to the jail.

"Sarge, take those horses to the livery-stable, get them wiped down, fed and have Carlos check the brands and find out who owns them."

"yes suh, Cap'n."

Having drew a crowd, Sheriff Walker was out front and concerned about the wound on his deputy's, Mary Lou's leg.

The Doc was sent for too and soon everyone was talking about us and after the dead bodies were taken to the undertakers, they all clamored to know what was in the two strong boxes. Soon a large crowd of townspeople had gather around and I was obliged to tell them where we had been and what happened. Murmurs, through-out the crowd and shaking of heads that something was now and finally being done about the riff-raff, the murdering and high-jacking of the silver and gold and other supplies.

Our new Mayor, as word had gotten around, was encouraged to say something. "Ladies and

Gentleman, please I assure you, you all will eventually learn of our trip to Pagosa Springs or I should correct that to say the Little Piedra, is where we were able to subdue this gang of outlaws, yet sorry to say three of them escaped, but we were able to capture this wagon loaded with gold and script that was initially intended as a back payroll for railroad crews and now will be distributed properly when the railroad paymaster arrives. We do not know much about the gang we were able to overcome and an investigation will be on-going. Now we are all tired from this ordeal, so permit us to continue to do our job and first of all get some rest. Thank you folks for allowing us to serve you. Please go about your business now."

As the crowd dispersed, the Doc had already arrived and she directed both Chen Lee and Mary to go to her office so she could cleanse the wounds and apply sterile dressings to ward off any infection.

Inside the jail, the Marshall directed his crew of volunteers to go home, get some rest and a good dinner, and thanking them for a great job...

Let's see now, just exactly where are we in this? *I thought of all the clues we had already found, plus capturing and killing most of Squires gang, but who's actually the real boss?*

Squires must be taking orders from someone and that someone will now be damn mad that the payroll was lost. So what could possibly be his next move?

Sheriff Walker walked into my office as I was pouring myself a short shot of Overholt. "Seems you did damn good Marshall, proud of you. Who was it exactly that was able to get away, did you recognize any of them?"

"Only two," as I poured the Sheriff a drink, "It was Sam Squires and Tim Taylor from the old gang I used to run with, but have no idea who the third man was. But if he's running with Squires. I'll eventually get him too."

"You have quite a history with Squires, Marshall, how did the bad blood developed twixt you two?"

"Sheriff, I never did like the way Squires was always terrorizing people and had no qualms about killing, but it was in Missouri when I got pardoned that Squires tried to rob the local bank, and to make a long story short, I shot and killed his brother and they didn't get away with the money."

"So how did he manage to get out here, or did he have information where you were going to to follow and exact his revenge on you?"

"I have absolutely no idea Sheriff, and frankly could care less. I have sworn to uphold the law as a United States Marshall and that's exactly what I aim to do, no matter who I may have to take down or get killed trying. End of story Sheriff."

"Fine, so what's your next move Dan?"

"Don't rightly know just yet, need to give it some thought, but I have a feeling it's getting close to the wire. Something will break soon, I'm sure."

"Well, I'll leave you with your thoughts Dan, hope you get this mess figured soon. Have a good day now, my friend."

As I continued to ponder my next move, it just sorta figured to be a big mess, had lots of clues but nothing seems to add up. Well, I think I'll have a talk with Da Yung Lin, see if he has anything worthwhile to say or if he'll say anything at all.

"Hello Da Yung Lin, how do you like my little jail?"

"This is a hell-hole Marshall," I was surprised to hear him speak so clearly in English.

"What you mean is that it is a real jail that no one can break you out of, but that suits me. Now I'm figuring several charges to put you on trial for...you have anything you want to say to me at all?"

"Not a damn thing Marshall, and don't you worry none, I'll soon be out of here and have your scalp."

"Fine suit yourself, but tell me one thing, why did you want to kill little Sara Jane, then after that failed you arranged to have her meet you in that old line-shack and have sex with her again, or did you plan on killing her after you had satisfied yourself on a young helpless girl?"

"Go to hell Marshall, I'm not saying another word."

"No problem, but don't plan on busting out a here soon. Whoever tries will have one hell of a time, you can bet your bottom dollar on that." At that, I left Da Yung Lin in the dark in his cell.

Glenn and Charlie were upstairs in my office again as I climbed back up the stairs and locked the barred cellar door.

"Thought you two would have eaten a good meal and be getting some rest now. What's going on?"

"Uncle Augie, we were just concerned about you and who's going to watch your prisoner, and continue to take his meals to him. He's crafty as can be and I'm sure he's gona try to escape."

"Funny you should mention that honey, as he just finished telling me that same thing."

"Marshall, well I've been thinking," Glenn intervened, "there's only one possible way for him to escape from your jail and if I'm not mistaking it's probably being not only planned right now, but actually is being worked on as we speak."

"What the hell Glenn, how can anyone escape from my jail? What's your idea?"

"Marshall my friend, think about it. With all the underground networks now throughout this area, tunneling would be the only way. In the dead of night he would be gone."

"Now I'll be damned, I should a thought about that. Your right Glenn, but now we can set another trap just for that, and catch them as they bust through my rock wall."

"That's right Uncle Augie, we can beat them at their own game...then we need to take Da Yung Lin out of that cellar cell and put him upstairs in a cell without telling anyone; he just won't be there when they bust through, and we can be there waiting for them."

"That's right Dan, then we can blow up the shaft they've dug to seal it off and repair your rock wall, and the cellar cells are good as new again."

"Damn my old hide, I should have thought of that as I was having it built..just never crossed my mind; but you having some experience in mining, it just came to you...I need to thank you both."

"Actually Dan, it was Charlie here that thought about it, she gets the credit for sure, and I'm sure they are digging now and probably have been nearly since he was brought in and it's possible they could try to bust through this very night."

"Well, we won't take any chances, but I'm going to wait till night fall before moving him to an upstairs cell here."

"Glenn, will you and Charlotte round up the rest of the crew...including Chen Lee? I've got an idea how to handle this and turn the tables on this escape. Tell them all to be here about seven this evening."

"Not a problem Uncle Augie." Charlie chirped. "It'll be good to get rid of this element here in Durango; well, I know this won't get rid of all of it right away, but at least other would-be-gangs may think twice before invading our town after we do this."

"Yes, word spreads fast when a bunch are taken down. Then again, there's always that dumb element that wants to try it out, you know." Glenn added.

That evening by seven and after, all my loyal deputies were gathered in my office-jail, and even our Doc Valerie Nichols was present. I presented my plan to them of which they all agreed upon and Doc offered to use her stethoscope to hear if anyone was actually digging.

"Doc, how in hell do you use that contraption?"

By way of explanation Doc put the two ear things in my ears and held the other end up to her chest..."What do you hear Dan?"

"Well, I hear thump thump thump, What The hell doc, but how can it tell if anyone is digging?"

"Quite simple Dan, you just put this end up against the wall downstairs, that I have to my chest now and you should be able to hear digging quite a ways off. It magnifies any sounds you put it up against."

"Well, don't that beat all, hell of a contraption, but now that I think on it, I did hear of that afore. Should we try it and see if anyone is digging now?"

"Sure Dan, lead the way."

"Valerie, I can hear what I think sounds like digging not to far away. We'll damn sure be ready for them now. Come on Da Young Lin, your going upstairs right now."

"What is that damn thing Marshall, what you think you hear?" Da Yung Lin blurted.

"Never you mind, but you damn sure won't be escaping tonight or any other night, you are my prisoner that won't escape or be killed before you go to trial, and you'll pay through the nose."

Later, that night our trap was set and with the stethoscope we could tell they were only a few feet away from the rock wall and it really wouldn't take a hell of a lot to break that down as no mortar was used. The river-rock had just simply been embedded against the dirt wall, then cracks filled with mud.

I had dispersed my crew in various places to be able to command all aspects of capturing and jailing these would be escape artists. The tunneling was no-doubt a good idea, but Charlotte had thought about it and suspected the tunneling would be done from the Chinese-laundry. Chen Lee and Sarge were to go through the tunnel from their end, so as to prevent them from running back as soon as they saw us in the cell waiting for them. We had them from both ways.

As it turned out fortunately, it happened just that way too. We now had four Chinese tunnelers locked up and kept Da Yung Lin separated from them. Glenn had some cement mortar in his last supply wagon and he suggested we use it to fix the rock wall in the two cellar-cells, and even use it for the floor, easier to clean plus they couldn't dig out.

So, here we are again, not knowing for sure what our next move should be. Squires and two of his henchmen are still loose and no telling how many more may have already been able to join him. The lure of fast easy money was one hell of a temptation, even for many law-abiding citizens.

I accidentally ran into Sophie Blessing on the street and I asked her, "Sophie, how you doing now that your the boss of The Palace and even being a mine-owner? Any problems yet?"

"None so far to speak of Dan, The Palace is still doing about the same without as much riff-raff hanging out; but I haven't visited the mine yet, though my ownership has been established with all the mine workers and they don't seem to have a problem with me as long as they get paid... Say Dan, you and I do need to have a talk, any place we can go that won't be so open to just anyone seeing us?"

"How about the jail Sophie, or do you want to meet some-where out on the trail where eyes aren't watching our every move?"

"Yes, that would be better Dan. Can you meet me tomorrow morning about eight, say, uh, well where you found me that time with a broken axle on my wagon?"

"Will do Sophie, have a good day now." As I tipped my hat and walked away.

Now I wonder what she has in mind, something is brewing, but I need to be on the look-out for bushwhackers. Thoughts running through my mind, still not making complete sense. *Is Sophie somehow involved in these robberies and killings, or has she learned some information that would help end this gang-war. Well, guess tomorrow morning I'll find out what's on her mind.*

Walking into the office, I caught Noah and Sara Jane in a tight embrace and kissing, it caught them off-guard and two young red-faced kids standing in front of me.

"Hi kids," with a chuckle, "It's alright, it's been a long time, but I do remember what's it's like to be young and in love, and still am with your mother Noah. So how is your learning of shooting coming along, oh yeah, the both of you now. Just re-member, as I'm sure Charlie has been teaching you, never draw without shooting, but never shoot unless you know what or who is shooting at you?"

Both Sara Jane and Noah gathered their wits about them and shook off the embarrassment.

"Pa, I think were doing fine and we do talk about and remember the things that both you and Charlie tells us about firearms. I'll be sixteen in a week Pa, is that to young to be a deputy?"

"Well now boy, you are a good size for your age...but why would you be in such a hurry to pin on a deputies badge?"

"Well Pa, Sara Jane and me want to get married soon as possible and I want to be able to support her, have our own place and such."

"Doesn't really surprise me son, but have either of you talked this over with your Ma Sara Jane or have you mentioned this to your Ma Noah?"

"No Sir, kinda wanted to hear what you say first off."

"I'm not one to have much say about marriage, look how badly I treated you and your Ma son, not meaning to, just didn't use my head. Marriage is a two-way street and if your Ma hadn't of been the kind of loving person she was, we wouldn't be together now. May I say, you two younguns need to talk about this yourselves more before talking to your mother's. Learn the responsibilities toward each other, get a job and save your money to start off with; and yes son, at sixteen you are at least a couple of years to young to be a deputy."

"Yeah, guess your right Pa, but Sara Jane and me will someday be married; and we have talked about what we both would like to do. I wouldn't want to be a deputy forever, we have plans of owing a horse ranch, to breed horses and Sara Jane would like to be one of them horse doctors."

"Now that's right nice son, and I believe you'll do it, and I'll help you do that as much as possible. Now get along with you two, but you still need to be on watch for varmints right now till this mess is over...got it?"

"Yes Pa, talk to you later." As Sara Jane and Noah left the office arm in arm.

Hard to believe those kids are growing up so fast, I messed Noah's childhood, now he's half-grown and 'bout ready to be married...

CHAPTER 17

The Shot from no-where

Meeting Sophie, I had my doubts of any useful information, but I didn't want to pass up any possibilities, and also was aware of a possible ambush again; so I got there early to scout the surrounding area. Finding no one or any good place to set an ambush up I dis-missed that from my mind. I decided to strike a small fire and put on a short pot a coffee, that I always carry in my saddle bags on the trail. Shortly I heard Sophie's horse and buggy on the trail and also heard or thought I heard another horse too. *Now who could she have brought with her?* Sophie arrived alone, no other horse or rider and that put me on edge again. *Now who could that be, was I being set-up again?*

"Good morning Sophie, lite down and enjoy an Arbuckle's with me. Good to see ya, but did you bring someone with you, I thought I heard another rider behind your buggy?"

"No Marshall I didn't and sorry I didn't hear another horse. My buggy squeaks terrible as you heard I'm sure."

"Well perhaps I was hearing things out of place...anyway let's have the cup of coffee and let me know what you have in mind."

"Daniel, oh ah sorry, Marshall I don't have a lot to tell you but it's been bothering me for sometime now and just this morning as I was leaving Sheriff Allen stopped me and inquired of my early morning ride. I told him that my rides were too simply get away from it all for awhile.

Now Marshall what I need to tell you, must be done quietly, I don't even like to say it out loud, so lean closer I'll whisper...and I'm scar..."

A shot rang out and Sophie slumped in her seat and blood started flowing from her neck.

"Sophie, Sophie, what the hell..." I jumped down from the buggy with gun drawn, but not another sound was to be heard. I scouted around a few minutes and noticed where the ambusher had taken his shot...but nothing was left behind except the horse tracks. I followed them a short ways, but needed to get back to Sophie. Tied my horse behind the buggy and carefully laid Sophie down the best I could and started back for town.

Now what was so important that she wanted to tell me in a whisper? Did she even suspect someone had followed her?"

Arriving in town, people were just starting to get about, yet no one really payed any attention to me as I went straight to Doc Valerie's. Lifted her in my arms and carried her in.

"Doc, Doc, got an emergency here," I kicked open the door to her living quarters and laid Sophie on the bed that Sara Jane had used when she was sick... "Doc, you here?"

Doctor Valerie Nichols burst through the door with satchel in hand, not saying a word and reached in her bag for her stethoscope. "Dan, she's alive, breathing is shallow, but she is alive...I'll need to operate immediately, run get Sara Jane and Daisy, I'll need both of their assistance."

I left the Doc, running as fast as these old legs could carry me. I reached the jail and hollered loudly all the while knocking frantically on the door. Noah opened up, looking puzzled, with Sara Jane next to him.

"Pa, what's going on."

"Sara Jane, quick your mother needs you, go now. Noah run get you ma and tell her to go to the Doc's."

Neither of them asked any questions, just did what they were bid...

Time was of the essence right now, yet I had to stay here to guard my prisoners; surely someone may try to take advantage of this situation. The Sheriff knocked and I let him him,

"What's going on Dan, I've heard a bunch of commotion, someone said Sophie got shot? Is she dead?"

"No, the Doc said it's an emergency and needs to operate immediately."

"Well, I'll be damned, who the hell would want Sophie dead?"

"Most anybody that's part of these gangs, maybe they think she knows to much. But who would know where she was going this morning?"

"Don't know Marshall, well sorry gotta be going now...Hoping things work out for you, and I'll be talking to you later." With a wave of his hand, Sheriff Allen departed.

Now what was that all about? He didn't even mention he had talked to Sophie earlier this morning at the livery-stable before she left to meet me. Well, forget that for now...need to plan my next move about Sam Squires. Just hope Sophie recovers, perhaps she knows who would try to kill her, and if she dies who would inherit The Palace and the mine?

For some strange reason I kept thinking of the Anasazi Cliff-dwellings too... *What part of that is important? We only found the burned holster and gun-belt with the initials Q.T. and I experienced a strange dream or was it a nightmare. I know Q.T. Stood for Quentin Taylor alias Josh Clever, who turned out to be Hadley's mining partner. Now, about that dream or nightmare...what on earth could that mean, if anything? Do I need to go back there for some reason? Am I missing an important piece of the puzzle? Questions continually nag at me; the cliff-dwellings are a couple of days ride but something keeps drawing my mind back there.*

Alright, damn it to hell, I'm going, if for nothing else but to get it out of my mind. Need to talk this over with Ethan and maybe even Glenn.

I decided to go to Doc Nichols and check on Sophie.

Doc was in the outer tent-office as I entered. "Afternoon Doc, how is our patient?"

"Still sleeping and under pain medication, but I think she'll be alright, but I think she'll never be able to talk again...that bullet damaged her larynx quite badly and I just don't have the skills or knowledge to repair that."

"Well Doc, you have done the best you can, no one can fault you for that."

"Thanks, but we do need better facilities than what I have here Dan. We need a clinic or even a hospital with separate rooms for recovering patients and most importantly we need a sterile operating room."

"That would take some doing Valerie and a heap a money, but I'll mention it to Glenn.

"Glenn just left here a few minutes before you came in, said he was going to talk to Charlotte."

"Thanks Valerie, good day to you now."

As I walked into Charlotte's nest I noticed the Sheriff going into the Doc's, obviously to check on Sophie too.

Glenn was leaning on the bar, talking to Ti Ling and Chen Lee over a drink; walking up to them I noticed a few eyes following me from a table off to my left..they were strangers and appeared nervous when I walked in. Yet I acted like to pay them no mind for now.

"Afternoon ya'll, need to talk you, including Charlotte, is she around?"

"Afternoon Marshall, Charlie's upstairs changing, reckon she'll be down shortly." Glenn volunteered.

And as I looked toward the stairs Charlie was coming down, dressed in a beautiful dress that made here look even more beautiful and her hair done up that shimmered as she walked.

"Hello Uncle Augie, what brings you here so early?"

"Charlie, my dear, permit me to say you are breathtakingly beautiful. Glenn my boy, you are a very lucky man for sure."

"Indeed I am Dan and yes she is beautiful beyond measure. Ethan I'm sure is a proud father."

"Oh, will you two please stop it, I'm the same as I always am, just got a new dress is all. Mercy now, stop it."

Everyone laughed and I glanced over at the strangers sitting at the table and could hear one of them making some ugly remarks...Glenn looked at me and I nodded back and we walked over to the table.

"You got something to say stranger? Say it loud for all to hear."

With a twisted smirk on his face and winking to one of his partners he said, "Just wondering how much for that tart just came downstairs. I know it'd be worth about a dollar, but I'd give her two."

Glenn was about to take a swing, but I held him back, Charlie came over to the table and said, "Mr. let me see those two dollars, you even got that much?"

"yeah Missy, I got more'n that, you got change for a five dollar gold piece."

"Sure have Mister, let's go upstairs and you'll want to give me the whole five before I'm through with you. Best time you'll ever have and if I'm not, it'll be free."

Glenn and I both was about to interfere, but with a wink from Charlie stopped us...

"Come on Mister, never mind them, you'll be my first customer today." As Charlotte reached out and took the strangers hand and led him upstairs to her room; but before going in made a hi-sign to Ti Ling.

As soon as the door was closed, Ti Ling told Glenn and me not to worry, that they had planned for a situation such as this. Joe would be going up the back stairs and Charlotte's balcony door was not locked. Nothing would happen as Charlie will give him a drink with a Mickey Finn in it...and play as if he's a fine specimen of a man, get him undressed and into bed, and by that time he'll be passed out.

We laughed about this and had another drink which eased our mind's to a great extent.

Ti Ling further told us that Charlie would stay up there until he woke up in about an hour with Joe standing by all that time. When he started to wake up she would act like she was getting dressed and tell him what a fantastic lover he was and insisted he wanted her to have the whole five dollar gold piece.

He of course would not believe this but she would show him just enough breast that he couldn't refuse...and say, Now you don't remember...as soon as you were finished with me, you fell asleep with you still right on top of me, I had an awful time crawling out from under you ..Oh, I'll never forget you.

"Quite a set-up Glenn, and his buddies will tease him, so there's no way he'd say he didn't have a good time, after being upstairs with her for over an hour."

"Well I just hope it works then. Still it bothers me to see her have to do this."

Finally we looked up to see her coming down the stairs with that stranger following behind with a big smile on his face. His buddies slapping their legs and hollering at Ti Ling to set them up again and a double for the lover boy...

"How was it Butch? You spent a damn long while with her."

"Boys, I'll tell ya I gave her the whole damn gold piece...but we need to go now, a bit late as it is...Boss will be angry as hell."

Glenn was near fuming, but understood...and as the trio left, saying they would be back, Charlotte leaned over and quietly informed them that Butch talked some in his sleep. Let's go in the back room and I'll tell you.

"He didn't talk in sentences but he kept saying the Cliff's, and gold and payoff...none of it made sense to me, but perhaps it does to you Uncle Augie."

"Yes, it does Charlie, and it's something I've been dwelling upon for a while now. Thanks Charlie, your a bigger help than you realize."

"well what the hell does it mean Dan?"

Glenn, ever sense Sarge and me spent some time at the Anasazi Cliff-Dwellings I've had some strange feelings and now I can add up a few things. Glenn how would you like to go with me to those dwellings?"

"Hell yes Dan, as long as I've been here, I've never gone there yet, so curiosity is killing me now, and as what you're suggesting may also lead to evidence of the gangs."

"I'm going too, heard about them and they sound incredible, but anything that may help to lead us to evidence of these gangs, I want in on and I think Joe would want to go as well. Ti Ling is perfectly capable of running this place." Charlie asserted.

"Very well then, I'll need Ethan to stay here to watch the prisoners and he'll be damned mad about that. We'll leave in the early morning, it's a two day trip just one way, and we'll be gone from five to seven days, if we have no problems, so we need to gather supplies accordingly."

Next Morning supplies gathered on a pack mule plus each person had a few of their own necessities and they were off, with Ethan fussing, but willing to do a job needing to be done right by making sure the prisoners were kept alive and safe for trial.

Their first two days and one night was uneventful and as they looked down upon these fantastic dwellings of the ancient Anasazi, they were simply overwhelmed, by the magnitude and beauty of it.

"We'll camp here for the night." I stated

"My God," Charlotte exclaimed, "this is totally amazing and I understand that just one day the inhabitants just suddenly disappeared or vanished in some way."

"I think were all amazed Charlie." Glenn added, "Since I've been in Durango I've learned quite a bit about them, I'll tell you sometime, but there have been other inhabitants living here since the Anasazi, that were called the ancient Hopi. They have quite a story too?"

With that we settle down to make camp for the night and cook some vittles. Daisy had made both biscuits and a loaf of bread, to go with fixings for a venison stew. This we need to eat right away as the meat would not last another day without some cold storage or smokin, also the vegetables would start to wilt.

As darkness crept upon us the sounds of nature invaded our ears, yet the strangest sounds came from the cliff's down below; and the wind pick-up and seemed to blow through the open doorways and windows which created a song, singing over and over to follow The Wild Wild Wind. Was this actually happening or was I again dreaming? Could anyone else hear it? Listen closely now, hear it? Wooooowo, wooooowo, the wind blows, it's telling us a story.

I was totally caught up in this, captured by the wild whistling wind...

Beside me, Charlotte set down. "Uncle Augie, do you hear that? The Wind is singing to us. It's trying to tell us something...Listen."

"Yes Charlie, I didn't think anyone else could hear it as I do...it's so beautiful, yet scary at the same time, and look it put everyone else to sleep. Perhaps it's the ancient spirits of the Anasazi, trying to tell us something. It's claimed that ghosts of the ancients still roam through those cliff-dwellings and I'm not about to deny it."

CHAPTER 18

Cliff-Dwellings

Morning came quickly and the wind seemed to have abated with the dawn of a new day, as the early morning sun peaked over the mesa, giving off an illustrious kaleidoscope of symmetrical colors beyond imagination...the Cliff-Dwellings changing patterns as the sun moved from east to west, shadows seemingly to make you feel that people are moving about.

We finished breakfast and started walking our horses down to the valley below, keeping a sharp eye out for possible intruders or at the least strangers that normally would not be there.

Finally, arriving at the base of these magnificent structures, we stood dwarfed and felt so insignificant in their presence and I truly felt humbled. I'm sure the others felt the same way as they too were staring in awe, saying nothing.

It took a strong will to break away from this, but gathering my wits about me I told our little search party to spread out and search for any possible clues of gang activity or camps. A three hour search revealed nothing, and as we neared the end of the mesa dwellings, I recalled we had not opened up or search through any of the Kivas, and I had to explain what they were.

"Uncle Augie, come here, I think I've found something...it's kinda strange though as it has a door on top of another door."

"I think you have found something Charlie," as we all rushed over to where Charlie was standing. "Let's open that door up all the way." Then suddenly I recalled I had been here before. Yes, this is the place that girl led me too and I had that dream...It was trying to tell me something then, but I simply was not thinking straight then.

Now, a sound from within the darkened Kiva, the wind started blowing, it was talking again. I listened ... then another sound, like groaning.

"Glenn, light that torch there by the entryway, there's someone in here and can't see worth a damn."

With the lighted torch we slipped inside the Kiva, but it was a large Kiva and the light did not glow so well as to make light enough to see clearly; so I started to walk the inside perimeter of the Kiva and with another sound that was in anguish I saw a body lying on the dirt floor...

"Cap'n, that you sur, it's me Sarge, I been awaiting fer ya."

"I'll be damned Sarge, wondered where you got off to again without telling me. Seems you turn up in the damnedest places ever. How bad ya hurt Sarge?"

"Not sure Cap'n, but I's a mite thirsty."

Charlotte knelt down and lifted Sarge's head and gave him water. "you'll be alright Sarge, we're here now and we'll take care of you."

"An Angel from Heaven Cap'n, she'll do to ride the river with."

We carefully lifted Sarge up and carried him outside, but Charlie threw a cloth over his eyes, so the sun wouldn't blind him...but we placed him in the shade of the Kiva.

"Here Sarge, a little more water, tell us when your feeling better now and feel like talking."

"Hell's sake, I most often feels to like talking, but mostly no bodies 'round to hears me." Sarge sputtered with a chuckle.

"Alright Sarge, wana take that cloth from your eyes yet...and first off can you tell us who did this to you?"

"No surs, causes I never did to seen those cusses, but I heerd a lot...the gold and silver is stashed right here sur."

"It is..damn Sarge, where about?"

"Don't rightly know dat Cap'n, but I eard dem a talking. I was already been da beat up some." Sarge tried to move and we found a couple of his ribs broken, so I cautioned him to stop moving...just lay quiet.

"Sarge, were going to remove your shirt and bind you tightly around your ribs, they must have kicked the shit out ya Sarge, ya got a few broken ribs. Oh sorry Charlie."

"Oh hell Uncle Augie, you know I'm used to that talk. Never you mind."

With grunts and groans we got Sarge bound up, and he started talking again. "Cap'n, ya needs to look for a second door somewhere's, thas where they stash the loot."

"Hmm, second door? Charlie what did you say at first when you found this Kiva, that it had two doors?"

"Yeah, the other door is right underneath the first door like a cellar. Ya'll didn't notice it?"

"Damn Dan, yes here it is." Glenn exclaimed. "But I think it's gona take at lest two of us to lift it up."

With great effort we lifted the door and revealed a stairway to a cellar, a second Kiva, torches were available on the walls so we lite a couple and was astonished at the amount of mining sacks filled with what turned out to be gold dust on one side and sliver on the other side, in the middle was a couple a wooden boxes filled with currency and script.

"My God," Glenn exclaimed, "there must be hundreds of thousands of dollars worth here, if not millions."

"Is there that much money in the whole world?" Charlie was beside herself.

"So, it seems this was their stash, to obviously be divided up whenever the big man said so...more money than they could ever count or haul away."

"Just who in the hell could be the big boss?" Glenn added.

"Well presently that doesn't matter, but we will get him sooner or later, if no other way than just right here when he comes for it."

"Uncle Augie, that could be a very long wait, depending on who it is and just think if someone of the gangs come by and sees that other people, like us, has been here and found their stash, they'll for sure be on the lookout."

"Yeah your right Charlie, so we certainly have to be on the look-out ourselves; we'll need to figure out a plan. Anyone have any idea's? We can't haul this loot away without at least two wagons and we don't even have one."

"Dan, do you think we'd have time to move it to one of the pit houses and then cover our tracks completely?"

"Good idea Glenn, but along with that same thought, how about only moving part of it, then they'll think someone of their own gang has stolen it and high-tailed it out of the country. Just maybe it'll start a fight among themselves."

"Hell yes, lets give it a try anyway... but I think if we move just the two boxes of script and currency, that'll be enough to start accusations and arguments, and hopefully start fighting.

"No telling when the gang will be back around here to add to their loot or just to check on it...I'm surprised they don't have somebody around to kinda guard it, as it is. Seems kinda sloppy of them, but then again that might draw unnecessary attention to it."

"We need to stop talking about it and just do it Uncle Augie, no telling when someone will come around."

We worked into the night, those two boxes were mighty heavy and we had to pack them about fifty or sixty yards, it was more like a tug of war for us...but we finally accomplished our task; and as tired as we were, we just slumped into the pit house ourselves after we carried Sarge with us. Tomorrow morning early, we would wipe away all our tracks leading to and from the pit house and Kiva.

Up at dawn, no coffee or breakfast, as we knew we may have limited time to finish our task and as it turned out we were right; riders appeared withing minutes after we had saddled our horses and we put Sarge in back of Charlotte and left the same way we came in. Went to our old camp of the night before...They would discover our tracks to this point and from here on we needed to hide our tracks and double back to observe their reaction that someone had invaded their stash in the sub-Kiva. They would also find out Sarge was not dead and no where to be found.

We found a place about a half mile from our initial campsite atop an escarpment looking down on the valley floor and the mesa, giving us sufficient cover not to be spotted easily. Yet we could observe their movements and actions quite clearly; however, from our vantage point we were unable to recognize any one person.

Yet we could see their surprise, their pointing at our tracks, gesturing obscenely and hollering, even though we were to far away to hear. The few that entered the Kiva, came back out pointing fingers at one person and then another, just as we suspected. Trust between the outlaws had vanished completely. We decided to start back towards Durango, but taking a different route than when we came as our tracks would still be visible in many places. Further, when we camped for the night we did not want to be visible to any of the outlaws that may possibly try to track us, unless they took a very wide track off the main trail.

Again, the second day we slogged into town bone-weary, tired, yet felt some feeling of accomplishment. We needed to get a couple of heavy-duty wagons and two teams of horses, plus extra men with guns to ride as guards before we start back to the cliff-dwellings to retrieve the stolen loot. We pulled up to my office-jail and the Sheriff was there to greet us...

"Hello Marshall, any luck on your trip?"

"You might say so Sheriff, yet it seems we're no smarter now than before we left."

"I see you found Sarge, is he alright? Where did you find him, somewhere's along the trail?"

With a jerk of my head, something popped in my brain. "Sheriff, how did you know about Sarge?"

"Well now, not sure, guess someone mentioned him to me, an come to think of it, it was probably you before you all left."

"Don't think so Sheriff, anyway, guess it doesn't matter now. But he does need some attention from the Doc again."

"Someone nearly kicked the shit out a him and left him for dead to rot." Glenn volunteered.

"Need help getting him down from behind Charlotte, some man of the small crowd asked?"

"Yeah, thanks, be gentle with that ole coot...think he has a few broken ribs." As three men came forward to carefully carry Sarge to the Doc's place.

The Sheriff followed the Marshall into the office, being very inquisitive of their trip and what they learned. Ethan, of course, was there and poured a cup for Dan, "Sheriff, ya want a cup of Arbuckles, just made it fresh?"

"Ah, well no, but I'll take a shot a whiskey if that's to be offered."

"Don't serve whiskey here Sheriff, but I have a couple a questions to put to you Sheriff Allen.

Let's see now, you've been here for sometime and all this time never learned anything at all of what the hell's been going on... Sheriff, you were my commanding Officer in the Army, you sent me out on details and scouting patrols and if I hadn't of come back with some pertinent information for you each time, you'd politely dress me down in a military way. Now Sir, my question to you is just what the hell have you been doing? You just hang out in the saloons drinking and bragging and from what I have heard mostly lies to build yourself up like some wartime hero."

"Ah, well now Captain, I meant no harm to anyone; and my pay here is not even what it was in the Army... well I just wanted people to like me and look up to me now like they did in the service. It's hell getting old and worn-out Marshall."

"I'd like to understand that Sheriff, but had you devoted your efforts towards doing something about these gangs of outlaws running wild, you most likely would have got the recognition and applause deservingly. I give you no excuse Sheriff and something is sticking in my craw about you that I can't put my finger on right now; but if it comes to my mind, and if it's against the law I will arrest you the same as I would anyone else. Now please go and get your whiskey, I need to talk to Ethan."

With head bowed in indignation Sheriff Allen Walker, also known as Major Allen Walker, slowly walked out of the Marshall's office and started walking up the street, dragging his feet as if one step after another was just too much.

"By the Jesus Dan, I never thought you would have talked to the Major like that. What's going on?"

"Ordinarily Ethan, I never would have, but things are just beginning to make sense to me and it includes our not-so-honorable Sheriff Walker. Settle down and I'll give you my thou..."

A shot rang out, Ethan and I went to the door and opened it to see what it was all about, In the middle of the street Sheriff Walker stood, arms akimbo, legs straddled. "I guess it's showdown time Marshall, ya finally figured it out. Was hoping to light out before this happened but I see it's not in the cards. I'm calling you out!"

234

"Sheriff, you don't need to end it like this, ya know damn well what'll happen, throw down your gun, and come on in."

"Can't do it Dan, you know that."

By now a crowd had gathered and I had no choice but to step out into the street. "We don't need to do this, come on, throw down your gun and come-on in."

"Stand your ground Marshall, it's the only way this can end, and you know that to be true. It's either you or me." As the Sheriff pulled leather, so too did I.

In the blink of an eye, a life was forfeited. What a waste, as the sheriff was once a good man and perhaps could have been great. I stood there transfixed as I saw him slowly kneel down then fall backwards with his gun drawn, but not fired. Ethan ran to him, the doc walked over too and examined him...

"Dan, the Major had unloaded his gun, not a shell in it; it's like he wanted you to kill him."

"Yes, I kinda figured something like that, but wasn't sure. He didn't want to be exposed to ridicule, that would have killed him worse than my bullet did."

It cloudy over quickly and started raining, the undertaker got men to carry the Sheriff to his parlor. Murmuring and gossip among the crowd as what the hell happened but at this point I didn't feel like making a public explanation. They all witnessed how the sheriff kept prodding me and left me no other choice but to draw and shoot...

"Dan, I'm just a bit mystified myself, tell me what the hell is going on." As we walked out of the rain into my office.

"Ethan, to make a long story short, Sheriff Allen was the leader, I couldn't pick out the signs right-away, but they were there from his actions and a few of the things he asked me and some things he said from time to time. Further, Sophie was in on it too, her and the sheriff actually were the main bosses. I just could never understand how Sophie or the sheriff could permit Sara Jane to be mixed up in it... The thing about it is that they both were getting old and wanted to have themselves a bit of a nest-egg and thought they could get away with it for awhile and they did for quite sometime. Their stash is located at the cliff-dwellings, but we hid it by moving it to another place out there, or part of it anyway. That also reminds me now that Sam

Squires is still on the loose and no bosses to tell him what to do or not do. If he doesn't already now what has just transpired, he soon will and will be getting wagons and teams together to load and move what he can, but he's greedy as hell as you know and he'll want to take it all. If this rain doesn't let up soon, he won't be able to do anything same as us.

The wind picked up to near gale-force and the rain plummeted down harder and harder and reminded me of the day Daisy was shot and later of the funeral and how it started clouding up that day. *Here I am Daisy, I hope both you and God can forgive me, I am standing here looking down on your grave and cursing my ways that I brought you to this end...I promise you I'll raise Noah as you would have me to...he's found a girl and will marry soon, she's a beautiful girl, you remember Sara Jane that one day I brought her home...well anyway, not much else to say, but please remember My Darling, I've always loved you.*

Very touching Daniel, almost made me cry," Sam Squires butted in. "I had other plans for you, but guess now is a good time to put an end to this and you can lay beside your beloved Daisy. Rest in peace Marshall."

Sam Squires drew and fired putting a bullet into the Marshall's shooting arm...but the Marshall wasn't even wearing his gun.

Then another voice rang out, "Sam Squires, your a polecat for sure, you wanna try that with someone with a gun."

Squires turned quickly, drew again, but a bullet found it's mark and Sam fell dead.

"Noah, Oh my Good God Noah...

ABOUT THE AUTHOR

Rebecca Ra'Chel lives in Iztapa Puerto, Escuintla, Guatemala where she engages herself in the quest of research and study of the ancient Mayans.

Rebecca further still prefers to remain a type of recluse, shuns parties, and other groups of people, yet a one on one chat she can handle quite well. She has a hybrid Wolf named "Prince", a loyal Akita, "Bubba" and a colorful Appaloosa named "Just Plain Sam."

Rebecca was born in Oregon in 1989 and her parents relocated to Santa Barbara, Ca. When she was still a toddler. Both of her parents were killed by a drunk driver on her 8th birthday. Grandfather from Texas then raised her. He became her mother, father, counselor, teacher and preacher, but most of all was still her grandfather with a BIG shoulder to cry upon. He bridged the gap left by the passing of her parents. Rebecca is married with two wonderful children.

She started writing poems and short stories at age 9, as she used that conveyance instead of talking. Rebecca is a degreed anthropologist, cenote diver, adventurist, sports fan, plus being an avid fisherman, hunter and horseback rider. You could often see her jogging on the beach, with Prince & Bubba, running right along beside her.

She loves writing and hopes you will enjoy her first novel "Portals of Time," A Woman's Shamanic Visions as well as her sequel, available soon, "Beyond the Portal," A Woman's Shamanic Quest. And now a western genre "The Wild Wild Wind," is her first attempt at penetrating the old west in all it glory, and loves the research.

www.beccara-chel.info

Books by Becca Ra'Chel

Western
The Wild Wild Wind

Sci-Fi
Portals of Time: A Woman's Shamanic Visions

www.ingramcontent.com/pod-product-compliance
Lightning Source LLC
Chambersburg PA
CBHW051149030726
47504CB00004B/1111